Stronger

ERICA MARSELAS

This story is dedicated to anyone that's ever been bullied, that's ever been beaten down, and felt lost. Scared. I want you to remember you are never alone. That you really are stronger then you believe. Keep fighting through the darkness because there is light at the end of the tunnel.

"I'm going to tell you a story—about a girl who learned how to come out of the shadows, discovered her inner strength and rose above the hate. She just needed a boost from a person she least expected— someone that also needed her. Together they became stronger—once they learned how to stand up for themselves."

CHAPTER ONE

"Nobody saw me. Nobody wanted me. Then you stormed into my life and flipped it upside down. You saw me. You wanted me. I just have one question: Is it really me *that you wanted, or the person you thought I could become?"*

Brooklyn

My alarm rings obnoxiously beside me and I slap down the snooze button. I groan and bury my head under my pillow, not ready to get up. It's Monday...again.

I don't detest the idea of getting up in the morning because the weekend is over.

It's because I have to go back to that place where people see me as *nothing* and don't know who I truly am.

My alarm beeps again and I toss my pillow across the room in a huff. "Fine, I'm getting up," I moan to the clock and turn it off. I wish I could just go back to sleep until graduation—when my future will begin. Till then, I have to make it through another day.

Tossing my blanket to the floor, I make my way to the bathroom to start my day. I catch my reflection in the mirror and run my hand through my tangled mess of red

1

hair. *I'm a disaster.* Grabbing my brush, I smooth out my rat's nest and tie it back in a ponytail before I slip on my glasses. Like every morning, as I stare at the pale, freckled girl in the mirror, I ask myself if I should put more effort into what I look like. Then I shake my head and remember it didn't do me any good in middle school, so it wouldn't matter now.

Brooklyn Turner will always be the so-called nerd everyone labeled me as.

There are worse things to be called though. So what if I get good grades and happen to love to learn new things, being challenged and also value my education?

When I was young, my mother instilled in me that I could be whatever I wanted to be. But I should make sure I have the brains and knowledge to back up my dreams. *"You can either spend three hours getting yourself ready in the morning to "pretty" up or spend those three hours studying. Because looks only get a person so far, an education will get you everywhere."*

It would take me till after seventh grade, the roughest time in my life, to understand her advice. A time where I wanted to give up because all but one friend turned their backs on me. They believed the words of the bully who had been out to get me since the first time she laid eyes on me. She made every day a living nightmare. I was slut shamed because I developed early, slammed into lockers, and insulted by every name in the book. Online and in the halls. I spent most of my days crying and wondering what it was I had done wrong to be outcasted. Still to this day she tries to get to me. As much as it hurt, I soaked up my tears and realized I didn't need to stand out and be popular. I needed to succeed, focus on how great I'd be one day, and show them all they didn't break me.

I've let myself fade into the background. I avoid social media, I've blocked numbers and stayed out of my aggressor's way. I've let myself get lost in the shuffle and

Stronger

I just ignore the world around me while I earn my A's. I've enjoyed it here ever since.

High school is almost over. I'm getting out of this town and never looking back as soon as the final bell rings on my high school years.

But first I need to make it through another Monday.

My pen taps on my desk as I listen to Mr. Marshall talk about the post WWII era. Mr. Marshall, who also happens to be my French teacher, is my favorite teacher in the whole school. He's young, down to earth, and treats everyone equal. It also helps that he's easy on the eyes. *Very easy.* If only I was a few years older.

There's a familiar unease that bubbles in my belly. I get it every time I'm in one of Mr. Marshall's classes. And it has nothing to do with the fine specimen with the firm ass and the veins that bulge in his arm every time he writes on the whiteboard. *No.* The unsettling knots in my gut are all due to Hunter Evans, the school's football star. I turn to look at him and catch his piercing forest green eyes roam over my body and a smirk cross his lips. Goosebumps form on my arms as the nervousness unravels in my stomach. It's like he's plotting and planning my untimely demise. I'm waiting for people to come out of the walls and throw eggs and toilet paper at me while everyone else laughs at my embarrassment. Though when his traveling gaze comes back to mine, he's smiling. There's this shine in his eyes, but I can't put my finger on what it means. He gives me a wink and my cheeks heat. I quickly look away and pick up my textbook, hiding away from him.

Why is he smiling and winking at me?

Most people avoid looking at me or pretend they don't see me. He used to be one of them, but as of late, he's always staring at me in class. I try to ignore the hairs standing on the back of my neck and focus on Mr. Marshall's voice, trying to learn something, as Hunter continues to glance my way.

The school bell rings, freeing me from him boring holes into the side of my face. In my haste to make a quick retreat, I throw all my stuff in my backpack, not caring that I'm squishing the bag of chips at the bottom.

I just need to get out of here.

I'm two feet past my desk when Mr. Marshall's smooth as honey voice, laced with his lingering French accent calls me back. "Miss Turner, can I talk to you for a moment?"

My shoulders sag, the sweet taste of freedom now further away. I spin around and notice Hunter leaning against Mr. Marshall's desk. My heart beats wildly wondering why he isn't leaving and going to be the middle of my conversation with my teacher.

I give them both a weak smile, but my eyes focus on the stapler instead of on them. "What did you need to talk to me for?" I ask, trying to keep the hesitation and nervousness out of my voice.

"I was wondering if you would be able to tutor Mr. Evans here. He needs a little extra help with studying and sadly, I don't have the time to assist."

My eyes widen horrified, glancing up at the crazy man. "Me?" I squeak.

Where did he get the idea I would want to tutor, anybody?

"Yes, I was hoping my prized student would be able to lend a hand. If anyone could help Hunter, it would be you." Mr. Marshall smiles at me with his warm chocolate eyes.

My own eyes fall back to the stapler, finding it much more interesting and hoping it will tell me how to escape the room without saying yes. I've never tutored anyone before, much less the jock who is probably missing a few of his brain cells. I don't know if I should because I have a feeling this is going to come back and bite me in the ass. But I also know I'm not going to say no to Mr. Marshall.

I shrug, relenting. "What is it that I need to do?"

"Well, Hunter here needs to improve his grades if he wants to keep playing football to the playoffs and have a chance of getting a scholarship. He's slacking off in French as well, so maybe a couple tutoring sessions will help. Would that be something you would be able to do?"

"Sure, I don't see why not."

I'm going to need an appointment with a shrink because I've lost my damn mind.

"Thank you, Brooklyn," Hunter says with the same bright smile he had given me earlier. "I promise to be a good student." His hand reaches out and touches my arm.

My skin tingles where his fingers touch, and my heart skips a fluttering beat.

I'm not sure what to make of this, but I like it.

Before I can shrug him away so I don't turn into a pile of mush, his hand falls back to his side. The knot in my stomach is tighter and bigger than before, and I'm still flustered by his touch. I nod. "Okay. I guess we can set something up later."

"Alright. Great. Now that's all settled, I expect better grades from you, Mr. Evans, from now on. There's no way I could believe Miss Turner isn't teaching you anything." Mr. Marshall chuckles and claps the running back's shoulder. "I'll see you both tomorrow."

I give them both a quick smile before darting out of the room.

My best friend, Riley, waits for me at the bottom of the stairs outside school, holding her flute case in one hand and her cellphone in the other. Riley is a band geek, but she's not *geeky* looking in the slightest. She has gorgeous blonde locks and sparkling blue eyes. She's what I think most of the boys would be after. And with her looks, she fits better with the cheerleaders than with the nerds. Riley is pretty but likes to keep to herself, which keeps her from socializing with others. And she *hates* girls—well, besides me.

I've been friends with her and her brother Elijah since I was four. I always had a crush on Elijah, and he was someone I also considered my best friend. He had braces till he graduated high school along with these cute large black-rimmed glasses which made his blue eyes pop. His cheeks were always freckled, and he used to keep his hair long. He was by far the definition of nerd, being class president, and the school valedictorian. *Like me.* But he was hot.

We dated for two months the summer before my sophomore year, then he left when he joined the Air Force. We obviously broke up knowing the distance between us would never work. In the end, I think it was a good choice because we were better off friends than being boyfriend and girlfriend. We write each other occasionally and he's now dating some girl he met on base.

I haven't gotten close to anyone since him. But it's not like anyone has tried either. The next person I date, I want to have those romance novel tingles—like the ones

Hunter gave me today when he touched me.

"Where have you been?" Riley asks, calling me back from my mindless memories.

"Sorry," I shake my head, "I got held up with Mr. Marshall. It looks like I'm going to have to tutor someone."

"Who?"

"Hunter Evans," I say miserably. No matter if I like the way he smiles or the way it felt when he touched me, I give him an hour before he gets on my nerves.

"Get out of here! He's like the hottest guy in school."

There *may* be a lot of truth in her statement; his body alone looks like he walked out of an Abercrombie and Fitch ad.

"And obviously not the brightest since he needs me to tutor him. How hard is History? Okay, I get not understanding French, but history*, so easy*." I roll my eyes. "Bet he's going to try and bribe me to do his homework."

"Well, get something in return if you do. You need some extra dough for when you run off to Stanford." She giggles.

"I'm not doing his work!"

Riley's lips press together in a tight smile as she glances behind me, and I turn my head, wondering what has captured her attention. Coming down the stairs two at a time is Hunter. His ash brown hair whips around in the wind as he heads our way.

He gives me an award-winning smile as he approaches me. "Brooklyn, I'm glad I caught up to you."

"You are?" My voice squeaks and I curse myself for being so affected by him.

"Yeah, I was hoping maybe we could start studying tonight? We have that French quiz tomorrow."

"I already have plans."

It's not a lie. Riley and I had already made plans to

go shopping today. Well, she's shopping, and I'm being dragged with her against my will. She always tries to play dress up with me, but I won't have it. I like to be comfortable and able to breathe. I want to move in my clothes, have a taco for lunch, and not worry about my stomach busting out.

Okay, that's just an excuse. I do like pretty clothes, but I guess I've forgotten how to look pretty in them when a certain bully always made me feel less than I was.

"But definitely tomorrow if you want. The quiz should be fairly easy…" I put out an olive branch, though I hope we can forget this whole tutoring thing by tomorrow.

His smile falls, and he stuffs his hands into the pockets of his letterman, "Oh. That's fine. No biggie."

Why does he look so *gloomy?*

"We won't be out late though," Riley pipes up and I spin to look at her, begging her to shut up. "We should be back around five. Plenty of time for a quick study session, right, Brookey?"

I hate when she calls me Brookey.

I glare at her, trying to set her on fire. I mouth 'what are you doing?' and she just grins and nudges her head back at Hunter. I try to put on my best smile as I turn back to him, all while thinking where I could hide Riley's body while we're at the mall.

"Suuure. I guess that will be fine."

God, I'm such a pushover.

Hunter's winning, cheeky smile is back, and you would think he had just won the lottery. "That works for me. I need all the help I can get. Thank you again. Can I get your number?"

"My number?" I stutter, my brain not comprehending why he would want my number. His hand touches my shoulder again, and the tingles are back, feeling as if I got hit by a bolt of lightning. His light chuckle pulls me from the tremors. I step back, needing to be far away from his cosmic force.

"Hey, I just want to be able to call you so we can figure out where to meet." His laugh ceases and his dark greens reassure me of no ill intent. I hate how much I don't trust anyone anymore.

"Right." I breathe out a sigh of relief. "Give me your phone and I can put it in for you."

"Awesome." He pulls out his cell from his back pocket and hands it over to me. Brushing my finger to open the screen, I find a picture of a little girl with her arms wrapped around a Pug.

"Cute picture," I mumble while heading to the phone icon.

"My little sister and our dog." My eyes peek up at him and his genuine smile is breathtaking. Also, swoon. What boy in this school would have their sister and dog as a screensaver? I was expecting a half-naked girl or a football team logo.

Without saying anything else about that, I type in my number and call myself, so I have his number. Once I feel my phone buzz I hand it back to him. "We good?"

"Yep. I'll see you later, Brooklyn." He grins and gives me a wink before walking away to the parking lot.

"What the hell was that?" I sneer at Riley, who's smiling like a complete loon. I grab her arm and yank her away from the departing figure.

"Oh, come on. The hottest guy in school wants to hang out with you. He was pressing for you to study with him. Why would he do that if he didn't care? And he was looking at you with goo-goo eyes."

"Shut up, no he wasn't. He's only desperate to keep playing football. Now, no more talking about it, so I can try to enjoy shopping with you."

"Girl, I'm getting you into a skirt to show off those legs. You're going to make him want to drag his tongue up and down them." She laughs, and I shove her away from me. She stumbles a bit, but it doesn't cause her to stop giggling.

Yep, I'm going to have to find a way for a bunch of designer shoes to fall on her head.

"I doubt he wants anything to do with me besides getting a better grade. I think he gets twice the action than you do during the summer."

"You have no idea if you don't try. I remember the old you who used to wear—"

"Will you stop?" I cut her off, placing my hand over her flapping lips. "I'm not dressing up to study with him. I can safely say that this man only wants me for my brain and not my looks…"

My hand drops from her mouth and she's still giving me a cocky smirk. "We'll see."

I flop to the couch, exhausted from the two hours I was dragged around the mall being my best friend's personal dress up doll. Riley is a pushy broad, and I find myself just doing what she tells me to get her off my back. The mini skirt she bought me will send my daddy into an early grave if he sees it. Granted, I can admit I do look good in it, but there's no way I'm going to wear it for Hunter. He'd more than likely laugh at me for trying too hard.

Plus, I have no interest in trying to impress him.

Okay, maybe I do a little bit.

Gripping my phone in my hand, I convince myself into calling him about studying for tomorrows quiz.

I don't like to break promises, although I shouldn't have gotten myself into this one.

Scrolling through my list of contacts, I find his name and hit send and pray he doesn't answer. Unfortunately, after the second ring, he picks up.

"Brooklyn?" My full name rolls off his tongue and sends shivers down my spine. But why is he calling me by my full name when nobody at school uses it, not even the teachers?

"It's Brooke. Not even my parents call me Brooklyn unless I'm in trouble." I babble and wonder why I'm telling him all this. It's not like he cares.

He chuckles. "Well, I like Brooklyn better."

"*Well,* if you want me to help you study, you'll call me Brooke."

"Yes, ma'am," he says, but laughter still echoes in his voice. "Does this mean you'll help me study tonight?"

"Yeah, I suppose."

"Thank you, *Brooke.* Where can I meet you?"

"I guess you can come to my place. I know you probably wouldn't want to be seen with me in public." I try to make it off as a joke, but it's the truth. Nobody wants to be associated with me.

He's quiet for a moment, the only sound coming through is his heavy breathing. My mouth pops open wanting to end this awkward silence but he finally speaks again.

"I'll be at your place in ten," he says, and the line goes dead.

Pulling the phone away, I stare blankly at the screen that tells me the call has ended. I didn't even tell him where I live, but maybe this is his way of telling me he won't show up.

To my surprise, no more than ten minutes later, my doorbell rings. My mother comes out of the kitchen, drying her hands on a hand towel. "Wonder who that could be?"

"It's for me. I'm helping someone study."

"Oh?"

I give her a weak smile without answering and move to the door. I open it slowly and standing before me is Hunter with a lazy grin on his face. He's changed into a pair of gray sweatpants, a black Nirvana shirt, and his backpack is slung over his arm. His brown hair is wild and untamed, looking like he just rolled out of bed or just finished having sex. Knowing his reputation, I'll say sex.

But goddamn does this look make him hot.

"Hey, are you going to let me in?"

"Wait. How did you know where I live?"

"The school directory. Can I come in now?"

The school directory? What the...?

"Um, right." I accept his ridiculous reason and move out of the way to let him in. He walks in, and his head twists back and forth as he checks out my house. My mother is wearing a wide grin and I wonder what *that's* about.

"Mom, this is Hunter. I'm going to be helping him with French and History. Hunter this is my mom." I wave my arms between the two, feeling all kinds of awkward.

"Mrs. Turner, it's a pleasure." He reaches out to shake my mother's hand. His preppy boy smile shines brightly, and I think I'm going to need sunglasses. My mother graciously takes his hand, giving him a proud smile in return.

Who knew he had manners?

"It's good to meet you, Hunter. Will you be staying long? You're more than welcome to join us for dinner."

My eyes go wide, screaming at my mother to hush. But she ignores my panic and continues to stare at Hunter. What is with everyone trying to push me into this man's arms?

Hunter briefly glances my way, I'm sure sensing my

12

panic, before turning back to my mother. "Maybe another day, Mrs. Turner. I ate right before I came over."

Thank the lord. Because there's no way I could've eaten in front of him. I don't want to have to deal with him longer than I need too.

"Alright, I'll let you two be." When Hunter looks away she gives me a wink and mouths 'he's nice,' before going back to the kitchen. I roll my eyes, having no idea how I'm going to explain to her that this means nothing.

"Sorry about that," I mutter and lead him over to the couch.

"Don't be. One day I will stay. It smells like your mom can cook. I couldn't tell you the last time my mom actually cooked." He shrugs and sits down on the couch, pulling out his French book.

I sit down next to him, as far away as I can manage without having to sit on the arm of the couch.

He chuckles, shaking his head with a smirk. "I won't bite, Brooklyn. I promise."

"Brooke. It's Brooke," I grumble, but inside I love the way my name sounds coming out of his mouth. He nods but doesn't say anything else as he opens his textbook.

We quickly fall into what will be on the quiz tomorrow. He actually listens to me and writes down everything I tell him to, and then repeats back in perfect French dialogue. He asks a couple of questions about the accents, but he doesn't need to. Because as I listen to him, I'm wondering why Mr. Marshall thinks he needs a tutor in French.

"Hunter, you know this. I don't think you need me," I tell him and toss my French book to the coffee table.

"Um…" His eyebrows knit together, and his nose scrunches up before he turns away from me. "I've been trying since I was told I need better grades. You know the team needs me." He shrugs and then closes his book.

13

When he turns his eyes back to me, he grins, the confusion—or was it worry?—leaves his face. "An A is better than a B or C any day, right?"

"Yeah, I guess." I bite on my finger nervously, not sure what to do now. Instead, Hunter figures it out for me and begins to read the excerpt for tomorrow's quiz out loud.

I take the time to admire him as he talks. I can't say why I'm counting the prickles of his facial hair which is trying its damnedest to be a beard or why I think he has the cutest nose, but I am and I do. He doesn't seem all that bad, and I haven't seen a trace of asshole yet, but I fear—

"Brooke?" My mother's voice calls me out of my trance and I have no idea how long I was staring at him.

My cheeks heat in embarrassment and I look at my mother. "Yeah?"

"Your father will be home shortly, and dinner is ready. You're still welcomed to join us, Hunter."

"Mom—" I hiss through my teeth and I wave my hand under my neck signaling her to cut it out.

Hunter looks my way and I freeze my wild hand movements to make it look like I'm fixing my hair. He chuckles and turns back to my mother. "It's okay, Mrs. Turner. Thank you again, I should be heading home anyway."

Oh, Thank goodness.

"Alright, it was nice meeting you, hun. When he leaves, can you set the table, Brooke?" I nod and she heads back to the table.

Hunter collects his books and shoves them into his backpack. "Thank you, Brooke, for your help."

I helped?

I nervously scratch the back of my neck, knowing I did nothing but stare at him for the last forty-five minutes. "I didn't do anything. Sorry, we didn't have more time." My eyes close momentarily, trying to figure out what the

14

heck I'm saying. More time? Nuh-uh. "But I think you'll be fine for tomorrow." My eyes pop back open giving him a half smile. I stand from the couch to urge him to the front door.

"I know." He laughs uncomfortably, as we walk outside to the front porch. "Are you free tomorrow after school?"

"Tomorrow?" I gulp. "Are you sure? I told you, you don't need the extra help."

"There's still History," he points out and I sigh, knowing we didn't get to that subject yet.

"Yeah. Sure." It's not like I'll be doing anything.

"Great. Thank you for doing this, Brooke." He touches my shoulder and leans over to give me a quick peck on the cheek.

I'm taken aback by the gesture, but unable to produce words before he walks away. My fingers brush my cheek, where a little bit of wetness from his kiss still lingers.

What the hell was that? And why is my cheek tingling?

I try to tell myself it means nothing and it in no way means more than a thank you. I watch as he gets into his car and starts the engine, my hand still on my cheek. When he notices me, he gives me a wink as he pulls out of the driveway. I somehow manage a tiny wave before turning and running inside.

The smell of chicken and bacon halt the thoughts of Hunter that have been circling my now exhausted brain. My mother places the casserole in the middle of the table and then walks over to me as I set down the last place setting.

"He seemed nice," my mother muses and I roll my eyes at her persistence.

"I guess," I mumble and grab the napkins from the center of the table.

"What do you mean you guess?"

"I don't really know him, but let's just say he doesn't keep good company." I hope she'll know what I mean and drop it.

My mom's lips purse together, and she nods. "Alright. Well, will we be seeing more of him? Because you can't judge him alone on the friends he keeps."

Why not?

I fight the urge to stomp my foot, but she's right. *He's* not that bad, but it doesn't mean I trust him yet.

"He's coming over tomorrow, or we'll go to the library. I give it a week before he's had enough of me."

"You know, Brooke, you're a very lovable girl and it's okay to have friends outside your little circle…"

"I know, but I don't think he's going to be one. He just needs better grades to keep playing football. Can we talk about something else now?" I beg her, seconds away from putting my hands together and falling to my knees.

"Of course, dear." She brushes my hair back and I sigh in relief that I won't be interrogated further.

"Bonjour," Mr. Marshall addresses us as we sit down for class. "J'espère que vous êtes tous prêts pour le quiz d'aujourd'hui." *I hope you all are ready for today's quiz.*

I feel the usual pair of green lasers bore into the side of my head. My head snaps to Hunter's and he greets me with a lazy smile, his stare not faltering. I give a quick smile back before turning my attention away from him.

Mr. Marshall comes by to pass out our quiz. The paper slips onto my desk and I'm finding it impossible to look away from Hunter's lingering eyes. It's not till Mr.

Marshall grabs his attention that his gaze drops from mine. Mr. Marshall says something to him that makes him laugh and hold his hands up in defense.

I'm curious to know what that was about, but instead, I try to focus on the seven questions in front of me. We have to write out everything in perfect translated French, and then a bonus question where we make something up of our own.

I'm finished in record time and bring my test up to the front. Two feet behind me is Hunter, also handing in his quiz. "You were right, it was easy."

"Yep." I nod. Suddenly I visualize his lips on me again and I scurry away to my desk, so he can't see my cheeks redden. I'm a freaking mess.

The rest of the class, I sink into my seat and hide in my textbook. Hunter continues to look at me and I don't understand why he's paying me so much attention. It's as if my boobs have grown two sizes bigger or something. I remember when it happened in seventh grade and all the boys would point, stare, and drool. A certain girl went on to make fun of me afterward, eventually making the boys turn against me. I was somehow shamed as a slut because my body changed faster *and larger* than all the other girls. I used to think I was beautiful, and then my self-esteem was torn apart and stomped on. It's one of the events which changed me and made me realize I will only trust a few people ever again.

Although, Hunter seems different from the crew he keeps company with.

I wonder if he's thinking about the cheek-kiss he gave me. Did he like it as much as I did? Does he think he made a mistake and he's hoping I don't rat him out to his friends for his lips touching a nerd?

Because cooties are still an issue in high school, I chuckle to myself.

The bell finally rings, and I dart out of the classroom

without another look in Hunter's direction. I'm making my way to my locker when a hand brushes my back and the prickle of facial hair tickles my ear. "I look forward to our study session later, Brooklyn."

"Wha?"

I don't even get the full word out before he's gone, down the hall. I stand frozen as I watch him high five his buddies, John and Dan while I'm left confused by what just transpired. Moving toward my locker I continue to study Hunter's interactions with his friends. He's laughing as Dan shows him something on his phone and I wish I could feel that happy while roaming these halls. This is where being popular has its benefits; you're everyone's friend and all you have to do is roll out of bed in the morning and be blessed with the perfect day.

A locker slams shut next to me, causing me to jump, effectively ending my spying. "Hey, vermin." The vile voice belongs to the one and only Kara Adams. Standing next to her is her best friend and follower, Emma Williams.

Kara is the one who has been making my life hell since seventh grade. She hates me and the feeling is mutual. Emma just joined in on Kara's hate wagon being the little plastic minion that she is.

"Don't look in their direction. We wouldn't want to taint those boys with your creepy stare. I mean, I get why you look, they're a prize you're never going to get. Must suck." Kara hisses as she steps in front of me, and the smell of her overpriced perfume makes me gag.

"Trust me, there's nothing prize worthy about a couple buffoons who lose more and more of their brain cells after every game. It's why, sadly, I got picked to tutor Hunter. He lacks the capability to get good enough grades to keep playing."

"Poor Hunter." Kara places her hand over her heart and pushes out her bottom lip in a fake pout. "Having to deal with your face. Well, spare him as much as you can while he's at school. Oh, and word of advice, just because *our* Hunter is known to have gotten around, doesn't mean he would ever be desperate enough for you."

I roll my eyes and close my locker before walking away from them. They giggle behind me, thinking they got to me, but surprisingly, they didn't.

My mind wanders again to Hunter's faux pas kiss, and think that maybe for even a second, he saw me as more than nerd Brooke, but as his Brooklyn.

Oh, for pity sake, Brooklyn, get a grip on reality.

Erica Marselas

CHAPTER TWO

"Never question how beautiful you are.
To me, I can see how well your beauty shines. It's
your smile, your eyes, your skin, the aura around
you, which light up the world.
But it's your heart and your soul that makes you
stand out, making you dazzle."

Brooklyn

Over the last week, I have to admit Hunter has grown on me. A lot. He's not the dickhead or dumbass I thought he would be, and he's been willing to learn and listen to what I have to say. I expected him to be disinterested and give up after the second day, but here he is, day seven, in my living room.

Nothing more has happened between us since he kissed me on the cheek the first day. No other attempts have been made, and neither one of us have brought it up.

Riley is convinced he has the hots for me, and all I can think is she's losing all her common sense from blowing into that damn flute of hers all the time.

Although he continues to stare at me, he's *only* overly nice to me when we're alone together. In the halls at school, it is as if I become a ghost. Deep down inside my gut, I get a funny feeling about the whole thing. He

21

either likes me and is ashamed or this is going to end up being some cruel joke. Build me up to knock me down again. He's good friends with my number one enemy, Kara Adams, so my trust in him is already shaken.

Hunter and I are in our usual spot on the floor with our feet tucked under my coffee table, backs pressed against the couch and our French books are open on our laps. We're studying for tomorrow's quiz and I still don't understand why he needs my help because he speaks it better than I do. But his history knowledge is off, along with his grammar techniques and spelling. We had to write a paper on the cold war and I believe I would've seen fewer mistakes if a kindergartner had done it.

Okay, it wasn't that bad, but… it's good to know he's not perfect with everything.

When I handed the paper back covered in red marks, he was upset and shut down for a bit. I thought after that I was going to be rid of him, but the next day he showed me his revisions and told me how thankful he was for the help. I do think I'm going to have to tell him we can skip the French and I can help with his English assignments instead.

The familiar feeling of holes burning into my neck is back, and when I look up, Hunter is once again staring at me.

"Why do you keep looking at me? Do I have a hideous pimple on my face or something?" I finally snap, slamming my book closed, having enough of this one way staring contest.

He shakes his head and his hand reaches over to my face. Before I can process he is even touching me, he pulls my hair tie out of my hair. "Vous êtes tout simplement beau et devriez laisser pendre vos cheveux." *You are simply beautiful and should let your hair flow.*

I swear I feel my eyes popping out of their skull, shocked and confused by his comment. He gives me a cheeky smile, knowing I understood him, but it doesn't mean I understand *what* it is he's doing. His hand reaches up again, this time pulling off my glasses. I reach for them and he holds them further behind his back.

"What are you doing?"

"You have such pretty eyes. Why do you hide them behind glasses?"

"Because it's part of my secret identity. You know at night I become superwoman," I scoff. "Why do you think? I need them to see…"

"Why not wear contacts?"

"I don't know. Can I have them back please?" I reach for them again and it's like I'm playing a game of keep away. I could just lunge for them, but I want to avoid landing head first in his lap.

"I just want to have a look at the real you. I bet this is how hot you look when you go to bed at night. Relaxed and yourself. It's like you don't want the real you to shine through." Hunter runs his finger down my cheek, causing goosebumps to prickle on my skin. "You're really beautiful, Brooke. You should show it off more."

"So, my glasses and ponytail make me ugly?" I snarl, seconds away from punching him in his face. Though I'm sure his hard chin would do more damage to my hand than my knuckles could do to his face. What the hell is his game?

"I didn't say that," he says firmly. "You're gorgeous no matter what. You grabbed my attention as is. I just think that you hide behind baggy clothes and throwing your hair up because you don't want to try something new and that way others won't see you, but I see you."

Why has he suddenly become the male version of Oprah? Although, he's hit the head on the nail.

"Well, thanks. But can I have my glasses back at least? I'm blind without them." I reach out for them again, my hand making a gimme motion.

23

He grins as he hands me back my specs. When I go to slide them back on my face, he grabs my hands, stilling me and kisses me.

Time is at a standstill as I realize what has happened. Hunter Evans kissed me...again… But this time, on the lips.

I'm vaguely aware of his chuckle in my shocked state. I'm expecting people to jump out of the woodwork telling me I'm being punk'd, but in a blink of an eye, his lips are on me again and his tongue pushes its way into my mouth. I don't resist and part my lips to let his tongue explore my mouth. I've been kissed like this before when I dated Elijah, so I know I'm not a terrible kisser. Well, according to him.

I clear my mind as Hunter's arms wrap around me and pulls me to his chest. My glasses fall to the ground beside me and my body molds to his. I feel like I'm floating. I'm going to enjoy this even if it ends up being a sick game.

When Hunter pulls away from me, his nose brushes with mine, and those lasers he has for eyes, look as though they're smiling. "I like you, Brooke."

He likes me? *Me?* I can't help the million questions running through my head about why someone like him would like me. I'm not his type—at all. We're oil and water, fire and ice. Utter and complete opposites.

"Why?"

He chuckles, and his hand runs down my cheek. "Why? Because I find you mesmerizing. There's something about you that calls out to me. I tried to ignore it—"

"Because liking the school nerd isn't allowed?" I pull out of his arms and wrap mine around my body, putting up a protective barrier.

"That's not it. It's more because I didn't understand what I was feeling. This last week has opened my eyes to you. You're always so quiet, hiding behind this shy exterior."

"Nobody likes anybody who is different. I would much rather blend in with crowd than be ridiculed for standing out."

"I get that." He moves closer to me and I don't shy away. His finger runs down my cheek again making my goosebumps have goosebumps. "But you don't need to hide from me. I want to get to know you. I want to become *more.*"

"More? More how? Friends?"

"Well, I thought we were already friends." He smirks and his lips replace his fingers movements. "More than friends. I'd like to date you…"

My heart stops and I think I must be in some alternate universe. "I think you need to lay off the steroids. You've lost your damn mind."

He backs away and places his hand over his heart, wearing a teasingly shocked expression on his face. "You think I take roids? I'm hurt. I don't take anything, Brooke. My feelings are real. I'm not blinded by anything."

How can this person I thought was a dumb jock only a week ago, turn into the guy that makes my heart flutter and my temperature rise?

"What would all your friends say?" I ask, knowing that his friends would not be cool with us dating, but it would feel good to stick it to them all.

"It's none of their business." He sighs and runs his fingers through his messy hair. His eyes dart around the room, obviously trying to come up with an answer. When his eyes land back on mine, he reaches over to grab my hand. "But maybe it'll be better to keep this between us."

"You *are* embarrassed by me, aren't you?" I snatch my hand away and slide away from him.

I should've known it was too good to be true.

"Listen, it's nothing like that. But I like our bubble

and everyone will try to come and burst it. Just for a little while; can we keep it between us?" His eyes plead with me and I might be wrong, but he looks sincere.

The referee is pulling out the red flag and blowing his whistle loudly at me calling a foul play, but I'm blatantly ignoring it with a nod of my head. "Okay."

Welp, you only live once, right?

Who are you kidding, Brooke? What the heck are you getting yourself into?

"Good." He leans in, and his lips part to kiss me, but I put my hand to his mouth, stopping him.

"How do we date if no one is allowed to see us?" He grabs my wrist and moves it away and somehow manages to scoot in closer to me.

"Less study time, more talking, movies, *kissing.* We'll figure something out. I promise. But let's get back to kissing." His warm breath tickles my lips as he inches back in to kiss me, but I turn my head stopping his attack—again.

"One last thing…"

"Anything."

"Don't hurt me." I stutter my plea. My biggest fear is getting egged on Prom night like in *Never Been Kissed.* "Don't let this be some sick joke that you go back and laugh at me behind my back about. If it is, I beg you, stop now. You don't seem the type that would go out of his way to hurt me, but please know my daddy has many guns in this house, and he's a man that acts first, asks questions later, if you do."

I close my eyes and visualize giving Hunter a chance and it turns into me getting egged or dog food poured on me as the whole school watches and he goes into the sunset with someone like Kara Adams.

"I won't hurt you…" He kisses me lightly on the lips. "I promise."

And for now, I'm going to try and believe that

Stronger

Hunter and I had spent the rest of our study session making out. Man, can he kiss. My head is still spinning. It's no wonder girls are all over him, hoping he'll come banging down their doors. Even hours later, I'm still fanning myself when I think about his lips and his tongue dancing with mine.

Once my mom and dad came home, Hunter left for the evening with the promise of seeing me tomorrow. I'm still wary of him because it's all too good to be true. He doesn't want to show me off as his girlfriend and that does sting, but then again, do I want the drama that would come once everyone finds out that we are dating? All his friends are assholes and I'm sure they would go out of their way to make my life hell.

God, I'm the cliché secret girlfriend.

"You haven't stopped smiling since I've been home. It's so nice to see." My mom says as she puts a plate of taco shells, seasoned beef, and salsa in front of me. My mouth salivates at the deliciousness. I love Taco Thursdays.

"Well, I guess maybe things are changing." I shrug and put together my taco with all the fixings.

"Would this smile have to do with that boy who left our house with the same cheeky grin on his face?" My mom pushes looking for gossip, making me forget who the teenager at the table is at the moment.

"Yeah, he kind of asked me out." I bite my lip and look back down at my plate. A sudden rush of embarrassment heats my cheeks.

"Really?" she asks gleefully, with a single clap of her hands. She might be happier than I am. I'm sure she's thinking that her little girl is blossoming into a woman.

"Yeah."

"Well, I know I can't speak for your mother, but I would like to meet him, have a man to man talk with him," my dad pipes in, wiping his lips with a napkin.

"So, you can embarrass me?" I groan and sink into my seat. My taco is staring at me waiting for me to eat it, but my stomach is now filled with anxious knots.

My father has a knack for embarrassing me; sometimes when he does it, he doesn't even realize he's doing it. One time a whole bunch of popular girls came into an FYE and my dad was singing in the middle of the aisle to some One Direction song. They saw me despite me hiding my face behind a Beyoncé CD. I was made fun of for days about my dad's antics.

Don't even get me started on what he used to do to Elijah.

Can I hide under my bed and not come out till I graduate, now?

"No, but I know what teenage boys are like, and I want to make sure he knows what *not* to do with my daughter."

"Max, leave her alone. He's just giving you a hard time, honey." My mom playfully waves off my father. I look at her like she's nuts. She has met the man she's married to, hasn't she? The man that pledged over the years no one would ever be good enough for his baby girl.

"Um, I remember the hard time he gave Elijah and you both have known him since he was little. I know dad put him under the scope because he couldn't look me in the eye for two days after that." I run my hand down my face and know there's no way out of this. "Just please go easy, I like him."

I fear my dad wanting to have some kind of "*keep*

your hands off my daughter or I'll cut them off talk" might deter Hunter's interest in me. It's hard enough to accept that he even wants *me*, so the last thing I want is my dad to scare him off.

Or have it used or spun around to be used against me later.

I hate thinking that this is only some crazy scheme he has with Kara and the rest. I wonder if I should do what they do in the movies; try to win him over and show him how hot I truly am and make him fall madly in love with me.

I need to stop watching 10 Things I Hate About You and Pretty in Pink on repeat. Television and movies really do give you a false sense of reality.

I need to go into this relationship with Hunter, thinking the best. I know there was nothing fake about that hard on he was pushing into me or the way he was kissing me.

"Mom. Can we go shopping this weekend?" I ask her, knowing that she would love to play dress up with her only daughter, something I never enjoyed doing.

I'll beautify myself and make him proud to be seen with me.

'Mission: Brooklyn Turner; from nerd to hottie' is what Riley dubbed our weekend. She's been dying to do this to me since middle school, wanting me to go back to the real me, the person I was before bullies destroyed me.

I vaguely remember that girl. I guess I have missed her. If anything, I'll get the old Brooke back. The girl that had confidence. Maybe, if I'm honest, this is more for me than it is for him. This might just be the push I needed. I am going to college soon, then the working world. I have to stand out because Hunter is right, I have been hiding.

I've been dragged from store to store by my mother and Riley over the last two days. Riley said, "*You need to go in with a bang. Shock value works a lot quicker in getting attention than the gradual small changes. Blow him and everyone else out of the water. Show off what your mother gave you.*"

I also got contacts today. Before, I'd stayed away from them because the thought of sticking something in my eye was a no-no. My eyes would flutter so bad at the incoming contact, I didn't think it was going to be possible. After many—many tries, I got them in, and it's such a relief not to have to wear glasses anymore.

I'm exhausted, but the mission was successful. I'm ready to go to school, proud, and feeling sexy, maybe for the first time ever. Though there's still a voice in the back of my head telling me I'm not good enough.

I've texted Hunter all weekend while he was spending time at his parents' lake house. I refused to tell him what I've been doing because I want to blow him out of the water when he sees me again. Maybe we could reenact what we did on Friday this afternoon. My whole body heats from the memory of his lips and hands all over me and then my mother's embarrassing talk afterward. Hunter had come over to hang out, but instead, we spent the whole time together making out. We were supposed to watch a movie, but the disc never made it into the DVD player. We were so lost in each other, I didn't hear my mother walk into the room, catching us in the act. I was just thankful it wasn't my dad. My mother made him leave soon after and then she proceeded to give me the safe sex talk. I had to remind her that she already gave me this talk when I was with Elijah. She didn't care and wanted to refresh my memory.

"Condoms are a must, Brooke. I'm too young to be a grandmother and a widow because it would kill your father, you getting pregnant so young. And don't give it up because you think you have to. If he doesn't appreciate you, honor you, he isn't worth giving it up to."

As much as I want to trust Hunter and hope that he is *the one* to share that *moment* with, I don't yet. I hate this nagging feeling that maybe not everything is on the up and up, and it's starting to eat me up inside.

Shaking it off, I fluff my red curls one more time and admire myself in the mirror. Today will be a good test to Hunter's resolve. I want him looking at me all day, forgetting about all the bimbos that fawn over him all the time. For him to remember I'm his girl, whether anyone knows it or not.

"Welcome back, Brooke," I mumble to myself. "Go show the world what they've been missing."

CHAPTER THREE

"I want you to know who I am and see that on the inside I'm actually just as scared as you."

Hunter

"Why didn't you invite us out this weekend, Hunter? You always do." Kara pouts as we stand at our lockers waiting for the first bell to ring.

"Because it was meant to be family time." *And because I didn't want to.*

She lets out a deep breath and crosses her arms. "Fine, but next time remember me. It's bad enough that your weekdays are now taken up by the dweeb to study. I don't get why you have to study *every day*."

I steady my temper that's boiling inside of me, so I don't snap at her for calling Brooke a dweeb. I don't understand Kara's problem with her. Actually, I don't understand her problem with half the students in this school, but if I want to keep my 'reputation' I let her think what she wants.

Once I leave for college, I hope I can cut them all out of my life because I won't need them anymore. They all think I'm going to Michigan or Duke or VA Tech to play football. All those schools want me, but football isn't my end goal. I want to do more with my life. I've also applied

33

to Stanford, Harvard, Terry College, and the University of California. My SAT scores are the highest in the school, something I don't think Brooke knows, and my grades are steady A's and B's. However, I can't help but wonder where Brooke is going. I don't know what will happen to us, but I've spent enough time pining over her to hope that it goes further.

"You *have* to be kidding me." Kara snarls, pulling me from my thoughts. I turn my head in the direction of where Kara is looking. When I see who she's looking at, my jaw drops to the floor.

She looks amazing, stunning, *fucking* hot.

Brooke is walking through the hall, her arm linked with Riley's. She's wearing a pair of tight black jeans that accentuate her ass and make her legs look as if they go on for miles, along with a gray cropped sweater that shows off part of her flat stomach. Her amber hair is down, curled, and flows over her chest and back. Her glasses are gone too, and you can see her shiny, honey colored eyes. The eyes that caught my attention in the first place. She was beautiful before, but she's irresistible now. It's the first time I've seen a genuine smile as she walked these halls instead of counting the tiles. I can see she's a little bit nervous about the heads turning to look at her, but she's playing it off well.

"Does she really think dressing like that is going to make people like her, or will make guys think her ugly mug is cute now? She, of all people, knows it doesn't work."

I'm confused about what she means by that, but I don't have the energy to ask her. Knowing Kara, it's something her imagination has worked up.

"She looks good, Kara. Why does it matter to you anyway?" I turn back to her but keep my view of Brooke in the corner of my eye.

"Looks good?" She scoffs. "*Please.* She's probably

doing it for your attention, Hunter."

I know that she is doing it partly for my attention, and boy does she have it. This is the Brooke I've been dying to see.

"So what?" I shrug and slam a book into my locker.

"*So what*?" Kara sneers. "She thinks she can be one of us, and that's something that can *never* happen."

"Or you can just leave her be?"

"Since when do you start standing up for the vermin in this school?" Kara glares and crosses her arms over her chest. "She needs to be put in her place and remember where she belongs."

I shake my head, annoyed, and pinch the bridge of my nose from the oncoming headache she's giving me. "Is it worth the unnecessary drama? She hasn't done anything, so what's the big deal? Plus, right now she's helping me stay on the team. You should be thankful."

"Whatever." Kara slams her locker and storms off down the hall acting like the bitch she is.

Brooke is still standing at her locker and I make my way over there. She freezes when my lips brush her ear. "You look ravishing today, Brooklyn."

Brooke turns around and smiles at me. I notice her eyes dart around the halls before they steady on mine. "Thank you, Hunter."

"I can't wait to run my lips all over you later." I give her a wink and leave her gaping as I turn to walk down the hall.

I spend first period writing a note to Brooke. I want her to know how I feel about her. It's so juvenile, middle school, to hand her a note, but I feel like I need to reassure her that I won't hurt her. The look on her face when she asked me not to hurt her affected me. She doesn't trust me, but I can't blame her, I wouldn't trust me either.

Mr. Hall is driveling on about electron configuration and everyone is taking notes, so I won't look too out of place as I write away. If John or Dan saw me writing this kind of note—to any girl—they would hang me by my balls and call me a pussy. But they would be the last two people next to my brother that I would listen to advice from on women. Sure, they know how to get ass, but none have ever been with a girl longer than a week. They're jackasses, so I had to go to my dad for advice. It was awkward but informative.

He'd said, "If you want to keep a girl, tell her the truth of how you feel. Don't act tough and pretend nothing bothers you. Make her feel special. You don't have to become overly sensitive or even a 'wuss.' But give her some clear insight into what you're thinking, and don't listen to a thing your brother says."

> *Dear Brooklyn,*
> *I can't stop thinking about kissing you, knowing now you're mine.*
> *I know keeping our relationship a secret isn't easy and not something you want, but I like the idea of a bubble. You and me and no one else. It won't be forever, I promise.*
> *Anyways, just know that I'm not going to hurt you. I want to spend every moment trying to make you feel special.*
> *When I first saw you, you took my breath away. You were down to earth, sweet, but hidden.*
> *You were stunning then and today when you walked through the hall, I almost had a heart attack. That girl I saw today is the real you. You used to walk through the halls, with your head down, avoiding looking at people. Today you had your head up and you gave off a light and*

walked proudly through the halls, never hiding once. That's how you should always feel. I want to keep you feeling that way, even if tomorrow you go back to baggy clothes and that gorgeous hair tied back up, I hope that you still hold that head up high.

You're an amazing girl, Brooklyn. I'm glad you're mine.

After school today, I'm going to kiss you so hard, so powerful, your head will spin.
-H

When I arrive at French class, I slip my note onto Brooke's desk. She looks at me curiously before picking up the twice folded paper. I mouth for her to 'open it' as I slip into my seat.

Mr. Marshall is writing on the whiteboard and I keep my eyes on Brooke as she opens the note. I see her cheeks heat up as she reads each line. She turns her head to me and mouths 'thank you.'

She pulls out a sheet of paper and scribbles something on it. Her eyes glint over to me and she has a smile curled on her lips as she folds the paper up into a tiny square. She places it on the corner of her desk as Mr. Marshall starts talking.

I'm dying to know what her reply is, but there's no excuse for either of us to get up without looking obvious. Instead, I watch her as she chews on the edge of her pen and curls her finger around her hair.

"Remember class, next week's test counts for fifteen percent of your grade. Make sure you study so you're ready." Mr. Marshall addresses us all as the bell rings and everyone makes a mad dash to the door.

I walk over to Brooke and take the note off her desk, flipping it open.

"Hey! Who said that was for you?"

"I'm assuming." I shrug and read her note written in her perfect cursive.

> *I'm glad that you're mine too. I look forward to every kiss and every touch. I hope I can make you as happy as you have made me these last few days. Oh, and along with the new clothes, what I'm wearing underneath is new too—tiny and lace. xx B*

A note so simple, yet enough to make my dick twitch. I wonder if she would let me take a peek at what she's wearing under those clothes. I don't want to push her to have sex till she's ready, or till I'm ready. I want it to be perfect for her and not feel like she has to in order to keep me. I want so much more with her and she needs to know it before we get to that point. But would there be anything wrong with maybe just looking?

When I look up, she's already moving out of the classroom, giggling. I shove the note in my back pocket and go after her down the hall. As I walk behind her, I watch her ass sway and wish I could grab it. This afternoon feels like an eternity away because all I want to do his touch her and feel those wet pink lips on me.

Thankfully, there's a deserted part of the hallway under the stairs in D hall I know she's about to pass.

When she turns into the stairwell, I notice there are a few people walking by us. Anyone could catch us with what I'm about to do, but it's not enough to stop me. I grab her arm and she squeals as I push her up against the wall. "Tiny and *lace,* huh?" She's mid-giggle when I crash my lips to hers and kiss her so feverishly, so intently, that afterward, both our lips will be swollen. My erection pokes into her stomach, my hand twists in her hair, and my other hand grabs a handful of her ass.

She wanted my attention and now she has it. The end of the school day is too far away, I want her to myself. Desperately.

I pull myself away from her, we're both breathless, and her eyes are glazed over with lust. She liked my attack. I brush her lips softly with mine and savor the moment. "You're so beautiful, Brooklyn. I want to spend the rest of the afternoon with you on my lap, kissing every inch of your skin that I can."

"But we have a test to study for—" She pants, sinking her teeth into her lower lip.

"We'll be studying French kissing. It should count. It's important for our future."

"Is it now?" I nod. "Very well then. I'll see you at three." She gives me a peck on the cheek and then pushes me out of the way to head to her next class. Now, I need to run to the other side of the school to try and make it to my class on time.

"Hey baby, how much?" I joke as I pull up alongside Brooke and Riley as they walk home.

"I don't know. How much you got?"

"I think I could spare a couple bucks."

"A couple bucks?" She scoffs and flips her hair back, "I'm worth more than that, buddy."

"How about I throw in something extra special for you and maybe give your friend a lift as well?"

Riley leans into Brooke and whispers something in her ear. "Shut up!" Brooke laughs and shoves her shoulder away.

"She'd be happy to go with you. But her friend is going to keep walking the fifteen steps to her house." Riley pushes Brooke to my car, and waves to us as she walks away.

Brooke walks to the other side of my car and gets in, dropping her backpack at her feet. "I would have driven you both home if you waited." After history, I asked if she wanted a ride, but I would be fifteen minutes or so. She turned me down and told me she would see me later.

"It's okay. I can't expect you to be able to do that. People would see and I only live half a mile away." She tells me, looking out the window.

I don't say anything, knowing she's right. That's why I wanted her to wait, but I don't want to admit it out loud.

"You hungry?" I ask, changing the subject. Her head turns from the window and stares at me, her eyebrows knitted together.

"I guess a little."

"Good, I've been wanting chicken. It's a little of a drive, but I know this really good hole in the wall restaurant that makes the best fried chicken. If that's okay with you?"

"Yeah, that's fine. I figure you know the best places for food."

"I do. You won't be disappointed." I grin and head for the highway. It's about a twenty-five-minute drive to the restaurant and it will give us about an hour in the car together round trip. I'm hoping I can get her to open up a bit more than if we were at her place; where I would get distracted thinking about her lips and the tiny slip of lace she might be wearing.

"I'm going to be sorta blunt, Brooklyn, but why the sudden change? Did you only do that for me? Because I don't want you to think you had to."

She sinks her lip into her bottom lip and looks at me. "I did it for me and *maybe* for you too. You did say you liked me better with my hair down and no glasses. Easy fixes." She turns back to stare out the window.

"Well, don't go changing on the inside, okay?" I tease and reach over to take her hand, but she still won't look at me.

"Are you sure you wouldn't want that?" she mumbles and slips her hand out of my hold.

"What? That's the last thing I want. I like you for you. I've told you that. Brooke, I never asked you to change your hair or your clothes." I stop because I guess maybe in a way, I did, but it *isn't* what I wanted. "I would like you even if you were wearing a sack."

She turns her head back to me and crosses her arms over her chest. "But would you have grabbed me in the hall today or wrote me a note if I didn't? Would you still say I was ravishing?".

"Yes!" I say without hesitation. "I told you in my note what I thought about this." You came into school on Riley's arm. You were laughing, looking around without a care in the world. Confident. Sure, my note might have been differently written, maybe I wouldn't have kissed you in D hall because you wouldn't have teased me about what underwear you were wearing. But I would have stopped you to tell you how amazing you are."

I can tell she's studying me—trying to gage me like a human lie detector. We stop at a red light, and I take the moment to kiss her fully on the lips. She grips the back of my neck and pulls me closer, a small moan escaping her mouth. I pull away with a laugh when the car behind us honks. I hit the gas and surge forward.

"Do you believe me?"

"Yeah, it's just all new. You're someone in a hundred years I never thought would talk to me and now we're dating...in a way...and besides Riley, you were the first person to see that I'm more than a nerd, that I'm actually a human with feelings. That I'm more than what is on the outside. But also, I'm trying to understand, even though you see me, I'm still being hidden away."

She's right. "Fuck!" I slam my hand on the steering wheel. I feel her staring at me, but she doesn't say anything as I find a place to pull over. Once the car is in park, I turn to her and notice the uncertainty in her eyes. "Brooke, when I said I didn't want anyone to know, hiding you wasn't my objective." I pause and drop my head, trying to collect the words I want to say because this isn't coming out right.

Because you dip, that is what you wanted. You don't have the guts to be honest with your friends.

"I just know how my friends can be. They've done a lot for me, but I know they're assholes and wouldn't understand. I want to get to know you. As corny as it all sounds, I want to be at a place where we're stronger together and what they say or try to do won't matter. You already don't trust me."

Which is true, stronger together, better together. If we have that, nobody can bring us down.

"That's not—" I place my fingers on her lips to keep her from continuing.

"It's true, Brooke. You're waiting for the moment for this all to be fake. That I'm going to do something to you that will end up hurting you. It's written all over your face. My dad's a lawyer, I've learned to read people. But it's okay. I get it. If it was reversed, I might think the same thing."

And you have no idea that I know all about being a loser and the outcast.

"But you can't grow to trust me, if you have people talking in your ear, trying to put the other person down. Until you can trust me, completely, I think it's better kept to ourselves for now."

"I get it, but why are you friends with people that would want to try to destroy what you have?"

"Because they were there for me when I needed them the most. Let's just say they got me out of a dark place." I sigh and run my hand down my face as I remember a time that was so dark, that I can't bear to live again. I needed to survive and being friends with them is the only way I know how not to be that low again. "I don't know how to explain it. I know they're not perfect, but they're my friends."

"Okay. I can handle what we have for now. Because you're right we should try to get to know each other first. It's nobody's business but our own." She says it like she's still trying to convince herself.

"Can you tell me why you decided to hide in the first place?" I ask wanting to change the subject back to her.

"You mean, you want to know why I became an unpopular nerd?" She narrows her eyes and glares at me.

"No, Brooke…" I want to plead to her that's not what I meant, but then I see her smile. I chuckle, knowing she's trying to make me squirm, and I lean over to kiss her. "Actually, what I really want to know is how you became so perfect and let's say…unique? I don't know how you got the label as a nerd, but I don't think just because your gifted that you should qualify."

"I like to think I'm unique, but I've embraced being a

43

nerd. Listen, how about you keep driving so we can get our chicken and I'll tell you why people like you," she boops me in the nose, "and I, don't usually get along."

"Sounds like a deal." I settle into my seat and pull back onto the road as Brooke begins her little tale.

"Well, a long long time ago, there was a place called Woodbine Elementary. It was a place where I was somewhat normal. This so-called nerd had lots of friends and got along with everyone. Then evil came in, in the form of middle school."

I laugh at her narration, and when I glance over at her, she's giggling too. I'm sure she knows she sounds ridiculous, but I'm just glad to see her smile and more relaxed with me now.

"Anyways, I lost many of my good friends because they ended up at different middle schools. You also add a bunch of new kids and friendships changed. In seventh grade, I got a lot of attention from boys because...I...um...*changed."* Her cheeks flush, and I'm sure it has something to do with the huge rack she has. But I won't say anything. "There was this one girl." Her lip twitches with a snarl at the memory. "She was the little queen bee, the girl that got everything she wanted. She came in, basically sitting on a throne, and had people carry her around."

"So, she was a bitch?"

"Yep. I guess that's the best way to say it. She wanted my friends and the boys that paid attention to me and not her. She started a bunch of rumors about me. Would harass me online along with a bunch of her followers. I would get humiliated in the halls, things stuffed in my locker and backpack. I was called fat, ugly, geek, slut, and so on. I became a laughing stock overnight. The people I thought were my friends no longer were. I had hoped that after the summer it would be over but it wasn't. So instead, I buckled down and started to worry

44

about school and, in an instant, became classified as a nerd because my grades were better than everyone's, and well, they still are." She looks over me gloating, and I let out a small chuckle.

"I knew the only way to win at this point was to one day be better than them. I started wearing bigger clothes to hide, so no one could say anything about trying too hard or being a 'slut.' I didn't care about doing my hair anymore because one time, the "bitch," put gum in it. I didn't want to cut it short, so I cut the piece out and put my hair in a ponytail, so it wouldn't be as noticeable.

"Then in the eighth grade, me and her got into a huge fight because I 'supposedly' stole the new kid from her. I was asked to show him around the school and, well, when he didn't pay her any attention, she blamed me. Granted, he and I never talked again either. She got pissed and tried swinging at me. She missed, and I ended up punching her. I broke her nose and ended up suspended while she walked away without even a slap on the wrist. After that, I learned to avoid her and tried to blend in. I needed to survive."

I nod, knowing all about how it feels to need to survive. "Who was this girl?"

"It doesn't matter," she answers quickly. Too quickly. But I let it go when I see the wall she's putting up again. "That's basically my sad tale. Now you know."

"I'm sorry that happened to you." I pause for a moment and reach over to grab her hand. "Brooke?" I'm not sure how to phrase what I want to say that won't make me more of a jerk that I am.

That I myself am a coward.

"What?"

When I glance into her honey eyes, I realize I can't tell her yet. Maybe I can change, and I won't ever have to, but I fear that I don't know how. "Will you come to my game Friday night? Maybe you and me can sneak away somewhere afterward?"

"I don't know," she says looking down at her feet, and I think she picked up that my question is not what I had intended to say.

"Please?" I stick out my lower lip in a pout. "You have to see the one thing I'm good at."

"Hey, no pouting, you're good at other things besides football." She giggles and pushes my lip back in.

"Like what? Because I know it's not the English language."

"Hmm," she taps her finger against her chin and looks to the roof of the car, pondering. "Kissing?" Her eyes fall back to mine and she bites her lip trying to contain her smile.

"I am huh? Well, we were supposed to be working on our French kissing," I prompt, wiggling my eyebrows.

"Yes, but you decided your stomach was more important." She raises her eyebrow at me. "I have no idea where you put all that food. I've seen what you eat for lunch." She blanches.

"I'm a growing boy. You should see the workouts I have to do. They make you hungry."

Since we're out of Fairview, we don't have to worry about anyone seeing us. We grab our chicken and I find a park where we can sit and eat.

"What are we doing here?" She looks around the quiet park and I lead us to a picnic table under a couple of trees. There's a chill in the air, but overall it isn't too bad. It's better than trying to eat in my car and this way maybe it can feel more like a date.

"Thought we could eat out here in the fresh air." I wave my hand around.

"This is nice. It's so peaceful out here."

"Only the best for my girl." She blushes as red as her hair. I slip in next to her on the bench and put my arm around her. "I'll keep you warm too."

"I think the extra spicy chicken you got can do that." She jokes and lays her head on my shoulder. I press my lips to her hair and inhale the scent of her coconut shampoo.

Reaching into my pocket, I grab my phone, wanting to capture this moment of us and our feast. "Smile, angel."

Once we finish eating, I grab her and sit her on my lap. I waste no time diving my tongue into her mouth and kissing her as if my life depends on it. She's an amazing kisser. Her lips are soft, and she tastes sweet, like cherries. I love the feeling of her fingers scratching my scalp and the way her body molds in my arms. I always knew this girl was made for me. If only I had the guts to ask her sooner or had the guts to give her what she deserves.

We're making out for what feels like forever. My jaw starts to ache, and I might be leaving a handprint on her ass from gripping it so hard. My dick is hard as granite, to the point it hurts, and every time she shifts on my lap, it aches more. I'm sure she can feel it poking her.

I break away, both of us panting and flushed. My hand travels down her leg, wishing I could feel her smooth skin hiding under her pants. "Do I get to see that something tiny and lace?"

Because thinking of that is going make your dick throb any less, Evans?

"I should've known as soon as I wrote that, it would be all you thought about. Boys." She rolls her eyes for extra measure.

"Don't blame me. You teased me, of course, it's all

I've been thinking about." I wiggle my eyebrows at her and run my finger over the button of her jeans. "Just a peek?"

"Umm—" Her arms fall from my shoulders and she wraps her arms around her chest, closing up again.

"What's wrong?" I smooth back her hair, trying to comfort her. She looks troubled and I hope I didn't push too hard. and I don't mean with my dick. She knew I would ask, as she said, I'm a boy. I'm a boy that wants her. "Do you not want to show me?"

"It's not that." She looks down at her lap, but I won't have her hide away from me.

I lift her chin, but she avoids eye contact with me. "Look at me. Please?" She closes her eyes pained and takes a heavy sigh before looking at me again. "Tell me what's up." She needs to be able to tell me things. I know it's only been a couple days, but I need her to know she can talk to me like she did earlier.

"If I do show you, I don't want you to think that I'm ready to do all *that*." She blurts out in one long breath. "I wanted to shock you today and, well, what happened in D hall was proof that I did." A small smile crosses her face. "And, well, what's happening to you now—" She shifts again on my crotch and I still her body, so I don't end up exploding. "I think I know what you're thinking…"

I can't help the laugh that leaves me and I feel her body visibly relax. "I'm not going to make you do anything you don't want to do, Brooke. We've only been together, for what? Five days, kind of, but I think I've shown you that I'm not a complete douchebag. *Buttttt*….it doesn't mean that you don't turn me on, or I don't picture you in your underwear, or…." She shoves me hard in the chest making me stop the list of my daily visuals.

"I get it. I get it." Her eyes twinkle with laughter and mischief. "Fine. A little peek and I hope you know, this is me trying to trust your ass." She smirks and moves off my lap to stand in front of me. She looks around the deserted park then back to me.

She unhooks the button of her jeans and rolls them down. My mouth goes dry as she exposes her hip bones. I adjust my junk, afraid it's going to bust out of my zipper, knowing I'm getting close to the prize.

I gulp when I see a string of neon green on her hips and then the top of the lace triangle, but it's gone in a flash. She's already pulling her pants back up, giggling like a mad woman.

"Hey, that was too quick." I protest and slide off the bench, wanting to beg her for more—to touch her.

"I know, but that's all you get for now." She sticks out her tongue and skips off towards the car.

She's going to end up teasing me to death, I know it. I rush to catch up to her, throwing our trash out along the way.

"You do know, that it wouldn't be any different than seeing you in a bikini, right?" I'm acting like a sulky child, but I don't care, I wanted to see it all.

"Then you better take me swimming." She kisses me on the cheek before moving into the car.

I know there's a double meaning there, but I choose to ignore it. I'm hoping I can get her back home, so I can get more alone time with her before her mom and dad get there.

CHAPTER FOUR

*"I'm starting to see your hidden truths, and I
happen to like them more than the lies you cover
yourself in."*

Brooklyn

My time with Hunter has been amazing. Every day
he writes me little notes, telling me how sexy I am, or how
much he likes me, or about how much he enjoys being
with me. When we're alone, we spend more time making
out than talking. But when we do talk, it comes so easy.
We can spend hours texting when we're not around each
other and not run out of anything to say. I feel like I've
known him forever. I've opened up to him about some of
my past, something I've never done with anyone before.
He's told me a little about his life before he came to this
school, but I sense he's not telling me everything.

I go to his games but end up hiding in the back of the
stands, to avoid being seen by Kara. But even in the back
row, I get a sense of pride watching my boyfriend, number
50, play his favorite game. He also makes the uniform
look *good*.

He never fails to spot me in the crowd and make a
wordless gesture to me, whether it's pretending to toss the
ball to me, or a simple wave; it's his way to let me know

he still sees me, even if I'm still hiding out. The small wordless gestures mean everything to me and might be one of the few things that help keep our undercover relationship going.

Especially when he calls me Angel.

Now, after two weeks of dating, Hunter has been summoned to the dinner table with my parents. I begged my dad to let it wait till we dated for a while and got to know each other more *before* he tore Hunter into tiny pieces.

Riley's been over at my house for the last two hours trying to *doll* me up for tonight. Which means she wants to go through my closet and try on the new clothes I bought last weekend.

"I don't know what you're worried about. Like hasn't he sorta already met your dad?"

"Yeah, but my dad hasn't quizzed him or asked for his left kidney in trade for dating me, yet."

Riley laughs as she steps out of the closet wearing my Kimchi Blue Scarlett Fit flare dress. "God, how did you end up with better clothes than me now? You have to let me borrow this when I go out with Billy next week!" She spins around making the dress flair out.

"Of course, just um…don't *stain* it."

"Have some faith in me, will you? I'll have it dry cleaned if I do." She teases—or at least I hope she's teasing—before taking a couple selfies.

I fluff up my hair and dab a little extra gloss on my lips. I'm hoping after dinner we will be able to run off somewhere, alone, even for a little bit.

"Let me take a picture of you," Riley says as she grabs for my phone. "Now, give me some sexy poses."

"Why?" I shake my head and put my hand out in front of my face. She drops the phone and gives me a stern look that tells me to do as I'm told.

"Because I'm going to send them to your man. That

way he can see how hot you look."

"I do look pretty good, don't I?" I say cheekily, making her roll her eyes. But I do believe it. It might only be an outfit, but it's helping me find this confidence I had no idea I had. I'm wearing a flowy floral skirt with a thin long sleeve peach blouse. I'm dressed for the spring, but Hunter is always telling me how he loves to run his hands over my bare legs, so might as well show them off.

I pose for Riley, making funny faces, pouting, chewing on my finger and so on.

"Maybe you should go into modeling, Brooke, instead of Communication and Creative Writing."

"Maybe I can take it as another minor?" I shake my head and giggle because that's never going to happen. "But I have a feeling I wouldn't make it far in the modeling world. You, on the other hand, my friend, are going to an art school, so maybe you could do the modeling on the side."

She frowns, a deep pout transforming her beautiful face. "You're going to be so far away."

"Only an hour or so. We'll still see each other all the time you know."

"I know, but it's going to be odd. I can't just walk over here anymore." She pauses for a second. "Where's Hunter going?" she asks.

"I think he's still trying to figure that out. Must be nice to have a bunch of schools coming for you, instead of going to them."

"But what about you two?" she pushes and now I see what she's doing.

"I don't know. We've only been together two weeks. Plus, I think he would have to acknowledge publicly that I'm his girlfriend before I think about the future."

"Yeah, I get that. So, how much longer are you going to do this whole 'secret affair?'"

"Maybe two months tops?" I shrug and flop down to

sit on my bed. "I haven't thought much about a timeline. I'm getting to know him and that's what's important. I really do like him, Riley. Is it a big deal that nobody knows?"

Sometimes I go back and forth in my head and wonder if it's a big deal or not. I do like him, but at the same time it eats me up inside that not everyone can know that I'm his.

"Yes and no. I see some of his points, and don't get me wrong, I like the guy, but sometimes I wonder why he doesn't tell everyone. But all that matters to me is if you're happy right now?"

"Yeah, I am. It's just I worry about falling for him and he ends up never wanting to tell. Or it still ends up being some joke. I don't believe that it will. I think he shows me enough that it isn't, but he still hangs out with Kara. And I know that I can't trust her as far as I can throw her."

Riley comes over and slips her arm around my shoulder. "Let's not over think the what if's right now. Go with the flow. But I will add, he does seem sincere, Brooke. He looks at you like you're the only girl on Earth. I know you don't see it, but I do. I've noticed it since the beginning. He's nuts about you. Oh, and next time you come over and watch a movie, I'm going to separate you two, so I can watch it without all the slobber noises."

Hunter and I go over to Riley's house sometimes to hang out and watch movies. It makes the relationship feel somewhat normal when we can share it with someone else. Riley and Hunter get along well, and I'm glad that he accepts my best friend and doesn't act standoffish with her.

"Shut up, we weren't that bad." I wave her off, biting my lip to keep from laughing. "By the way, what movie were we watching again?".

Riley makes a gagging noise as she walks back into

my closet. My phone buzzes and it's a text from Hunter.

Hunter: You look like an angel. I can't wait to see you.

I can't wait to see you either.

Two hours later, I'm giving myself a once-over in the mirror before I head out to the living room. Hunter just left his house and will be here in the next couple of minutes. I pass my dad in the hallway on my way downstairs.

"Dad?"

"Yeah, honey?"

"Promise not to give him too hard of a time? Please? I know he's the first guy I've dated since Elijah, if Elijah really counts, but I like him…" I ramble and twist my hands in front of me.

My dad chuckles and wraps his arm around my shoulder. "I promise. From what I've seen so far, he does seem like a nice guy. But I'm trained to see bullshit. And if I think for one second that he's not good enough for my little girl…well, he's going to know. But according to your mom, he seems to really like you and she thinks he's good for you. I learned a long time ago, never to go against your mother's judgment. Plus, you do know that I tortured Elijah because he was so easy to rile up and I couldn't pass up on it."

"Thank you, daddy." I go to give him a hug, just as

the doorbell rings.

"You better go greet our guest. I'll be down in a second."

I run down the stairs, practically flying to the door. I'm a little nervous about tonight, but I'm more happy to see Hunter than anything.

I open the door and a smiling Hunter greets me. He's wearing a pair of black slacks and a button-down shirt, and his usual untamed hair is pushed back and brushed. In his hands, he's holding two small bouquets of wildflowers. He walks in and his eyes track over my body as I close the door behind him. "Hey."

"Hey, you look gorgeous." He kisses me and hands me one of the bouquets.

I blush as he acts like Prince Charming. "Thank you. Who are the other ones for?"

"They're for your mother."

Damn! He's racking up all the brownie points at the gate.

"Maybe you should've got them for my dad. He's the one you're going to have to butter up," I joke, and he laughs. "Whatever you do don't let him intimidate you. He's harmless. But I'm sure this isn't the first time you've met a girl's parents."

"Actually—"

"Hunter, the boy trying to take my daughter's heart. How are you?" My dad's voice booms into the room. My dad reaches out and shakes his hand.

"I'm good, sir. You?"

"I'm well." My dad studies him for a minute, pausing mid-shake. They both don't say anything, and I watch my dad raise his eyebrow at Hunter. He opens his mouth and closes it again. Hunter stands strong, not losing his eye contact with my father. My dad drops his hand and hums while rubbing his hand under his chin.

"Good grip, good eye contact…so far, so good. Now,

tell me what are your intentions with my daughter?" My dad crosses his arms over his chest, reminding me of Robert De Niro in *Meet the Parents.*

Thankfully, Daddy doesn't work for the CIA.

"I…um…"

"Dad! You promised!"

"I brought you flowers." Hunter holds up the bouquet to my dad, presenting him with a peace offering. I instantly start cracking up. Hunter laughs as well and looks over to me. "You told me to give them to him."

"Then she forgot to tell you it's my wife who likes wildflowers. I'm partial to sunflowers." He grips Hunter's shoulder. "Come, let's sit down. It seems my wife has gone out of her way to make some fancy meal for tonight. Something she found online. Should be interesting."

My dad sits at the left of the table and like the gentleman he is, Hunter pulls out my chair for me across from my dad. Once he tucks me in, he places the flowers he got for my mother next to her plate. My dad smiles and nods his approval as Hunter sits next to me.

I lean over to him to whisper in his ear, "And another point for you." He gives me a playful grin.

Seconds later, my mother comes out of the kitchen carrying three large plates. My dad gets up to help her and they place them down in the center of the table.

My mom went all out tonight.

"Geez, mom did you make enough! What is all this?"

"It's braised short ribs, mashed potatoes, and vegetables. I figured the football player needs the protein and veggies. I have more in the kitchen. Brooke did mention that you…hmm…*what* is it that she said?" She taps her finger on her chin.

"Mom, stop." I shake my head and my cheeks flush.

"Was it that I eat like a pig?" Hunter interjects with a smile.

"That's it." My mom snaps her fingers as she takes

her seat next to my dad. "Nothing wrong with that. Growing boys, that's what they do. My sister's two teenage boys eat her out of house and home. She's thinking about making them get jobs to start paying for their own stuff and putting locks on the cabinets."

"Yeah, my mother used to say stuff like that about my older brother. He never stopped eating," Hunter replies politely to my mother's small talk. He reaches under the table and takes my hand. "This looks really good, Mrs. Turner."

"Well, dig in. I hope you like it. I've never made this before."

My mom sits down and notices the flowers at her seat and then mine. "Thank you, Hunter. These are lovely." I swear she looks like she's about to cry.

"You're welcome, Mrs. Turner."

"You know, those flowers were meant for me, Terri," my dad teases.

Hunter and I choke back our laughter when my mother smacks him playfully in the chest. "Oh, you stop that. Now eat. I'm going to put these in water."

We portion up our meals and start eating. My dad and Hunter easily fall into a comfortable conversation about football and Hunter's last game. I know as they clamor away, that he's won my dad over.

Every once in a while, Hunter will caress my leg or gently brush it with his fingertips. It should make me feel anxious that he's touching me in this way, but it's relaxing. I love the way his little touches make my skin tingle and make me feel cherished.

"Did Brooke tell you she got into Stanford?" My father brags. He's been telling everyone the news as soon as I got word of my full scholarship last week.

I knew I was a shoo-in for Stanford. I didn't have any doubts, but when it came with a full ride, I knew all my hard work had finally paid off.

Hunter looks over at me and squeezes my hand. "She did. I couldn't be happier for her."

"I'm just glad I won't be sending you both to the poor house to be able to send me to college." I had already planned to get loans or financial aid, but now, at least, with this scholarship, I won't be paying back dues until I'm old and gray.

"You know we would have done anything to make sure you go, little one." My dad reminds me like he always does when the conversation of college comes up. "Hunter, what are your plans?"

He tears his gaze away from me and something flashes through his eyes as he addresses my dad. "I've been accepted into a couple places for football." He shrugs. "I would probably choose Duke, but I'm still on the fence about what I want."

"Well, Duke certainly would be able to let you stretch your education."

"Yeah, that's what I'm hoping for." He grins brightly at my dad. But then when he looks back at me, he appears pained. I wonder what that is all about?

"Your parents must be thrilled. Not many kids have colleges chasing after them." My mom gushes with a look of pride.

Yep, mom is aboard the Hunter wagon.

"Yeah, they are. But I'm not sure if it isn't just because they're happy that they're getting me out of the house."

"You have a brother and sister, correct?" my mom asks.

"Yeah, my brother, Aaron, is in college in Miami and my little sister, Heather, is in seventh grade. I think she's the one my mom and dad are going to have to worry about; she's very hyper and very dramatic—she wants to be an actress one day."

Hunter goes on to tell them about how his mom,

Debbie, is a realtor and his father, James, is a lawyer. My mom and dad probe into nearly every detail of his life. Hunter is relaxed as he answers all my parents' questions and doesn't appear annoyed or uncomfortable in the slightest.

He's certainly piling on the brownie points. I'm not sure how much more I could like him at this point.

"This is really good, Mrs. Turner." He dips his fork into his third serving of short ribs.

"Thank you, Hunter. It's so nice to have someone else to come eat with us and share my creations with. We don't get to have many of Brooke's friends join us for dinner…"

I glare over at my mother. *Thanks, Mom. Make me sound more like a loser then I am.*

I know her intentions are harmless in her sudden announcement, but sometimes she forgets her filter.

"It's usually only Riley and Elijah," she continues.

"Who's Elijah?" Hunter turns to me, eyeing me curiously.

"Riley's brother…" I glance down at my lap, not wanting to say more. Of course, leave it to my mother to fill in the blanks for me.

"Yes, he left for the Air Force a few summers ago. Riley and Elijah practically grew up in this house. Brooke even dated Elijah for a short while." She laughs, thinking she told a funny joke. "But when he joined the Air Force, they broke up, but are still good friends."

"Mom!" I hiss, narrowing my eyes at her so they scream for her to hush.

Hunter grabs my hand and squeezes it. I look over at him and give him a weak smile. I'm sure no guy wants to hear about their girlfriend's exes.

"He's coming in to visit in a couple of weeks. I bet you two would hit it off," my mom adds, and I just shake my head wanting to hide.

"I'm sure we will," he tells her sweetly, and he takes my hand again. I'm wary when I glance up at him, and I breathe a sigh of relief when he mouths, 'it's fine.'

The rest of dinner goes off without a hitch, and Hunter and I offer to clean up. We're both in the kitchen and as I put the plates in the dishwasher, Hunter comes from behind me and wraps his arms around my waist, nipping at the side of my neck. I turn my head to look at him and he takes the advantage to kiss me.

"I need to touch you, kiss you. See if you can escape. I mean, it is Saturday." He grins and runs his hand down my face.

"I think I could work something out. But wherever would we go?" I tease, knowing that we aren't going to the movies or bowling.

"You'll see." Hunter unwraps me from his arms and spins me around towards the dining room, giving my ass a pat. I look back at him and he has a wicked gleam in his eyes. "I'll finish in here. Go."

I roll my eyes and walk to the table where my parents are still sitting. My dad has his arm around my mom's shoulder and they're both talking quietly. They're both still so much in love with each other. My mom always has hearts in her eyes when she looks at my dad. That's something I want to have one day. Unconditional love.

My footsteps on the hardwood announce me, and they both pop their heads up to look at me. "What is it, sweetie?"

"Would you guys mind if we went out for a bit tonight?" I give my mom and dad my sweet smile and trust-me-eyes. I usually just have to tell them I'm going out, but I don't know if they had other plans to try and get to know Hunter more.

Who knows where my mom is hiding scrabble to have our pre-Hunter Saturday game night.

"Sure, I doubt you two want to be hanging around

us old fogies all night." My mom chortles. "Be home by curfew."

"Thank you." I give them both a hug and then skip my way back to the kitchen to grab Hunter.

Twenty minutes later we're in Hunter's car driving down a dark back road. I've changed into a pair of jeans and a sweater when Hunter told me where we were going would be outside. I would have frozen to death in my skirt.

"Where are we going?"

"You'll see." He grabs my hand over the console and presses his lips to my knuckles.

We soon arrive at Angler Beach Park. It's not much of a park per se, but it's a grassy area where you can go swimming off the docks in the summer. It's dark with only a few lights illuminating the area. The area isn't closed off, but I do wonder if we are allowed to be out here at night.

We walk out to the end of the dock and hang our feet over the edge. "Are you sure we won't get in trouble out here?"

"Nah. We just can't go screaming. I used to come out here by myself all the time at night to clear my head." He puts his arm around me and pulls me close to him.

I wrap my arms around his waist and settle my head on his chest. "This is nice." The light from the houses twinkle off the water and the cool crisp air smells good as it blows on our faces.

It's peaceful.

Our bubble.

"Stanford, huh?" I purse my lips at his random thought. I told him all about it a couple days ago, so why is he bringing it up now?

"Yeah? What about it?"

He shrugs and moves his hand up and down my arm aimlessly. "I was just thinking about us. We'll be in different states…" His words wander off as he peers up to the clear night sky.

"Oh, I guess it would be one of those things that we have to talk about when it gets closer. It's still a bit away." Is he honestly thinking of our future? I know it's normal to have hopes in any relationship you go into—nobody thinks of failing—but this soon into it? "Do you actually see us going past graduation?"

Going past next week, I muse.

"I do," he simply says and that's enough for me.

A chill runs through me as a large gust of wind blows off the water. Without asking, Hunter shrugs off his letterman jacket and puts it around my shoulders. "Thank you," I tell him as I pull it closed around me. I look up and kiss the line of his jaw. "I thought you needed to touch me and kiss me."

Hunter moves to lift me up and I squeal as he moves me to his lap. One wrong move and I'll go falling into the water. "Don't worry, Angel, I got you." He goes to lay back, pulling me down with him, and kisses me. His cold hands move under his large jacket and my sweater. I shiver at the contact. "I need to keep my hands warm," he murmurs against my lips.

It's not till my knees start to ache from pressing into the wooden boards for so long that I suggest we move to the grassy area. I'm sure his back has to be killing him from most of my weight lying on top of him.

Once laid out on the grass his hands are again on my bare skin and slowly making their way down my pants.

My body tenses, but I don't stop kissing him.

"What's wrong?" he asks, muffled with my lips still pressed to his.

"Nothin'." I'm going to trust it won't move past touching. For one it's too cold to get naked—well, I guess we wouldn't have to get naked, but it's not like I can't tell him no. The way he's squeezing my ass feels amazing. I wish his fingers would just go a little lower. His erection is rubbing in all the right places. Maybe I can do this? It does feel good.

No, it's too soon.

Hunter breaks away from our heated kiss. "Stop overthinking. Trust me, I'm not going to go further than touching you. If you need me to stop, I will, but when we make love…whenever that is…it won't be outside in the cold."

I nod, without saying a word, and kiss him again. We get totally lost and absorbed in each other. It's not till we start hearing other voices around that I push him away.

"Hunter?" The sounds could be in my head, but I'm not taking a chance.

"What?"

"Don't you hear that?"

"Hear what?" He chuckles and leans down to kiss me, but I put my hand on his face to stop his attack. I hear the noise again, and by Hunter's wide-eyed expression, he did too. "Come on, let's go." With lightning speed, he's on his feet and stretching his out hand for me.

We race back to the car, hand in hand, laughing. Once safely back in the car and out of possible trouble, Hunter suggests ice cream, even though we're freezing our asses off. Not wanting the night to end, I agree, and he turns the heat up in the car for me.

I scoop a spoonful of *Chocolate Deviousness* and put it to my lips. I moan, as the chocolate overload hits my taste buds and suck the spoon dry. Out of the corner of my eye, I notice Hunter shift in his seat, eyeing me. "What?"

"Noth—thing." He croaks and shakes his head. "Um, is it good?"

"So good," I moan again, taking another bite. I swear I hear him mutter 'she's gonna end up killing me' under his breath.

He clears his throat and scoops a bite of his *Strawberry and Raspberry Delight.* "So, um, if you could do anything when you grow up, what would it be?" He looks away from me as I take another bite.

"Are we playing twenty questions?" I giggle at his random life question.

"Sure, I want to know everything about you." I hear the sincerity in his voice as he brushes back a fallen strand behind my ear. I nibble at my spoon as I find myself falling for him deeper. He's always genuinely interested and cares about what I have to say and think. It's one of the most important qualities I want in a guy, and Hunter checks that box.

"There's not much you don't know."

"I don't know the answer to what you want to be one day. I have a guess, but…"

"I always had this dream of being a writer. Maybe write books or movies. What about you?"

He shrugs. "I don't know. When I was little I wanted to be a lawyer and follow in my dad's footsteps, but I kind of like the thought of maybe broadcasting or something with computers."

"Not the NFL?"

"Nah, I told ya, football isn't the dream, just the foot in the door and looks good on paper. Now tell me, what's your favorite flower?"

My eyebrows twist at his random question. "That's an odd one."

"Humor me." He smirks, and there's a mischievous glint in his eyes telling me he's up to something.

"I liked the wildflowers you got me, but I think roses. I don't know why though, maybe because each color has a meaning and they're pretty, but they can also be dangerous in a way if you handle them wrong."

"Is that your way of telling me to watch your thorns?"

"Yeah, mess with me, and I might cut ya." I giggle and use my spoon to make a slice motion at my neck.

"Hmm. I'll remember that." He winks and takes another bite of his ice cream. We ask each other some random ass questions as we finish our dessert.

"I kind of want more," I say as I put my bowl down on the center console. When I glance up at Hunter, I find him staring at me. "Why are you looking at me like that?"

"You got a little something right—" he leans into me and his warm breath tickling my lips, "here," he murmurs and licks my cheek from my chin to my nose, leaving a nice wet trail.

"Hunter," I squeal, giggling like crazy, and wipe off my slobbered face.

"I wanted to make sure I got it all." He grins, and as the street light above hits his face he looks so carefree. I don't think I've ever seen him look like this at school or around his friends, so I have a feeling this playfulness and this freedom is reserved for me. I could be wrong, but I'll take it and run with it.

CHAPTER FIVE

*"I might act tough and like everything is alright, but
the thing is, you can't see what's underneath. You
can't see the hurt that lingers from the years of pain
I have suffered. The surface is only just that—an
act—till I figure out how to crumble down the walls
I built around me and find out who I really am."*

Hunter

I'm rushing down the school hall before everyone
comes in this morning. I asked Brooke for her locker code
yesterday and when she handed me the paper with the six
digits, it meant more to me than she could comprehend.
She's starting to trust me, so I know I'm doing something
right despite the secrecy of our relationship. I want to up
my game a bit. She loves my notes, but it doesn't feel like
enough to show her what she means to me.

I get to her locker and slip a single red rose and a note
into her locker. It's not much, but my mom gave me the
idea of doing something small yet meaningful, rather than
trinkets and large gifts. So, I figured since she told me she
loves roses, it was something I could give her every day
to show her I do care.

That this isn't a game.

I hope she knows I'm trying.

With the items safely in place, I make my way to my locker to watch her reaction.

Laughter and murmured conversations echo down the hall as I wait for Brooke to arrive. I try to make myself look busy by opening my binder while I replay last night when I took Brooke to have dinner with my parents and little sister. Brooke was insanely nervous about meeting them, but my mother successfully embarrassed me when she hugged her and gushed, *"So, you're the girl my son can't stop talking about."* As I figured, both my parents loved her and my mom took her aside to talk. I never found out just what they talked about besides the fact my mom sang my praises. Or so Brooke said.

Maybe I should be buying flowers for my mom too.

My hyperactive baby sister, Heather, also adored Brooke and wants to go shopping with her to get fashion tips. Now, it only leaves my brother to meet her, but that asshole would end up embarrassing me more than my mom ever could.

I'm yanked away from my thoughts when I spot Brooke walking down the hall with Riley, looking sexy in a pair of tight jeans and a just as tight long-sleeved shirt. She gives Riley a hug before she skips off toward her locker.

Throwing her red hair over her shoulder, she spins her dial on her lock and then glances over her shoulder at me. Her eyes dart around the hall before blowing me a kiss. I happily return the gesture.

I love how every day she comes a little more out of the shell she was in. I always knew she was in there, the real her, that confidence. I would see it when she was out of school where she could just relax. I hope she knows she didn't have to change anything about herself for me to want her.

Because I've only wanted her since Freshman year.

I watch as she opens her locker and pulls out the rose.

She turns to me and mouths thank you before turning back to read the note.

"Hunt!" John yells slamming his hand on the locker throwing me out of my gawking. "What are you doing man?" He leans against the lockers beside me and looks across the hall where Brooke is throwing her backpack over her shoulder and moving down the hall.

"Nothing. What's up?" I close my binder and shove it in my bookbag.

"Um-hmm. Anyways, we're throwing a party tonight. Kara's uncle is gone again, so bring a bag, I'm getting you shit faced."

"I can't. It's my dad's birthday and I have to go to dinner with my parents."

It's only a half a lie. It is my dad's birthday, but we had just had the dinner yesterday. I would much rather just hang out with Brooke tonight than get drunk with John and the rest.

"Lame. Get out of it."

"I can't, dude. I already promised. Plus, my mom would kill me if I don't go."

"It's never stopped you before, and the old man would understand. Or is it hanging out with that fucking cow all the time making you a fucking wimp?"

"Don't call her that." My voice is deathly low trying to contain the anger bubbling in my veins.

"Oh, this is classic," John hoots and puts his hand over his heart. "You fucking like the bitch."

I slam my fist into the lockers, wishing it was his face for calling Brooke a bitch. "Shut the fuck up, asshole."

"See, you're getting all defensive over her. Are you dipping your dick—"

"No," I growl, ready to punch him out. "I don't get why you guys don't see she's helping me stay on the team? And believe it or not, I need the grades for my scholarship to Duke. Plus, she's not all that bad."

"Kara would love to hear this."

"I've already said it to her and so what? I don't need Kara's permission to be friendly with someone."

"Maybe not, but it's about respecting your friends and Kara hates her more than anyone in this school. We're *your* friends. Not her. We brought your loser ass into our group and made you into one of the stars of this school, remember? And we can kick you out. But trust me, if you want to hang with bottom feeders like Brooke, go ahead. You'll regret it and so will she." He shrugs, looking like a smug bastard.

"Is that a threat?" I squint my eyes, but my own pathetic fear rises over my anger. My past taunts me—a place where I was close to meeting my death because I was nothing. This is why they can't know. They'll stop at nothing to make my life hell, and not just mine, but Brooke's too. Especially Brooke's.

"No. It's just a promise. Anyways, I'll see you later. Maybe you can stop by the party when your done eating cake." He pats me on the shoulder and walks off down the hallway.

I slam my fist into my locker, hard enough to make the metal rattle and alert half the people down the hall to my anger.

And that I can't stand up for myself.

I'm one of the most popular kids in school, yet I can't separate myself from the outcast that got beat up every day before I moved here to get away. I've put on twenty pounds of muscle since then and can bench press my own weight, and yet here's John making me feel thirteen again.

Fucking pathetic.

Stronger

And just when I'm sure this day can't get worse, it does after second period.

> *Angel: Soooooo, Ian asked me out today.*

My hand squeezes my phone so tight as I make my way to third period, I think it might snap. My fingers stab the keyboard in my angry reply.

> **He did what?**

> *Angel: Asked me out.*

> **I got that. What did you say?**

Three little dots mock me then disappear, then reappear mocking me again. What the hell is she typing? My hands are clamming up as I stare at my phone while I stand outside of my class. Everyone is breezing past me to get inside and I'm not sure how I'm going to make it through this class if she doesn't answer me soon.

"You should take your seat, Mr. Evans," Miss Horvat sternly says beside me. I look up and she's eyeballing the phone in my hand.

I tuck it in my pocket and make my way inside with a nod.

I feel out of control thinking someone is going to steal her from me because they would be more than happy to show her off on their arm. I want to yell at her to tell him that she's mine—but she can't.

With my physics book out in front of me, my phone finally buzzes with what I hope is a reply. With Miss Horvat's back to me, I pull it out and open the screen, hiding it behind my book. I sigh in relief when the message reads, NO.

But what took her so damn long to type *that?*

Is that all you said?

Angel: Was I supposed to say something else? I told him no and that was that.

I'm unable to say anymore, not like there's anything else to say.

The next two periods go by in a blur, till I see her in French class. I arrive before her and sit at my desk when she breezes by me to hers. A small piece of paper falls out of her hand and lands right in front of me.

She takes her seat and keeps her eyes trained on me as I open the note.

*Meet me in D Hall
and show me again
why I told him No.
P.S. Thank you for
the rose and your
note, I loved it.*

Oh, Angel, I'll show you.

As Mr. Marshall yammers on, I'm thinking of all the things I want to do to her to show her. But I should stop because it's making things a bit uncomfortable in my pants. I shift in my seat and hone in on my girl. She's biting on the end of her pen as she watches Mr. Marshall write on the whiteboard. I wish I knew what it was about Brooklyn that makes me always lose focus. Maybe it's because I'm wondering how her lips would look around—

"Monsieur Evans, vous vous êtes réveillé là-bas?" *Mr. Evans? You awake over there?* My head snaps into the direction of Mr. Marshall who is narrowing his eyes at me and my classmate's chuckle. Including my pretty redhead who I was busy staring at it."Oui monsieur" *Yes, sir*. I give him my best smile and he shakes his head.

"vous étiez, hein?"*You were, huh?* He snorts because he knows just what I was doing. I don't know how many times he's told me to stop staring at Brooke and to wipe the drool from my chin. Hell, I owe him everything for asking Brooke to help tutor me. "Then you can tell me Quel temps fail il aujord' hui?" *Then you can tell me what's the weather like today?*

"Il fait froid avec une chance de neige." *It's cold with a chance of snow.*

He nods, "Très bien. J'aimerais maintenant que chacun ouvre son manuel à la page vingt." *Very good. Now I would like everyone to open their textbooks to page twenty.*

I tune out the rest of what Mr. Marshall is saying and stare back at my girl. The thirty minutes left of class crawl at a snail's pace. I just want to get out of here and kiss the shit out of Brooke. When the bell rings, I'm out of my seat like the place is on fire.

Brooke sashays in front of me, and I'm hot on her heels as I follow her to our spot in D hall. When the coast is clear I grab her hand and push her against the wall and ravish her lips. I want to show her how I feel and that nothing is going to tear us apart. Not John or Kara. Not even Ian.

She yanks on my hair and tilts her hips, so they push into my crotch which is desperate to break free. "God damn," I murmur against her lips not ready to break free from her.

"Mmmm, I'll say," she breathes and lays one last kiss on my lips before pushing me back.

"Does that prove to you now why you told the douchebag no?"

"Yeah. Your jealous side is kind of cute." She smirks

and draws her finger along my arm.

Glad she feels that way because I might be jealous to the point of insanity.

I close my eyes to reign in my temper before I explode on her for something that is only my fault. Taking a steady breath, I open my eyes again and run my hand down her cheek.

"It doesn't surprise me that other guys want you. You're beautiful. But the thing is, I know your mine and I'm yours. So I trust you to keep turning them down."

"Maybe." She winks and goes to walk away, but I grab her hand and spin her back.

"Maybe?"

"Mmm-hmm. I guess you've just got to trust me. Now go, before you're late." She reaches up on her tippy toes and kisses my cheek. "See you in eighth." I release her hand and let her run off.

I trust her, but that 'maybe' weighs heavier on me than it should. I know what she wants. I want it too. I just want her to trust *me* and for her to love me as I do her. That's when I'll know we can survive together through anything. Because we'll be stronger and united.

But is there anything truly wrong with our bubble and forgetting everyone else?

I'm steps away from my next class when Kara grabs my arm. "What's this I hear about you defending the vermin of this school *again*?" she hisses, and I roll my eyes, shaking her grip off.

"Kara, I'm not in the mood right now to deal with your bitching." I head for the door and she grabs at me again.

"God, Hunter what the fuck is wrong with you?"

"I could ask you the same thing." I bite back to meet her venom and push her off me again. "I don't have time to listen to you whine about whatever I'm sure John told you."

"I don't whine. I'm just saying how it is." She crosses her arms and looks away. When she looks back at me, she fake sniffles and rubs her nose. "We just miss ya, Hunt. You're always with her and now you're skipping the party."

Because she's the only person I want to be with, now, I want to yell at her. I should. Then I wouldn't have to worry about Ian hitting on my girl. Everyone would know she's mine, but for some reason, the words vaporize in my throat.

"I'm not always with her and as for this party I already had shit to do."

"Fine," she resigns, "will you at least skip with us next Friday?"

"I'll think about it."

I move into the classroom and Kara is right behind me as I take my seat. I pull out my binder and a pen wanting to forget about her breathing down my neck. Her desk squeaks as she scoots in closer to me and rests her chin on my shoulder. "I just think lately you're forgetting who you're loyal too."

"I haven't forgotten, Kara," I grit out and stab my pen into my desk.

"I would just hate to lose you for the dumb bitch. Because never in a million years will I be associated with her. I hate her, Hunter."

Who do you not hate?

"I kind of figured, Kara. But I do like her so can you let it go now?"

"No."

I pinch the bridge of my nose and am thankful when Miss V starts class. Kara scoots back from taking up my oxygen. I should spin around and wipe the smug look I'm sure she has on her face.

I'm tempted to do so when my phone buzzes against my leg. When Miss V's back is turned I pull it out and open the screen. There's a message from Kara and there's a picture of a bottle of vodka and pills. I hate that she knows that part of my life because once upon a time I thought I could trust her with the information. She acted as if she gave two shits when I told her, but maybe it was always meant to be a form of attack. I don't say anything and shove the phone in my pocket. I try to pretend it doesn't bother me, but for the hundredth time today, I'm left wondering what the right thing is to do.

I'm met with the smell of sweat and gym socks as I enter the locker room after school. I've spent the last hour beating the heavy bag until my hands were sore and I was about to pass out.

I had hoped hitting the inanimate object would rid me of the built up aggression I have, but it didn't. The thing with John, Kara and then with Ian have been circling my mind. I should just tell everyone I'm with her, but the darkness of my own fear clouds over again and again. I hate myself more with every passing second.

I grab my clothes out of my locker and head for the showers when a couple other guys walk in, hooting and laughing. My head peeks down the hall of lockers to see Ian and one of his buddies.

"You're going out with Brooke on Saturday?"

My ears perk at this information and I move in closer.

"Yeah. I plan to take her to places she's never seen before—if you know what I mean."

"I didn't think that girl was hot till a couple weeks

ago. I never saw that body hiding under those clothes she used to wear."

"Yeah, but have you seen the tits on her? I can't wait to motorboat those babies this weekend."

My blood boils and a surge of heat is sent through me. My nostrils flare and I'm clenching my teeth so damn tight they might crack.

His friend laughs and slaps him on his back. "I don't know. I've heard she's a prude."

"Forget what you heard. Look at her friend Riley, she'll give it up, especially after some beer. Brooke is just waiting to get broken in."

Who the hell does this asshole think he is?

I'm feeling murderous as they flap their mouths about Brooke's friend. My vision is blood red and when Ian's jackass friend leaves, I take the opportunity to make myself known. I might not be able to tell everyone Brooke is mine, but this dickhead is going to know for sure. In a cloud of rage, I approach Ian and shove him against the lockers.

"What the fuck, man?"

"I want you to get one thing straight. Brooke is my girl. You so much as utter her name, look at her, or even try to talk to her, I will pound your face. I should do it now just for the things you were saying about her alone."

"Your girl? Really? Since when do you date girls like Brooke?" His eyes dart around the room. He might be trying to act tough, but he's nervous.

My hand slams against the locker next to his face; he noticeably jumps and his face pales.

"What did I say about you saying her name?" I slam the locker again for added effect. "Next time you do—and in any form that will be your face. Understand?"

He nods, frightened as shit. Which adds to my crap factor because I should be doing this to John's face. The only difference is Ian here is a "bottom feeder" and I know he would do anything to stay out my bad graces. Sure, he *could* tell whoever and my friends *could* find out, but it's a risk I'm willing to take so he doesn't talk anymore drivel about Brooke.

"Good. Now get out of my face."

He nods again and ducks around me to grab his bag, muttering his apology as he leaves.

The second Brooke's front door opens, I grab her by the hips and plant my mouth on hers. Instinctively, she wraps her arms around my neck and we fumble our way back to the couch. I lift her legs and help her fall to the cushions below and crawl over her. My lips reconnect to hers and I push my heavy erection into her center. I admit I'm dying to have her, but now wouldn't be the time in the middle of her family living room.

"Hunter." She pants, the second my lips break from her. But I'm not done, and I nibble on the side of her neck which makes her giggle. "What's gotten into you?"

"You," I mumble into the side of her neck. I really don't know what I would do without her in my life now. "I just don't think I'll ever get enough of you."

My lips find hers again, and visions of losing her run through my mind. The last thing I ever want to do is hurt her, but I do every day by not confessing.

"Tu es si merveilleuse, spéciale et à moi." *You're so wonderful, special, and mine,* I whisper against her mouth.

"Hunter?"

Her nails run down my back and they scrape my skin

through my thin shirt. "We need to stop. My parents are going to be home soon."

I groan, not wanting to get up, but I somehow manage to do it. I flop back on the couch as she fixes herself upright and flattens out her wild hair. "Do you want to go see a movie?"

"Aren't your *friends* throwing some big party tonight?" she spits the words out so bitterly that they feel like a slap to the face.

"Yeah, but I'd rather hang out with you," I tell her honestly and her eyebrows knit together telling me '*yeah, right.*' "It's the truth, Brooke. I already told them I wasn't going."

"Alright," she pauses and hooks her finger in the collar of my shirt, "can I pick the movie?"

"How much of a chick flick are we talking about?"

"There's that Nicolas Spark—" I groan and throw my head back. She giggles and climbs into my lap. "I'm just kidding, what about that new Cumberbatch movie instead?"

"I can work with that."

Erica Marselas

CHAPTER SIX

"Words can be the sharpest of daggers.
They pierce through the heart with the greatest of
ease.
They leave the biggest wound
And fester in your mind on repeat."

Brooklyn

I'm standing at my locker after fifth period Honors English. Hunter is across from me, talking to Kara and Dan. I can feel his eyes bore a hole into the back of me. I casually drop my notebook, bending over, so he'll get a nice view of my ass that he always likes to grope.

There's nothing better than when he attacks me in the hallways to kiss me and his hands work over my body. He never fails to leave me breathless, aroused, and wanting. Every touch and embrace makes me think I'm closer to being ready for us to have sex.

I come back up and open my locker to find another single red rose with a note attached inside. My heart flutters like it did on Friday when he did this the first time. I put it to my nose and squeeze it to my chest, trying to contain my glee before placing it back in my locker. I pull out the note and open it up. The simple words make me feel like a princess.

81

*Talking to you and
seeing you smile, makes
my day.
Without you, I'm
nothing.*

I sneak a glance over Hunter's way and he gives me a wink before turning his attention back to Dan.

Kara swings her head towards me, giving me her usual bitchy stare before turning to Hunter and rubbing her hand along his arm as she says something to him. He shakes his head and I'm grateful when she moves her infected hand away from him. I stare at the rose in my locker and try to remind myself between the hours of 3:30 pm and 9 pm, and on some weekends, he's mine.

I slam my locker shut when I realize how stupid that sounds.

I make my way to the bathroom and examine myself in the mirror as this *new* Brooke. The one who's been hiding for so long. The Brooke I should've been if Kara didn't stomp all over her. I like this girl, and I'm glad to see her back. I comb my fingers through my hair and as much as I like it down, it gets in the way sometimes. I'm digging through my bag for a hair tie when the bathroom door creaks open and a second later Kara appears in the mirror behind me.

"I've been telling you for years, no matter how hard you look in the mirror you can't fix ugly." Her lips twitch into a snarl, matching the tone of her voice.

"What do you want Kara?" I huff, wishing she would just go the hell away.

"I'm just trying to figure what you're doing." She smirks, twirling her hair around her finger.

I spin around to face her, crossing my arms. "I have no idea what you're talking about." I hate that ever since I started tutoring Hunter, I've been on her radar again.

"You really think changing your looks, changes what you really are?"

"No, but I know it makes me hotter than you now. You could never stand that, could you? Must be driving you crazy," I snip, using some of the stored confidence I have to fight back.

It's the main reason I was her number one enemy in middle school. I had all the boys' attention and she didn't. Then her hate expanded from there. Once I made myself invisible, her hate moved onto other people. She would only pick on me on occasion when she was bored. But I guess now I spend time alone with Hunter and that kills her.

If only Hunter would tell her the truth and help kick her down off her high horse.

Her eyes narrow and she snorts. "Hardly. You can't fix pathetic nerd or that pig nose that your mother passed down to you."

I clench my fist to my side and a delightful flashback of when I punched her in eighth grade enters my mind. I also remember how mad my dad was when I ended up suspended for two days and Kara was the one that walked away looking like the victim.

"You do know Hunter is mine now. He's always been mine. And I'm sick of other girls getting in my way, just because he used to fuck everything in a skirt," Kara sneers, pointing her nasty, hateful finger at me, "and I don't appreciate your little mousy ass pining and drooling over him."

"I'm not pining over him." I don't have to pine over him, because I have him.

"Oh, please. I see the looks you give him. Everyone does. We all think it's hilarious. Hunter doesn't say anything because he needs those A's. And you do know if he doesn't get them, the whole school will hate you if he has to sit out."

"Whatever…" I push my way past her and she grabs me by my hair and pulls me back viciously. My scalp hurts from the yank and tears prickle in my eyes from the sudden pain.

"Don't. Whatever. Me. You. Stupid. Bitch." She pushes me to the ground. "Keep your eyes to yourself, don't even try to address him outside your study hours, and we won't have any problems."

"Fine," I grit out, the tears burning in my eyes. I hate myself so much for letting her get to me.

"Awww. Is the baby going to cry?"

I shake my head and she laughs at me. I wish she would just leave me alone.

"It's too bad I forgot my camera. I would like to remember this precious moment we just shared because it brings back old memories. Remember, stay away from him or next time I'll make sure the whole school watches you cry. I'll make it my mission to *destroy* you."

With a flick of her blonde hair, she walks out of the bathroom.

I wash my face off in the sink, wanting to rid my tears.

Why do I let her get to me?

"Enemies are made through words of hate.
A punch or a kick will heal.
But the mind will not let us forget the pain of other
people's words.
Lies start to become the truth when you're not
strong enough to shield your heart."

Stronger

The bell rings and I realize I've spent my entire lunch period in the bathroom. Riley is probably having a fit that I didn't show up. I'll talk to her after school. I need to talk to her anyways since Elijah is coming in to visit tomorrow.

The rest of the day goes by in a blur till I reach last period. I ignore Hunter, even though I feel him looking at me.

I don't believe Kara when she says they're together, but it doesn't mean her words don't sting and watching her always touch him doesn't help the burn.

I'm so lost that I can't hear Mr. Marshall talk, and the year 1850 is going right over my head. All the memories flood back from when Kara made my life hell. I hate that it's all coming back now when I tried so hard to forget, but the memories don't want to leave and are infecting my mind all over again.

"Brooklyn?" My head snaps up at Hunter's voice, and I check my surroundings and notice everyone has left.

When did the bell ring?

"You okay? You seem out of it," he asks, concerned, and I wonder if he actually is. He's good friends with the enemy. He sits back and watches how his friends make other's lives miserable.

"Um. I'm not feeling well. I'm going to have to cancel this afternoon." I gather my books off my desk and throw them into my backpack.

"I can still come over. Nurse you back to health. Shit, I'll even risk getting sick with ya." He smirks and brushes his fingers along my cheek.

"That's okay." I shake my head, making his hand fall. "You can't get sick right now, anyways. You have a game

Friday night, Can't miss that." I rise to my feet and try to give him a reassuring smile to play off my lie.

"I've played with a broken wrist, I can play with a cold. I'll take the risk as long as I get to kiss you." He wiggles his eyebrows and I want to curse at him for being so damn sweet at this moment.

"Better not. I'll see you tomorrow, Hunter." I move around him and head for the door with him hot on my trail. All I have to do is make it to the hallway and I become a plague, causing him to retreat from my presence.

"Did you get my rose?" Hunter grabs my hand, stopping me before I pass the threshold, and spins me around.

"Yeah, it was lovely. Thank you," I whisper, not being able to look him in the eye because I know I will crumble, and I just need to get away from him, away from this situation right now.

"Will you at least call me later?"

"Sure." I free my hand from his grasp and dash into the hall, hearing him call after me one last time.

Hunter: How are you?
You feel any better?

Hunter:
I can bring you over
some soup? Ginger
Ale? Maybe you can
force me to watch
"Sixteen Candles"

> **again while I help you
> recover.**

> **Hunter:
> I know something is
> up beside you being
> sick. You never don't
> answer me. But maybe
> you're sleeping.
> Just...whatever is
> going on, Brooke, I
> want to be there for
> you.**

> **Hunter: Will you call
> me?**

I didn't call him, and I didn't reply to his texts either last night.

Maybe I'm being a bitch, but I hate that he makes me feel like everything and nothing all at the same time.

I need a few days to get my head together. The only way I know how to do that is without Hunter telling me that it doesn't all matter or blinding me with his fiery kisses.

I told Riley everything after school yesterday and she agrees that I need the space. It's not all Hunter's fault his friends are assholes, but he's the one that can stop it. I need to figure out if this is worth all the hurt that comes with being a secret.

Why can't a girl like me just be happy?

Then I remember that I'm an embarrassment. I don't fit in his world. He was right when he said the Kara's of the world would do everything in their power to break us up. She's made it clear that I can't even glance at him without putting a target on my back.

It shouldn't matter what people say, but sadly in high school, it does.

I also don't feel comfortable enough to tell Hunter about what happened with Kara. It's not like he would do anything.

Maybe I should end it? But the thought of not being with him anymore is like a stab to the heart. I think he's sincere in his feelings for me, but I don't think his feelings outweigh his friends. I've been flying high for weeks and now one thing happens and it all comes crashing down around my feet.

I arrive at my locker and there's another rose inside, this time it's pink. I look around the area and with great relief, I don't see him around. I open the note and read it.

I miss seeing you. I miss
talking to you. I miss
kissing you.

I sigh deeply and shove the note into my bookbag. He texted me this morning saying he missed me and hopes that I'm alright since I didn't call him.

I didn't reply again. I know it's bitchy of me, but I'm sure I'll say something I'll regret. Maybe after tomorrow, I'll talk to him, and blame my aloofness on a cold.

That's even if he still wants me after I've avoided him for so long.

By fourth period, I'm not sure how I'm going to react when I see him.

Put on a happy face and run when the bell rings. Repeat again eighth period.

Although, my heart drops even more into the pit of my stomach when I see Hunter and Kara outside of the classroom talking, and she's touching his lower arm. Kara catches a glimpse of me and gives me a smug smile. She then turns her attention back to Hunter, giving him a hug before running off. I admit he looks somewhat annoyed by her affection as he walks into the classroom, but *again* he does nothing to stop it. I'm relieved he didn't notice me, and I duck in behind him.

Due to assigned seating, it makes it impossible to avoid his line of sight and his stare. I swear I have permanent holes in the side of my neck from his ever-persistent gaze.

I give him a smile but focus all my attention on Mr. Marshall and his perfect French accent. I close my eyes and pretend I'm sitting at a café, across from the Eiffel Tower. One day, I'll travel the world.

When the bell rings, I rush out of the classroom like it's on fire. I'm not quick enough though because I can hear Hunter's heavy footsteps behind me, and the smell of his Kenneth Cole body spray. "What's the rush, Brooke?"

"I need to meet with Mr. Fisher before class," I tell him and pick up my pace, but he stays behind me. I breathe him, basking in his scent because I'm realizing how much I miss it and it's only been a day.

"How are you? You haven't called or texted." He sounds genuinely worried, but I can't tell him the truth. He won't care.

"Sorry, I thought I did. I've been distracted…head cold and all..." I let out an awkward chuckle and point to my head like an idiot.

"I can tell," he answers annoyed. "Well, are we on for this afternoon?"

"I can't. I told you a week ago I have plans..." Elijah is coming to town and we're going out after school with Riley.

"Right." Hunter grabs my arm and stops my adventure to fifth period. We're nowhere near the privacy of our usual D hall spot. "What's going on with you?"

I look around the busy hallway and notice nobody is

paying us any mind. "Nothing…I just have a lot on my mind lately."

"Like what? Maybe I can help sort things out for ya…" he says sweetly and my sunken heart flutters from in my stomach.

"I'll be better tomorrow…" I give him a weak smile, hoping I'll have my racing thoughts sorted out by then. But right now, all I want to do is hide. Maybe cry because I don't know what to do.

A shrill laugh echoes from down the hall. Out of the corner of my eye, I see Kara and Emma walking down the hall with their arms linked together.

"I should go. I'd hate for your friends to see you talking to me," I snip, ruder than I intend, but I need to get out of here and I rush down the hall before he can say anymore.

I glance over my shoulder and watch him push his hands through his hair. Our eyes meet for a second and he looks frustrated as hell with me. Frustrated and sexy. His hair is standing on all ends and his brow is creased.

"Hunter…" Kara's voice squeals through the loud hallway.

I roll my eyes. Maybe he can pick up the hint of my irritation and get a clue. But who am I kidding? He wouldn't get a hint if it bit him in the ass. I turn my attention ahead of me as Kara and Emma grab his.

I'm surprised how disappointed I am when I don't see Hunter in eighth. Although, it changes to pissed when I hear that a bunch of seniors had skipped the last two periods.

Whatever.

He probably wouldn't have told me he was skipping, even if I was talking to him. I drop my head into the thick history book, trying not to scream out.

I just don't want to care anymore.

Stronger

After an afternoon of movies, bowling, and the mall with Elijah and Riley, we're having dinner with my mom and dad. I haven't seen Elijah since he graduated from the Academy a year and a half ago. He spent six months over in Iraq and got back a couple weeks ago. I'm so glad he's home and safe, however, I'm still trying to get used to his shaven head. Elijah used to have these long blond curls, now it's more like a q-tip.

Having Elijah around today was a relief. For the first time in a while, I've felt like myself. Relaxed and not feeling like I always have to be on.

"Toss me a roll, Brooke," Elijah asks from across the dinner table. I pick up a potato roll and toss it to him. I aim for his head, hoping to hit him square between the eyes. His hand reaches out capturing it before it hits.

"Ah, your reflexes have improved over the years. A couple of years ago, I would have got you." I laugh.

"I have to be prepared for anything these days. Even flying rolls." He takes a large bite out of the potato roll.

"You're really getting stationed in Germany, Elijah?" my mom asks, with a small pout on her face.

"Yeah, I'll be an aviation ammunition technician. It's pretty easy work so I'll use the spare time to explore…"

The rest of Elijah's sentence is cut off by the doorbell. "Who could that be?" My mom looks down at her watch. "Brooke could you go get it. And if it's a darn solicitor at this hour, I give you permission to tell him where to put whatever he's selling."

"Aww, Mom." I put my hand over my heart, and bat my eyes, "you're giving me the honor. I'm blessed." I giggle when my mom shoos me away with her napkin. I head to the door as the doorbell rings again. I peek out the side window and see Hunter standing there.

I open the door just a crack and stand in the opening. "What are you doing here?"

"I came to see you. We need to talk," he hisses, aggravation written on his face.

"Well, I can't talk right now. We can talk tomorrow."

"Why? Is it because you're sick?" he snarls, making me gulp. I've never seen him angry like this. "You can't be that sick since I saw you happily skip around the mall with Riley and some guy. A guy that had no problem putting his arm around you."

"Will you keep your voice down," I whisper-yell and look back behind me to see if we've gained attention. But I hear my father's boisterous laugh and know they're distracted enough for now. I turn back to him and narrow my eyes. "And if you must know, I was with Riley's brother, Elijah. And I said I was sick yesterday. Today I said I had plans."

"Elijah? Your ex-boyfriend?" His jaw ticks and I nod, holding my ground. How dare he act all jealous when he has his own fan club all over him throughout the day.

But he's jealous, Brooke, like he was with Ian, it's a good sign.

"He's just a friend now, and I've told you that."

"But he's the reason why you blew me off?"

"I didn't blow you off. I told you he was coming to town and I wanted to see my friend who I haven't seen in over a year. If anyone blew anybody off today it was you, when you skipped the end of the day."

"I only skipped because my girlfriend was giving me the cold shoulder and pissing me off."

I snort. "Please. You skipped with your friends. Everyone knows it. Now, I'm sure Kara is waiting for you, so if you don't mind." I go push the door closed and he puts his hand out to stop it.

"What does Kara have to do with this?" he growls.

She has everything to do with this. How does he not know that?

"I was told that you're together. It's hard not to believe. You two are *always* together and she's *always* touching you." I grit out through my grinding teeth.

"Brooke, you know I'm not with her," he says forcefully, and I can see the vein in his neck pulsing. "And I left with them today, but I didn't stay. I went to the mall to buy something for my little sister's birthday, and I saw you with him."

"It doesn't matter. As you can tell, I'm in the middle of dinner. I need you to go." I push his chest trying to get him from holding onto the door, but I might as well try to push a Mack truck.

"So, you are hanging out with him to hurt me because you think I'm with *her?*"

"I'm hanging out with him because he's my friend." I bark. "Now go."

"A friend you have history with." He narrows his eyes and takes my wrist in his hands lifting them off his chest. "He's someone you used to fucking kiss and today you were all over him. I'm not okay with that."

"I guess I could say the same thing about you and Kara." He drops my wrists letting them fall to the side and runs his hands through his unruly mess.

"I've never been with Kara….in *any* way…"

Yeah, like I believe that.

"Brooke?" My dad calls as he walks to the door. "Everything okay?" He looks between us, and I put on a fake winning smile.

"Yeah, Hunter just came to say hi, but he's leaving now."

"Nonsense, let him in, he can join us."

Hunter smirks at me. I close my eyes to steady

93

myself from screaming and open the door wide to let him in. Why, in this moment, does my dad have to get along with my boyfriend? "Thanks, Mr. Turner. Mrs. Turner's cooking always makes my mouth water."

I roll my eyes and walk back to the dining room while Hunter and my dad talk about what's on the menu.

"Hunter, have you met Elijah, Riley's brother?"

"No, I haven't," he says giving his best fake smile.

"Elijah is visiting home this week. The Air Force finally let him have a break," my mom says enthusiastically, glad to have him here again. Elijah and Riley have always been treated like my parents' other children.

Elijah stands to reach out and shake Hunter's hand.

"It's nice to meet you," Hunter says, sweet as honey, but I can see inside he's fuming by the fire in his eyes and the tension in his jaw.

"Same." Elijah nods, giving Hunter a look over. Elijah takes his seat and looks over at me, raising an eyebrow telling me he sees through Hunters charade. I shake my head, trying to tell him not to worry about it.

My mother makes Hunter a place at the table and, of course, it would be right next to me. He's sitting so close to me our shoulders are touching. I want to scoot away, but I would end up sitting on Riley's lap instead.

"You alright?" Riley whispers in my ear, putting her hand on my shoulder.

I turn to look at her, my eyes pleading for help, but I smile for the sake of everyone else around me. "I'm fine."

"Mmm-hmm," she mutters, but thankfully she doesn't push the matter and goes back to eating.

I pick up my fork and push my food around my plate. I'm so angry now that my appetite has vanished. All I wanted was time away from him and here he is playing nice with my parents.

I don't understand where he comes off being pissed

Stronger

I'm hanging out with Elijah. Someone who he knew has been my friend forever.

Does his big head think that nerds can't have male friends or something? Or friends, period?

Hmm...I wonder how hard I have to push my fork into his arm before he starts to bleed.

I'm thrown out of my need to hurt someone when Hunter's hand grabs my knee and squeezes. I look over to him, glaring, but he's too busy talking to my dad to notice. I push his hand away, but it finds its way back, higher up, and now brushing dangerously close to my sex.

I slam my hand on top of his to stop his movements. Hunter turns his attention to me, smirking like a jackass.

Maybe a fork to the eye instead will stop him.

"Stop," I hiss quietly.

He leans over and brushes a lock of my hair behind my ear, his warm breath tickles my neck. "I haven't touched you in two days. I need to feel you. Or am I too much of a distraction in front of your ex-boyfriend?" he seethes, and I twist the fork in my hand, my inner thoughts becoming very tempting.

"Go fill up Kara and leave me alone." I shove his hand off me again. His jaw tightens and I'm thankful he doesn't put his hand back.

"I have an announcement. I wanted you guys to be the first to know because you've been a second family to me," Elijah starts and everyone's eyes dart to him. He's wearing a huge smile on his face that touches his eyes, almost literally. Elijah has always been a happy person, but now he looks ecstatic.

"I met a wonderful girl, Sheri, on base six months ago. We hit it off, and I'm totally head over heels for her. I asked her to marry me and she said yes."

There's a collective sound of gasps and Riley is the first one to jump up to hug him. I'm next, followed by Mom and Dad. Hunter offers his congratulations from across the table.

"That's not all. I know it might be hard for you guys to pull off, but Sheri and I are getting married in Dublin. We want to do it in July before I get stationed in Germany. I want you all to be there. We might be able to work out something with the cost if you can find the time."

"I'm there!" Riley and I blurt out at the same time. We both fall into a fit of giggles and jinx each other.

"Of course, Elijah. We wouldn't miss it for the world," My dad chimes in as my mother starts to cry.

The conversation continues along the lines of Elijah's wedding plans, his new assignment in Germany, and how he met Sheri.

"You didn't tell me how you and Hunter got together, Brooke?" Elijah asks, changing the conversation from himself to me. Now I want to stab *him* with my fork as he digs for information with that cocky grin on his face.

Hunter grabs my hand and smiles over at me. I avoid snarling at him because now that he knows Elijah isn't a problem, he's going to try and kiss my ass.

"She was tutoring me for French and History. I fell for her instantly. We've been together for almost three weeks now, but it feels like longer...in a good way, of course." Hunter gives me a swift kiss on my temple.

"Yep." I agree, putting on my best smile, but all I want to do now is disappear under the table.

I'm thankful when the conversation changes and my dad starts talking about football.

"You're not fooling anyone, Brooke. I think it's time to talk to him," Riley whispers in my ear. I sigh, knowing she's right but that doesn't mean I want to.

Stronger

Dinner gets cleaned up and we all move out to the living room. I'm almost to the couch when Hunter grabs my hand, stopping me from a rerun of *How I Met Your Mother*.

"Can we talk for a minute? Privately."

I sigh and look back over at my family. Riley makes eye contact with me and nods, pointing her head to the back porch. "Fine."

I lead him outside and stand against the rails with my arms crossed. We stare at each other for what feels like an eternity until he speaks. "Why have you been avoiding me?"

"I haven't been avoiding you." I try to make it sound less like a lie, but my voice betrays me.

"Don't lie to me, Brooke. I want the truth. Do you want to break up, is that what's been going on? Because it's not that hard to return a text and let your boyfriend know that you're okay." I can see the hurt swimming in his forest green eyes. He hasn't done anything truly to hurt me. I knew what I was getting into when I said yes to being his girlfriend, but it's just all biting me in the ass at once where I can't deal.

"That's not what I'm trying to say. Not unless it's what you want."

"Of course it's not what I want. I just want you to be able to tell me what's going on."

I look up at the night sky, trying to control my tears from falling. "I've just had a lot on my mind lately. People trying to bring me down, just because I'm me, and sadly their words still affect me. I hate that they do."

"Who was it?" he urges.

"Doesn't matter because it's not like you would do anything. I shouldn't have let them get inside my head anyway."

"Why can't you just say it?"

"Because I don't think you're that dumb, Hunter. You know who."

"Kara? Right?"

"Ding. Ding. Do you want a prize for figuring it out?"

"No, I just want you to trust that you can tell me. I'm your boyfriend." He runs his fingers through his hair. I know it kills him to think I don't trust him. I wish he would understand how hard it is to trust someone completely when you're being hidden away. "Or do you think this is still fake or whatever?"

I don't think he's faking with me anymore, those thoughts left after a couple of days. He's proven himself to me that he likes me and cares for me. He spends most of his free time with me and the way he kisses me is proof enough of his feelings. If it was some joke or bet, I don't think he would be kissing me as passionately as he does. But I'm starting to think he's spineless when it comes to his friends and wonder what kind of magic they hold over him.

"What do you want me to think though? You're friends with them. Then I have to watch Kara always touching you or flirting with you every second of the day, and you do nothing about it."

"That's not true, Brooke. You have no idea what I say to her."

"Obviously not the words, get off," I snap.

His body sags. "I do, or I just shrug her off, especially ever since we've been dating. I didn't used to notice it, but now I do. As for flirting with me, I don't think she does, but that's how she's always been; her normal annoying self, and as I said earlier, I've *never* been with her," he says the last part firmly, and I can see in his eyes he's being honest.

"Fine," I mutter, resolving that I need to believe that, "but I'm supposed to be okay with her pushing herself on you and I can't do anything about it?" My voice raises, my temper flaring again. I knew I wasn't ready to talk to him about all this. In all honesty, I wish I could just ignore it all and make it go away.

"I'll make sure I handle those situations better because I don't want to upset you or hurt you, Brooke."

"Then why not say something about us?"

"Well, tell me this. If I did tell Kara and the rest, and one of them continuously said the same things they said the other day to you or worse, all in an attempt to break us up, would you be able to handle it? At least at this point? You already pushed me away because of it. I happen to know their tactics and I know you do too. They would push and push till one of us busts."

I stay quiet for a minute to think. I know if anyone would harass me every day, or have Kara do what she did yesterday, I would go mad. I would go mad, even if Hunter was on my side; there's only so much a person can take before it becomes too much.

Knowing how Kara, Dan, John, and Emma work, they wouldn't stop until there was nothing left of us. But how strong do we have to be for it not to happen?

I'm so confused.

"I don't know," I scream and throw my hands up in frustration. "I don't know, okay? Sometimes I'm okay with the whole thing then other times I hate it. I can't help but wonder if all of this is worth it?"

"Yes, it's worth it. I want you, Brooke. I don't want anyone to interfere with what we have, because losing you isn't an option for me." He moves to stand in front of me, not touching me, and his eyes plead with me. "This is why

I wanted our bubble. I'm more me when I'm around you than I am with them. You're confident, daring, and yourself without all them around. Even at school, when we have our moments, like in D hall, that's us with no worries. If everyone knew, I know all those moments would be lost because someone would interfere. I promised you this wouldn't be forever. I—" He stops and turns around again, putting his interlaced hands behind his neck and stretches. I can tell he's lost in thought and I stare at him as his back flexes, waiting for him to keep going.

When he finally turns back around to face me, his eyes are full of sorrow. "I don't want you to give up on me. I know my reasons might be selfish and you deserve better than that, better than me, but I can't let you go. I've never felt this way about anyone before." He takes a step toward me and lays his hand on my cheek. "The people that mean the most to us know about us. They're the only ones that matter because they'll be the ones to support us no matter what." He bends down and kisses my lips ever so softly and I about melt at the simple tenderness. "Please just have faith in me, that when the time is right, the world will know. Till then, I'm going to do everything in my power to make sure you're treated the way you deserve."

I smile because he does try to do that already. The roses were a step up from the notes and when we are alone, he does treat me like a princess.

I reach up and grab his face, pressing our lips together. His arms wrap around my waist, yanking me closer to him. His kisses alone can revive any woman from the brink of death, and now it's enough to awaken me to remember what we have. Our kiss deepens, my belly tightens, and I feel the familiar tingles between my legs. If my parents weren't inside right now I would…

Shit! My parents, Riley, Elijah!

My hands meet with Hunter's chest and I shove him

away causing him to go stumbling back. "What?" he laughs, I'm sure seeing the panic on my face.

"Everyone is still inside. I don't think they'll want to see us put on a show."

Hunter's eyes go wide when he turns to the French doors. Everyone is still in the living room, but I have a feeling someone will come looking for us soon.

"I guess that wouldn't be a good thing for your dad to see me *smooching* on you." He grins and puts his arm around my shoulder. We move down the porch away from the large windows and he pulls me down along with him into one of the lawn chairs.

I cuddle into his arms and rest my head back on his shoulder. As I admire the twinkling stars in the sky, I recall his words from moments ago, "When you said everyone important knows about us, does that include your brother?"

"Yeah, I texted him the Friday after you said yes to being my girl. Of course, the man-whore wanted a picture, so I sent one, and he agreed with me that you were fucking hot."

"The Friday after? But I was still geeky looking." My mouth drops open, gaping at the revelation that he showed me off before I found myself again.

"You were and *are* still hot. I told you that. But you know what makes you really hot now versus weeks ago?" I shake my head. "Your confidence. The clothes and stuff are what you *think* you were hiding behind. But it was mainly because you didn't put yourself out there for everyone to see. I told you, I saw the real you the moment I first laid eyes on you, and I was gonna try to do whatever I could to make sure I got to continue seeing it. That week before I asked you out, you were coming more and more out of your shell. And that's why I waited to ask you out because I wanted you to be comfortable with me. But you do know you could come to school Monday in a trash bag, and if you projected every ounce of confidence you have now, nobody would care about the trash bag you were wearing, because they would all see the girl I see; stunningly beautiful, funny, smart, amazing. Do you want me to go on?"

I shake my head and lean over to kiss him. My cheeks are on fire and I think I'm going to float away. That was the most truthful and yet sweetest thing anyone has ever said to me. It makes me realize this whole thing is worth it

I push my hand through his curls and rest my forehead on his. "Thank you."

When I get back inside, Hunter says his goodbyes, stating he needs to get back home. Once he's gone, Elijah corners me in the kitchen. "Everything okay?"

"Yeah, we just needed to talk."

"That's good. At first, I thought he was going to rip my head off when he first saw me, oh and the glares he was shooting, I about burst into flames. I've never seen looks so vicious, not even from our enemies overseas." Elijah chuckles and I shove his shoulder not being able to contain my own laughter.

"I'm glad you find it funny."

"I've had the jealousy bug hit me once in a while. It happens, but as long as you're happy that's all that matters to me."

"I am. Thank you, Elijah." I wrap my arms around his shoulders and hug him tight. We might have had a romance once, but what we had doesn't even come close to what Hunter and I have.

"Despite the glares though, I could see that he's in love with you." Elijah steps out of my embrace and picks up a can of soda.

Did he just say *love*? I highly doubt Hunter is in love with me. It's only been three weeks. I can admit that I'm head over heels for him, but love?

"I think you have lust and love mixed up…it's too soon. We have a lot of things to overcome before that," I babble and twist my hands in my shirt.

Elijah raises his eyebrow and hides his grin behind his soda can to his lips. "If you say so. But I know the look. I've been infected with the look."

"Enough about me. Tell me more about the future Mrs. Matterson."

Elijah smiles brightly at me and his eyes shine talking about his future bride. Is that how Elijah thinks Hunter looks at me?

"I can't wait for your wedding…Dublin, Ireland…" I say dreamily, excited not just for my friend but about seeing the Dublin Castle or maybe even the Blarney Stone.

"Dublin," he says simply and grins. Elijah is quiet for a second and now he has a mischievous twinkle in his eyes. "So, tell me. Am I going to need to add a plus one to your wedding invitation?"

CHAPTER SEVEN

"I might never be the only, but you're the only one I want. You've taken my heart and cherished it, now I want to give you the biggest piece of me—my love."

Brooklyn

"Do you have any plans tomorrow?" Hunter asks, stroking his fingers along my leg. We're in his car in my driveway and just got back from this huge arcade place a few towns over.

"No. My mom and dad are actually going to go visit my grandmother and aunt tomorrow, but I got out of it."

Thank god, because my Aunt Helen drives me mad.

"So, you have the house to yourself?"

I bite my lip and nod. "Do you want to come over after they leave?"

"Is that really a question?" His eyes glimmer wickedly, and I can almost see the visuals he's making in his head of what could happen with us alone all day. With a bed and no adults.

Okay, maybe that's just me and my imagination.

"Nope," I say with a shake of my head. He leans over, placing his hand on my cheek, and I'm finding myself lost in his kiss again.

We've been together for a little over a month now and though I can't say the words out loud, I've fallen in love with him. Hard. I'm not sure the exact moment it happened, but there's something deeper than the heart flutters and floaty feeling when I'm around him telling me it's love. And now I want to take the next step with him and give myself to him. Despite the one major hurdle we have left to jump, it doesn't change the way he makes me feel: cherished, cared for, and wanted. Every day he still brings me a single rose and a note without fail. He also blows off Kara and the others all the time now for me.

Which is, unfortunately, pissing Kara off and like she did a week ago, she confronted me again yesterday.

"I told you to stay away from Hunter, bitch," Kara growls behind me and pushes me into the lockers.

"I am," I lie, and she shoves me into the locker again.

"Don't lie to me, bitch. I saw you in his car yesterday after school."

"So? We're still studying, and you said not during school." Kara's face turns red and looks as if she's about to throw a tantrum. She knows I'm right.

"I'm going to destroy you, vermin. Just wait," she hisses and storms off down the hallway.

"Brooklyn?" Hunter's voice rouses me out of the memory, his mouth still hovering dangerously close to mine.

"Huh?"

"I lost you, angel. Where'd you go?"

I shake my head and push away the thoughts of Kara. "I'm here. Sorry."

"You sure?" I nod, and he goes into kiss me again when my phone alarm rings announcing my curfew. I grab my phone off the console and turn it off.

Stronger

"I should go," I whisper and go to take off his letterman he had wrapped around me after we left the arcade because I was freezing. Hunter grabs the inside of his jacket and closes it around me. "Keep it."

"What?"

"You should keep it. You might get cold again."

"But I've already stolen like two of your hoodies. I can't keep this too. This costs a fortune."

He shrugs and buttons the jacket up, wordlessly telling me not to argue. "I like the way you look wearing my stuff. Plus, you're my girl, you should have it anyways."

My face breaks out in a large smile, and I burst out into little giggles. "This isn't the fifties you know. Are we going steady now too?"

"We're not already?" he gasps, feigning hurt, and then kisses my cheek. "Get inside before you get in trouble."

"In trouble with my parents or in trouble with you?" I purr and chew at my lower lip suggestively.

"Me. Now go. Text me tomorrow when the coast is clear."

With a final goodnight, I get out of his car and rush up to my porch. Once my door is open, I look back towards Hunter who is waving as he backs out of my driveway. Once he disappears down the road, I enter my house, thinking about what tomorrow might bring.

"Good thing your father went to bed early." I jump a million feet in the air with a screech when my mother appears in front of me like a ninja.

"Geez, Mom, did you have to come out of nowhere to scare me?"

She smirks and crosses her arms, "Of course, sweetheart. Have to keep you on your toes. Now, I think me and you need to have another talk…"

"Mom! I don't need a sex talk again."

"I wasn't talking about that. I'm talking about not trying to get your boyfriend killed outside our house by your father. He knows you kiss, but he doesn't need to see it. I don't need to see it. But since you mention the other thing."

"Mom, stop."

"What?"

"You know what."

"Fine. But you do know you can talk to me about anything, right?"

"I do." But not in a million years am I going to talk to her about my sex life. Nope, not happening.

"Good, now are you sure you don't want to join us tomorrow? Your grandmother would love to see you."

"I'm sure."

Very, very sure.

"Alright." She grins and puts her arm around my back. "Nice jacket, by the way. Did he give you his pin too?"

"Huh?" I look at her confused, having no idea what she's talking about. Why would Hunter give me a pin?

"Never mind. Let's get you to bed, sweetheart."

My parents have left, and I've been digging around my closet to find the perfect outfit since the second the front door closed. I want something to scream, I'm ready, but also be okay if he just ripped it off me.

I catch a glimpse of myself in the mirror and the bright, neon green thong I'm wearing, calls out an idea to me. I remember how bad he wanted to see me in it and how hard he got when I teased him. I eye my phone in the corner and I know I *shouldn't* do it.

I *really* shouldn't.

They preach everywhere not to send sexy or nude photos to anyone because you never know who might get their hands on it. But I want to send him a message that I'm ready for sex. I trust that he wouldn't do anything against me with it, and I'll make sure that I don't show my face.

I pick up my phone and snap a hundred different poses. I send the one I like the most, where my hair perfectly covers my breasts, standing forwards in the mirror. *I look good.* I know these will make him drool and want to do unexplainable things to me. I hit send and go finish getting dressed.

It's only a minute later my phone buzzes.

> **Hunter:**
> **Holy hell, baby. You look hot. I think my heart stopped. Is that the tiny lace panties?**

> *That they are. I figured you deserved a better visual of them then the one I gave you last time. ;) Maybe I'll let you see them up close and personal when you get here.*

Before I place my phone back down to finish getting dressed my phone buzzes again

> **Hunter:**
> **I'll be there in five.**

My heart starts racing and I know that this is it. I grab my black silk slip dress and put it on. I picked this up with Riley the other day; there is no way my mother would allow me to have something this sexy hanging in my closet.

It hugs all my curves and the perfect V-neck cut that shows off my cleavage. But hopefully, I won't be wearing it for long.

I rush downstairs to wait for Hunter. But the doorbell rings before I can sit my butt on the couch. I should wait to open the door, so I don't appear eager, but he's already spotted me through the tiny window. I can see his goofy smile from here.

I fling open the door and Hunter comes barreling in. He grabs me by the waist, and his lips capture mine. The door clicks closed and I'm guessing he kicked it with his foot, but all I can think about is his hands moving around my body. His right-hand grabs a handful of my practically bare ass.

I grab the back of his hair and pull him away. His eyes are on fire with passion and desire, heating me to my core. "I want you, Hunter," I breathe.

His eyes shine bright and I don't think I've ever seen him this happy before. You would think I just told a kid we were going to Disney World.

"You sure?" his husky voice asks me and sends a shiver down my spine. I love that even in his state of desperate want, he still checks on me to make sure I'm comfortable

"Yes, more than anything."

Hunter takes a steady breath and kisses my lips ever so softly. "Let's go to your room."

Moments later, we are standing in front of my bed,

his hungry eyes looking me over. I eye the huge bulge in his pants and it makes me smile knowing that I can turn him on this much. He wants it as much as I do. He runs his hand down my cheek, over the swell of my breasts, to the hem of my dress. "You look stunning in this, Brooke. It's a shame it's going to have to go…but I'll finally be able to get up close and personal with those green panties."

I can't help the giggle that escapes my lips. "I think you have earned your full peek."

He reaches for the bottom of my dress and pulls it over my head before throwing it across the room. He stands back and looks me over. I suddenly become shy, but when a deep groan leaves his throat and he bites down on his knuckle, I know he's pleased.

"Fuck, you look better than I ever imagined. Are you sure you're real?" His eyes burn lustfully, as he looks me over. My body reddens under his stare. God, I want him badly.

"I'm pretty sure I am." I walk to him and grab the hem of his t-shirt, "I want to see you now." I say in the best seductive voice I can muster up. He nods, and I lift his t-shirt over his head and throw it in the direction my dress went. I grab the elastic of his basketball shorts and push them down along with his boxers. Once they're around his ankles, he kicks them off the rest of the way, sending them flying, and they land on my desk.

"Holy hell," I gasp at the sight of his erection. I knew he was packing, but *hello mama.* "Impressive, Mr. Evans," I tell him, pulling my eyes away from his dick.

"It's all for you, baby," he smirks and runs his hand down my face. "Brooke—I...um…" He stops and leans over to place kisses along my neck. "You're perfection. I'm glad we waited to share this moment. I know with you...um...it's going to be perfect," he mumbles as if he's embarrassed by his words.

Before I can tell him I feel the same, his hand moves south and grabs at the string on my thong. He starts to pull on it and I'm not sure what he's doing. His head lifts and a low growl leaves his throat, as he continues tugging at the string. "Rip, damn it."

I giggle. "What are you trying to do?"

"Rip your panties off. I've seen it done before…" he looks at me and his lips twist together, "in some movies."

"Movies, huh? Were there a lot of boobs in these movies?" I joke, but I can't help the nagging feeling in the back in my head that he's done this before. *But he sure is fumbling a lot.* I push it aside, knowing that I'm not going to ask at this moment, nor do I care to know.

"Yes, but none were as nice as the pair you have." He wiggles his eyebrows at me. "Now as happy I am to see these panties, I'm dying to get them off you. Can you lay on the bed?"

I nod and move myself to lie down. He crawls on top of me and hooks his fingers in the strings of my underwear before pulling them down my legs. My whole body turns maroon when he places my panties to his nose and inhales. He sniffs them once more before throwing the thong aside.

"Do you have a condom?" I gasp out, feeling my face flush more for asking. I shouldn't feel this flustered over it. I'm lying here naked in front of him for heaven's sake. But this isn't going to happen without one, and I feel stupid for not buying some before I had him come over.

"Yeah, of course." He bends down and grabs his shorts off the floor and digs into the pocket, pulling out the foil wrapper. "I came prepared." He rips it open with his teeth and I watch him roll the latex up his shaft.

He kneels at the end of the bed and looks me over. "You're beautiful. Now just relax, okay? I want to taste every inch of you." It's as if my whole body has been zapped by electricity and it's just his words alone making me tingle. I didn't think that was even possible.

My eyes close, and my head tilts back as I enjoy the feeling of his wet, warm lips, make their way up my legs, between my thighs.

"You smell and taste like cherries. It shouldn't be possible, but it is. It's home. My home." Feather kisses brush along my stomach, across my breasts, up my neck, and across my lips.

His tongue swirls with mine and my fingers curl around the locks of his silky hair. He lifts my legs, and I wrap them around his waist, securing myself and him. I've never wanted anything as bad as I want him.

"Do you trust me, angel?" Hunter breathes, his nose brushing mine. His eyes shine into mine with something that might look like *admiration?*

Could it be? But I'm not able to place it, as he asks me again if I trust him while his lips trace down my cheek to my chin.

"Yes," I whisper back, "please, I want you, Hunter."

"You have no idea how bad I want you, Brooke." My body tenses and my eyes close as he slowly sinks himself into me.

"Gah," I cry out, and I grip the sheets. It hurts and tears prickle in my eyes. I wasn't expecting this. All the air has left my body, making it hard to breathe.

"Relax," he whispers and brushes my hair back, "just look at me." My eyes fly open and I find myself lost in his green forest eyes. It's just us. Just me and him. Our perfect little bubble that no one can pop now.

My chest expands as I take a deep breath and then exhale it out. I do it again, still losing myself in the blaze that has been ignited in his eyes as he sinks more and more into me. There's still a slight sting, but the emotions overrun any kind of pain.

"You feel amazing, Brooke. Are you okay?" His forehead wrinkles with concern.

"Yes, move, please. You feel so good inside me." I flex my hips, wondering if it was possible to have more of him. "Take me, make me all yours."

"Fuck baby, you can't talk like that. I'm going to come before I even start stroking," he groans.

"Sorry," I giggle but he silences me when his lips capture mine once again.

What I feel for him is crazy. I don't know if I could ever explain it, but it's like flying and never wanting my feet to touch the ground again. He starts to move, his tongue stroking mine, and I know for a fact that I'm head over heels for this guy. The way he makes me feel, the way he fills me, I know this is something I never want to stop doing with him.

He rests his forehead on mine and as I look into his eyes, I try to tell him that I love him. His mouth is back to mine and I'm gone again, savoring our movements. Our souls now connected as one and forever bound together.

"Brooke, I don't know how much longer I'm going to be able to hold it," he pants heavily. "I'll make it up to you...I swear..." He tenses, his eyes are closed and his forehead crinkles. And he's never looked sexier than he does in this second.

The way he feels inside of me, his bare skin to mine is the best feeling in the world. My nails scratch his back, my legs tighten around him, he's mine, all mine. I don't want this to end, but at the same time, I want to be the one that makes him so excited that he can't last.

"It's okay. Let it go."

His mouth moves to my neck and he sucks hard, his ass muscles clench under my heels. My nails dig into his firm back wanting to mark him, claim him like he's about to do me. He lets out a strangled noise and his body quivers from his release. "Brooke...Brooke...Brooke..." he says over and over again breathless, staring at me—that look of admiration is there again.

Stronger

We embrace, with him still inside me. He kisses my face all over, making me feel so cherished.

He rolls over and pulls off the condom. Tying it in a knot, he drops it to the floor and then pulls me back into his arms. "That was…" he starts and words trail off. He shakes his head and I'm engulfed in his kiss again. "That was," he whispers, "mind-blowing."

"I know…"

"I'm sorry you didn't…" He frowns and runs his hand down my bare shoulder.

"It's okay. I still enjoyed it. There's always next time." I grin wickedly because I'm hoping next time will be in a couple of hours.

We hold each other, enjoying the bliss of our connection. Sated, happy, us.

"Did you make sure that nobody will be able to see that picture I sent to you today?" I ask nervously biting my bottom lip. I'd hate for those to get around. I trust him, but it's not that hard for anyone to maybe stumble upon them.

"Yeah, I have them saved in the protected part of my phone. It requires a password to unlock and you would have to know how to access it. I promise I won't let anyone see them. My eyes only."

"Protected storage, huh? Do you have—" He puts his hand over my mouth and raises his eyebrow to me. His way of telling me to hush before I start overthinking.

"No. I know what you're thinking and hell no. No one else but you. I swear. The app also protects our text messages. Dan gets nosey and sometimes sends random joke text messages to people. So, there's no way I would let him see your number dating or not."

I nod. "Good." I nuzzle myself into his chest. "So, is there anything else you want to do today?"

He chuckles and lays a kiss into my hair. "I can think of a couple of things. I wouldn't mind taking my time to figure how to do that *something* for you."

"I'd be happy to tutor you. I know just the thing to do."

CHAPTER EIGHT

"The world is a funny place. Question is, are you laughing? And if you are, can you teach me how."

Brooklyn

I'm still floating from the euphoric high from my weekend with Hunter. Then this morning, when I didn't think I could get any higher, he gave me a hug and a kiss on my cheek, in front of everyone instead of pushing me into an abandoned corner. Okay, it was only three others, but it was still something.

Now, I'm the sun and no gloomy clouds are going to cover my glow. I'm practically spitting out rainbows and unicorns from the happiness I'm projecting. Soon the animals will start to surround me and talk to me because I feel like *Cinderella* when her Prince found her, and the wicked ones were served their justice.

Speaking of the wicked ones, here come Kara and Emma alongside John, Dan, and my man. They're all talking and laughing as they command the hallway, and everyone splits like the red sea. I hate every one of them, besides Hunter. He's so different from them and doesn't know how much better of a person he would be without them.

117

I take a steady breath and approach the group, wanting to put my arms around Hunter. I smile brightly at Hunter and am saddened when I only get a half smile in return.

"Hey, Hunter," I blush when my voice squeaks. I don't know where the nerves came from suddenly, but I can feel my veins pulse.

This man was inside you yesterday Brooke, and you're acting shy now?

"Get lost, loser," Kara sneers at me. "Your breathing the good air, now scatter."

"Kara stop," Hunter starts but is cut off by Kara's glare.

"What?" she snaps and turns her evil snarl back to me. "Just because you tutor him, doesn't mean you get to talk to him...or us. I've told you this before vermin, now beat it."

"No. I can talk to Hunter all I want. Right, Hunter?" I look over at him, wondering why he's allowing this to still happen.

"Brooke...I'll talk to you later...please, I promise," he presses, begging with his eyes for me to leave, and my warm heart freezes.

He doesn't need to announce to everyone we're dating, but hell, he could at least acknowledge me like I'm human, a friend, anything. It would be a start and a sign that he is going to make us more than some secret love affair. Hell, I thought the kiss in the hall was a clear sign we were ready.

"See...he doesn't want to talk to you. It's bad enough he has to even talk to you in the first place," Emma pipes in while the guys laugh behind them.

"And hang out at her place that smells like a barn. I mean that's what you said, right man?" John nudges Hunter, with a devious smirk on his face.

I take a step back. I can't believe he would talk about

me behind my back like that. After everything we shared, he would go back to his friends and spend the time insulting me. I was always nothing to him, the butt of his jokes it seems. There's no way I'm going down without a fight. I think I hear him tell John to shut up, along with something else, but it's muffled, all I can hear is the sound of my blood pumping.

"Really?" I say shocked and with a snort. "A barn? That's not what you told me. I thought it smelled good, like *cherries,* and home," I mutter sarcastically. Remembering what he told me last night and all the times he told me I tasted like cherries.

"Brooke... I didn't…" Hunter begs, running his hands down his face. "Let me handle..." The rest of what he is saying is cut off by his friends who are whooping obnoxiously, and making pig sounds beside him, and going on about cherries.

Fine, if this is how he wants to play. I will be happy to tell everything. At this point, I have nothing to lose. My dignity already took a long walk off a short pier.

"I guess he forgot to tell you guys that we're dating. He comes to my house, kisses me, touches me. Tells me how much I mean to him." I cross my arms over my chest and they all break out laughing. I look at Hunter in his eyes and make sure I try to convey that he just took everything we had together and threw it down the drain.

"Shit. That's the funniest thing I've ever heard. He would never go with the likes of you when he can have perfection like me, right babe?" Kara says sweetly.

Hunter closes his eyes as if he's pained but still doesn't say anything.

How stupid was I thinking that once we had sex everything would change? That maybe he would be proud of me and stop thinking about what his friends thought.

"You're right." I give a fake brave smile not letting them break me. "There's no way I would want to associate myself with someone whose IQ is only going to lead them to scrubbing toilets for the rest of their lives. Good luck with your history, French, *and* English exams. It would be smart to figure out the difference between a verb and an adjective, Hunter. Maybe Barbie here can get you that B you need to keep playing next week, but I fear she's dumber than you, and might be riddled in STDs, so enjoy the sidelines." Kara's mouth drops open and Hunter gapes at me, wordlessly, and lost. I smirk at the pair before I turn and walk away, feeling satisfied, but at the same time devastated.

Vaguely I hear Hunter calling my name from behind me, but I ignore him and quickly find a place that I can safely break down, now that the adrenaline is gone.

After my breakdown in the bathroom, I wipe away my tears and decide I can't let him win. I've spent too many years of my life letting people walk all over me, being used for others' sick games to boost their self-esteem.

I thought Hunter was different. I didn't think if he saw or heard the things they do to me, he would just stand there. How wrong was I? As soon as he told me that we shouldn't tell anyone, I should have stopped it. But I wanted him. I had my blinders on, I convinced myself that our secret wasn't a big deal. The love that was warming my heart and making me feel like I could walk on air, evaporates. My heart is now a hot, boiling pit in my stomach, and my veins are like a raging river in hell as anger consumes my body.

I won't let him break me. In five months, I'll be out of this small corner of hell, go to college, where I'll make something of myself. Hunter will spend his life drowning and I refuse to give him a life jacket.

I skip the rest of my classes knowing if I see his face I might go ninja on him and chop him into little pieces. When I get home, I try to come up with a plan to get even with Hunter. I think of all the pictures he's taken with me on my phone. My proof that we were more. I could plaster the pictures everywhere; however, I know he would come up with some lie to say I photoshopped them.

My phone buzzes in my pocket as I dig deeper into my mind for a plan. My temper rises when I see a text from him.

> **Hunter: Where are you? You never skip class and we really need to talk. I shouldn't have let that happen…I fixed it…I promise…I'm sorry!**

I should ignore it, but my mind has been taken over by my rage, causing my rationale to leave the building, along with the rainbows and unicorns of love.

> *There's nothing to talk about. You've made it pretty clear where I stand with you. I won't bother you anymore just like you won't bother with me anymore. Also, sometimes nerds skip class too. I'm smart enough to not fall behind like someone else I know.*

His reply is instant and it only serves to make me angrier.

> **Hunter: Brooke, don't be like this. This isn't you. I'll come to you if you tell me where you went. We need to talk and I need to explain. It's not what you think...**

I roll my eyes. My hands are shaking from the adrenaline of my fury. His three text dots are dancing on the screen, as he types away on the other end, but I don't give him a chance to say more and send my final f-you before turning off my phone.

> *This is me. This is what you turned me into with your games. Go to hell, Hunter.*

I shove it in my pocket and head down the hallway. I usually hate when nobody else is home with me, but today I'm grateful for the silence. When I get to my room, I spot Hunter's letterman jacket on my bed. The jacket he let me keep after he *used* me, letting me believe we were something more.

Asshole.

I pick it up disgusted and take it to the kitchen to find what I need to destroy his prized jacket. The scissors I have won't cut through the thick fabric, but a carving knife will.

I figure I'll give his jacket back to him with some minor adjustments.

Nothing worse than a woman scorned.

My heart hurts, my soul aches, as my anger spurs on

my cutting. It's like I'm having an out of body experience. I've never felt so out of control before. Shit, I've never felt this angry before. Even all the shit Kara has thrown at me over the years, didn't make me feel like this. Maybe because she was always a bitch, she never tried to act like she wasn't.

All he had to do was defend me, call me his friend, but instead, he left me to be humiliated in front of everyone. I was his tutor for pity's sake. Why would it be so wrong that we became good friends? But nope, to Hunter Evans, I'm an embarrassment. Not special enough for him to stand up to his friends and claim me as something much more in his life.

We made love yesterday, or maybe I should call it as it was, fucking. All the perfect moments were all destroyed in an instant. I thought they meant something to him. That *I* meant something to him. Maybe I shouldn't have assumed things had changed, that I wouldn't be kept in the shadows. I should've have asked him and told him to stop. Should've, would've, could've. No matter what, he should have stood up for me, instead he let them insult me for their own amusement.

The knife starts another slash through the thick fabric. All my sensibility is thrown out the window. This isn't me. But the pain takes over. Hot, angry, tears, roll down my face, as I replay today's moments over and over again. Why couldn't I be more to him? Mean more to him than his brainless friends?

An hour later I put the altered jacket in a box and take a stroll to the brainless jock's house.

CHAPTER NINE

*"Life can be like jumping out of a plane.
You're flying high above the clouds, soaring
through the air free as the birds. Not a care in the
world, living life to the fullest. Then the next thing
you know, you forgot the parachute…
And it all comes crashing down."*

Brooklyn

I stand outside the gate that leads to Hunter's family palace remembering that time last year I came here because Riley forced me to go to "the party of the year." We were soon spotted by Kara and Emma and booted out of the house. They made sure everyone witnessed the two nerds being kicked out. John and Dan threw cups at us upon our exit as Hunter just watched.

He wasn't laughing or participating in our embarrassment, but he did nothing to stop it.

He never does anything to stop it.

Stealing a breath, I push open the gate and take the path to the front door. Hunter should still be at school, so I have attached a simple note addressing him about the return of his jacket on the box. I drop it on the porch and am about to make my getaway when the door flies open.

Hunter stands in the doorway, staring at me, emotionless.

"What are you doing?" He glances down at the box and back at me.

"Returning your jacket," I say simply, crossing my arms over my chest.

I should turn and leave, but I want to have the sick thrill of seeing his face when he sees what I did to his priceless letterman.

Hunter grabs the box and opens it. Once he sees the torn fabric, he closes his eyes tight and drops the box down to the ground shaking his head.

When he opens his eyes again there's a fire that ignites in his green orbs. "Why?" his tone is eerily soft and it doesn't match the anger in his eyes.

"It's what you did to me. Now we're even." My head cocks to the side, trying to muster up all the sass I can, but I feel my resolve and strength weaken under his intense stare. He needs to know what he did to me and he can't walk away without any scratches on his heart. Though my broken heart can never be replaced like his precious jacket.

Hunter and I stare at each other. Neither of us says a word, our eyes portraying everything that needs to be said. The longer I look at him, it makes me hate how good looking this bastard is and reminds me for a moment suspended in time, he was mine. I can't stay here any longer, my adrenaline is waning. I know the coward in me will return, folding at his feet, due to the flames his eyes are shooting at me.

I turn on my heel but don't make it far when his large hand wraps around my elbow, pulling me back. "Where the hell do you think you're going?" he seethes.

"Leaving, asshole." I bite back and try to free myself from his hold. It's no use. He yanks me back again and, in a flash, I'm being picked up, flipped around, and tossed over his shoulder.

"You're not going anywhere till we talk." Hunter marches into the house while I kick and hit his back and ass.

"Put me down, you gorilla!"

"No." He slaps me on my ass, hard, causing vibrations to run up my spine. "Keep fighting and I'll do that again."

I don't heed his warning and keep flailing around. "Put me down, you stupid jock." His hand gives me another powerful slap on the ass.

"Mother fucker. Stop that!" I scream, but he's not listening to me as he climbs the stairs. What the hell is he going to do to me? I think of all the possible scenarios of what could happen and no matter how much I detest him, I know he wouldn't harm me.

But do I know him at all? I did just destroy something that meant something to him.

He places me back on the ground and pushes me with his chest into the wall. His lips crash to mine without warning and he grabs my right breast and left ass cheek hard. I push my hands to his chest, trying to push him away, but my lips are busy using a different brain function, and I'm kissing him back.

Traitor.

His erection pokes me in the belly and that's when all the circuits start working together. I catch his lip between my teeth and bite, a metallic taste runs down my tongue.

"Fuck, Brooke. What the hell?" he snaps, his hand freeing my breast and touches his bleeding lip. I shove his chest hard with both my hands and it causes him to stumble back and lose the grip on my ass.

"What the hell? What gives you the right to practically kidnap me. Leave me alone. We're through, not that we were ever really something." I turn trying to find my way out of my prison, but it only takes him a second to capture me again and pin me back to the wall.

His right-hand holds my wrist above my head, his left gripping my hip, as he pushes his whole body weight against me.

"Stop fighting me," he grits out, "and listen, you stubborn, stubborn girl….I told..."

"Lalalalalalalala..." I sing at the top of my lungs, cutting him off. I don't care what he has to say, it's all too late.

"Brooke! Stop!" he yells over my mindless singing and I stop, and glare. Fuck him.

"No. I hate you! I trusted you! I let you have my heart and you stomped all over it. I hope you rot." I spit, still trying to free my body from his hold.

"Well, I LOVE YOU!" he hollers and takes a steady breath. "I love you, Brooke."

"HA! Love? You son of a bitch. You'd have no idea what love is even if Cupid shot his arrow in your ass. Now, get off me!" I scream, wiggling like crazy.

"I'm not letting you go till you calm down and we talk. Maybe I need to tie you up, so you will listen."

"Well, then you better tell your parents I'm moving in because I'm never going to listen. You already proved to me repeatedly what kind of person you are. You're a creep."

"And you're being a bitch," he growls, his lips pressing to mine again, my traitor lips are back kissing him with equal determination. My whole body is turning against me as it ignites and sparks tingles everywhere.

Hunter frees my hands and they drop to my side. I'm at a battle of wills of wanting to push him away or let him do whatever he wants to me. I decide to fight and push against his chest, but he doesn't budge at my fruitless efforts.

"Tut tut tut..." he mutters into my mouth, stopping my efforts. He wraps my ponytail around his wrist, pulling me away from his lips, and holding me so I can't move my head. "I told them all how I felt about you. That I'm in love with you. And I told them to fuck off, put them in their place like I should've done years ago, and simply put, I'm no longer friends with them. I should have never let today happen. I hate myself more than you know for letting it happen, and if I could go back and fix it I would," he tells me firmly and I roll my eyes.

"A little too late for that." I shove his chest, and tears burn in the corner of my eyes, remembering how much today hurt and how it sliced open my heart. "You should've said something when I was standing there. You talked shit behind my back. How fucking could you?"

"I never said anything bad about you. Hell, I've even told them I liked you plenty of times, but they didn't care. You know I don't talk shit behind people's backs. I know you know that. Brooke, I wouldn't do that to you," he says with deep conviction, and his eyes plead with me, but I don't care. I just don't care.

"Then you could've told them we were friends, anything, but you didn't. You threw us away. Now, leave me alone."

"No. I'm never letting you go. I. Love. You." His voice is strangled and he closes his eyes as if he were in pain. I move to shove him again and he tugs on my ponytail, stopping me. "And didn't I tell you I like you better with your hair down," he says changing the subject, and all I want to do is scream.

"Bite me!"

He mischievously grins at me before biting the base of my neck.

"Mother fucker, you bit me…" I growl and start hitting his chest again, "Agh, why won't you leave me alone?"

"I said I love you and I told them to fuck off and you haven't heard a word of it." He pushes away from me and

I'm now free from his hold, but my feet are glued to the spot.

"I told you I didn't want to hear what you had to say. I don't care if you announced it to the world that we were together. You should've done it a month ago when you kissed me the first time, but I allowed you to walk all over me. You had your cake and ate it too while I followed you like a lost puppy eating your crumbs. I want nothing to do with you because I refuse to be treated like shit so you can sit on some high school throne of popularity."

The sting of my words lace through his eyes; he opens his mouth and closes it again. He shakes off whatever he was about to say, and the sting turns scorching hot, wild, and dark. My breath hitches at the sight. It's the way he looked at me yesterday when he first saw me naked. Fuck, I'm in trouble.

"You might be saying all that, but seconds ago your body was telling me a totally different story. You want me just as much as I want you." He stalks back over to me and I start inching towards the door.

"That's called hormones. They don't listen to my brain." I reach the door handle and I try to open it, but I'm struggling unable to get the knob to turn. I'm pathetic, I can't even escape correctly.

"That's because you're supposed to be listening to your heart." He grabs my hand and places it over his heart. "I'm human and I'm weak. I know I messed up big time, Brooke."

I'm not going to listen to my heart, that's what got me in this trouble in the first place.

I scoff, "You sure did."

"I'm sorry." His voice cracks and there's a chink in the armor of this macho man, who's trying to cure what he did with kisses and hypnotize me with his dick. "I never wanted to hurt you. It was the last thing I ever wanted to do to you."

"I told you it was too late for sorry."

"I don't believe that. If you didn't want me, you would already be bolting out that door. You had countless times you could've, but you didn't."

"You held me against my will." I raise my eyebrow at him and glance down at our still conjoined hands. He lets go, and I don't move.

"You're still not running…" He pushes himself into me once again.

Why am I not running?

Right, teenage hormones…

"You destroyed my jacket…" He runs his finger along the buttons of my blouse. I'm pretty much a goner at the point. My body now has totally betrayed my brain.

"You had it coming. At least it wasn't your car."

He grins and shakes his head, undoing the top button of my blouse. My heart is racing trying to figure out his next move. His eyes are dancing lustfully, but there are storm clouds behind them too, plotting and planning his revenge.

"I told you I love you and you gave me sass." I shrug, not wanting to believe his declaration. He undoes another button of my blouse. His smile turns smug before his lips are on the side of my neck. "The heat coming off your body is anything but hate, Brooke. Tell me the truth, that you love me back."

"Never."

"Never?" Hunter rests his forehead on mine, his smugness striking me down like lighting; it's one of his many looks I can't resist. "Maybe I need to show you again, like yesterday, when you were yelling my name as you came."

My body is screaming, yes please, and my sex is throbbing in need. I want to hate him, tell him to fuck off, but he's taken over my soul. I hate that I still have all these feelings for him. But did I really expect them to just disappear? Maybe I can use this moment as a last fuck for the road? Who knows when I'll ever get laid again because it'll be forever before I open my heart again.

"Don't flatter yourself...it wasn't all that…" I roll my eyes and grateful that my smartassness seems to be awake.

"Oh really?" he slams his lips to mine, pushing me hard into the door causing it to flex with the force.

Our teeth are clashing, tongues dancing. This kiss is filled with irrational need and want. My hands tug on his hair, pulling him closer to me. I savor the way his mouth tastes. I want to believe for just a second that he does love me. That this kiss is telling me everything I need to hear. I want him, but I want to hate him too.

"You still hate me?" he mumbles against my lips.

"Yes," I purr, now pissed at myself for not conveying my hatred, but my lust.

He chuckles. "Is that right?" Hunter's hands grab my blouse, and in a nanosecond, he rips it open, sending buttons flying.

"What the hell, Hunter?" I glance down at the destruction he just caused.

I liked that blouse and it wasn't cheap.

"Now we're even for the jacket…" he snarls, as he pushes the torn fabric off my shoulders, and feasts at my cleavage. His hand wraps around me and unhooks the snaps of my bra, and he sends it soaring across the room. Before I can protest, he's picking me up in his arms and tossing me to his bed.

"Still hate me now?" he says cheekily, pulling his shirt over his head.

"Yep and you're still an asshole." I shrug, propping myself on my elbows so I can watch him better as he takes off his pants and boxers.

His dick springs to life and I can't control the urge to lick my lips. It's like *that* because of me and it's something

I can feel proud about.

"I might be an asshole..." He crawls onto the bed and grabs the hem of my jeans. He pulls them down along with my panties, repeating the act he did yesterday, "but your scent is telling me how much you want me."

"That has nothing to do with how I feel about you. Girls sleep with assholes all the time."

"You might be right." His warm wet lips trail up my stomach, to my breasts, before he hovers over my lips.

"But this asshole loves you and this asshole is sorry for everything." His eyes beg me to believe him.

A hard lump forms in my throat and I try to swallow it down. He keeps saying he loves me and it's something I've been dying for him to say, but I can't process it. I can't give him that piece of me yet, even though there's still a piece of me that's telling me not to deny it. But I'm wound up tight, and since I already gave him my virginity, he can scratch this sudden itch I have now.

"Stop trying to romance me and fuck me already," I snarl.

"Fuck? Fuck..." he says the word testing it out. "I'd much rather make love to you, Brooke."

I groan frustrated. "Fine if that's how you want to play..." I push his shoulders in an attempt to push him over. I'm thankful when he flips himself on his back. I straddle his hips and he's wearing an arrogant smile. Which only makes my frustration and my anger rise, but at the same time, makes me twice as horny as I was before. Damn this man.

Maybe when I'm done with him I could smother him with a pillow.

I slowly sink myself on top of him. I hiss as I expand around him, still sore from yesterday. It feels so good to have him inside of me again. This is what I needed.

"Fuck, Angel," he groans, "you're so tight."

I splay my hands on his chest, to hold me up, as I

start to bounce. Hunter reaches for my breasts and I smack him away. "No!".

"What do you mean no?" He reaches up again, and I push him away.

"You don't get to touch me. I'm going to use you like you did me," I growl and roll my hips wanting to feel every inch of him.

"I didn't use you, Brooke!" he yells and grabs my hips, stilling me. "I fucked up. I fucked up majorly. Why can't you see that I'm sorry?"

"Because you're spineless, an asshole, and you hurt me!" I yell back and kick myself for letting the tears fall down my cheek.

I just want sex and then to leave. Is that so hard?

Hunter wraps his arms around me and pulls me down to him. Holding me tight to his body. "Yes, I'm all of those things and I never meant to hurt you." His lips brush my cheeks, kissing the fallen tears away. "Please, don't cry."

"Stop." I push on his chest, not wanting his affection because I'm going to lose it more and I just want the final goodbye. "Just stop."

"What do you want from me, Brooke?" he pleads, and I grit my teeth, my temper flared because he knows what I want.

"I just want you to shut up and fuck me. If you can't do that...I'll go somewhere else." I snarl, and his eyes darken. He's angry and maybe even hurt. But I don't care. He shakes his head and looks away from me. I try to move, but I'm still in his death grip.

"Is that what you really want?" he fumes, his eyes still not meeting mine.

"Yes…" I hiss through my teeth and try to wiggle my hips.

Hunter rolls me over and pushes me into the mattress. Our connection doesn't break. His nose touches mine, and his eyes bore into my me. His anger is gone and now he looks *pitiful*. "You're mine, Brooke. I'm not letting you go." He pushes his lips to mine and they mold together in a searing kiss.

I grip his hair, my nails scratching at his scalp and tug, pulling him back. "The best way for you to show me that I'm "yours" would be for you to fuck me harder," I grit out.

I know you have it in you, Hunt. Just one last time.

But do I really want us to be over?

Brooke, don't even question that now. Let the inner freak out and get your orgasm. Use this boy for sex. It's only fucking sex. It means nothing.

He rips himself out of me causing me to flinch in pain. He sits on his knees and runs his hands through his hair. "Get on all fours." I do what he says and get into position. His hand runs down my back and then down my thighs and legs. "This what you want, Brooke? For me to fuck you?"

"Yes, how many times do I have to tell you?" I snap, turning to look up at him.

"About as many times as I need to tell you I love you and I'm sorry."

"Oh, my god...stop," I groan frustrated. I don't want to hear it.

"No." He lays a smack on my ass, sends tantalizing vibrations to my already aching core.

"You might not like me very much right now, but I do love you, and I'm going to enjoy every second out of you...like it's my last." His voice hitches, but it's like it spurs him on, and he turns into a man possessed. For a moment, everything between us is suspended in time, forgotten as I enjoy the feeling of us connecting as one for the last time. It's rough, yet at the same time he's treasuring me, and making me feel wanted. Loved?

No, it's not love! This is lust. But I'll take it.

I somehow manage the strength to rise on my elbows again. As soon as I do that, he hits something, and all my muscles tighten. He does it again and again. Holy hell, he's hasn't hit this before.

"Shit!" I scream as I slide forward on the bed.

"This still what you want?" he grunts, each thrust is deeper and harder than the last.

"Yes, yes…" I scream. I'm gripping the sheets for dear life. I close my eyes tight trying to absorb the mix of pleasure and a little bit of pain.

"You feel so good. There's no way in hell I'm giving you up. You're mine…" He huffs out, deep and throaty like he smokes ten packs a day.

"Fine, whatever. Just don't stop."

"Never, Angel. Never."

Every muscle in me contracts and I yell out his name. Hunter follows behind me, calling my name. I fall to the bed, my orgasm leaving me exhausted and powerless. Hunter crashes next to me and scoops me into his arms. I rest my head on his chest, listening to the rhythm of his racing heart. For this second, I'm content, in this bubble of ours, wanting to believe nothing is wrong. Even though everything is still a mess and nothing is solved at all.

And I have to wonder if it's even worth trying to fix.

CHAPTER TEN

*"Free your demons. Free your pain. Free
yourself from all the things you've locked up. Once
you're done, I'll be here to hold your hand and help
you glue back together all the things that were
broken because you were always meant to fly."*

Brooklyn

My eyes are closed and my head rests on Hunter's
chest as he brushes my hair back. "I love you," he
murmurs, kissing the top of my head.

The words are like a bucket of ice water being poured
all over me, remembering everything that happened hours
ago. Does he truly believe just because we had sex,
everything would be alright?

"I should go," I say knocking us out of our post-
coital bliss. I sit up and toss the blanket off me.

"Why? If you're worried about my folks they won't
be back till later. They're at some function. Stay." He
grabs my hand, but I shake it off.

"I can't…" I sigh. "This shouldn't have happened.
I'm sorry." I get up and go in search of my clothes. I find
my pants, but I spot my blouse by the door, in shreds.

Great, just great.

Hunter bolts out of bed, snatching the pair of pants out of my hand and tosses them back to the ground. "Why are you running?"

"I'm not running, Hunter. Me and you are like oil and water. We can never work out."

"That's bullshit." His angry voice booms and bounces off the walls, causing me to jump. "What do I need to do to keep you in my life, Brooke? What do you want from me? I told you, I told them off, and how I felt about you." He takes a deep breath and his voice softens. "I know I let you down today because I let my own fears get to me. I've been living on their damn coattails for so long, I forgot that I have a voice. As they said something to you in the halls, I should've just taken you in my arms and kissed you. But even after I told John to shut the fuck up and I would hurt him for trying to hurt you, it's like you checked out."

Well, that is true.

"Then next thing I know you were looking at me like you hated me, and I was this vile creature. I shut down, feeling my world collapse around me. It wasn't till you walked away, that I came back and I realized I'd fucked up and let them have it."

"You were trying to get rid of me before that. Telling me you'll talk to me later."

"Because I had planned on telling them this afternoon about us. I've spent the whole weekend trying to figure out how to do it, so in return, they wouldn't hurt you. Then I don't know—I just…" He yanks on his hair so hard I see strands bunched in his hand.

"I'm a fucking coward, Brooke, and I knew that from the beginning. But you're right. I wanted my cake and to eat it too. I wanted you so fucking bad. I wanted to tell, but each passing day, I would wuss out more and more. It might have not seemed like this was killing me, acting a big game, but it was. It killed me to let you down…"

Hunter hits his chest with his fist and tears well up in his eyes. One slips down his cheek.

I'm bewildered that this star football player is crying in front of me.

"Sticking up for myself or others was something that wasn't allowed if I wanted to be in their clique. I thought that losing people I thought were my friends would be one of the worst things that could happen to me because I didn't want to be alone or made fun of ever again. They even threatened me to a point where I knew that's just what would happen if I did go against them. I'm an idiot because while trying to protect myself, I hurt you. I'm so sorry that I wasn't doing right by you. But now I know better and losing you would be a much worse thing than trying to keep a couple of fake friends around. I love you, Brooke. I know you don't believe me right now. That's my fault. I let you down, didn't defend you correctly in that moment, I get it. What I've been doing was inexcusable. But give me a chance to prove myself before you go throwing me aside like I mean nothing to you." His voice cracks from all his pain and anguish. This isn't the same guy thirty minutes ago trying to overpower me with his macho energy and sex. He's now a lost boy afraid of his own shadow. I've seen Hunter's softer side, but this is like a different person.

I look down at my feet and wrap my arms around my naked body. "What do you know about being alone or getting made fun of?" He's never told me anything about his past before he moved here. Minor details, but nothing specific. "You've been the golden boy of high school since Freshman year. Everyone loves you, girls fall at your feet, so excuse me if I don't understand what you want with me?" I glance back up at him and I see how shattered and defeated he looks in this moment.

I watch as he turns around and grabs the sheet off his bed and wraps it around me. He guides us over to the edge of the bed and sits, pulling me down on his lap. He firmly holds me by my legs to keep me from making an escape and stares at me. That's when I see it, the same look he gave me yesterday when we made love. I wasn't sure what it was yesterday, I thought maybe his admiration, or his getting lucky eyes, but now I know it's love.

"Before I moved here, I was a nobody at my old school. I didn't fit in and I was always living in my brother's shadow. He was popular, I wasn't. I was an oddball, the weirdo in Elementary school, from kindergarten, and it followed me all the way to middle school. I hid and never tried to make any friends. They made it clear I was nothing. They would beat me up nearly every day after school. There was always a bunch of them, so I couldn't fight back. I kept it from my parents for a while because they never hit me in the face. Then one day, they beat me so bad, I ended up in the hospital with a broken jaw, broken ribs, and arm."

"Oh my god," I run my hand down his face and kiss his forehead. "I'm sorry. What happened to them?"

My question causes him to snort. "My mom and dad went to the school, but there was nothing the school could do since it happened off grounds. So, my parents called their parents, but they refused to believe us until my dad threatened to sue them. The kids did stop beating me up, but the insults didn't stop, it only got worse. It sucked. I tried not to let it get to me, but after a while, I started believing I was worthless. My mom got me a therapist because I was so miserable. I knew if I was popular that none of this stuff would happen. Aaron never had a problem with other kids, so I couldn't understand why I was hated as much as I was. I was so depressed back then and they would taunt me about taking my own life because it would just be better if I died, so that's exactly what I tried to do. I took a bunch of my mother's pain pills, with a crapload of vodka. I just wanted the pain to end.

My mom found me in time and I had to have my stomach pumped. After that, the therapist thought a new start would help."

My heart breaks in half. Even with everything that happened to me, I was never brought down that low. No wonder he was afraid. He was in a dark place and I can't fully blame him for not wanting to go back there. Fear and pain are major enemies. The things that happen when we're younger stay with us for a lifetime.

"Why didn't you tell me?" My voice cracks from the tears I'm trying to choke back.

"Because I was embarrassed, ashamed, and I didn't want you to think less of me than you already did." He nuzzles his head into my neck. "Also, I was hoping that I could finally stand up to them. Change. Be better. I couldn't and I'm sorry." His voice drips with his shame, breaking me more.

"Hunter," I whisper and brush his hair back.

"There's more." I nod and let him continue. "Well, all that was the reason why we moved to Fairview. New school, new life, right? I was already the new kid, so I was an outcast already. Oddly enough the day before I met John and Dan, I thought about joining you and Riley at the lunch table."

My jaw drops. "You're lying."

How different everything would be if he had.

"I'm not. I lost my nerve because I didn't think you would like me. You were so pretty, even with your glasses and your ponytail, mind you. You were laughing at something Riley said, and you were wearing these jean overalls that were a little too big for you, with a black and white shirt." He gives a small laugh and my cheeks heat.

He remembers what I was wearing from Freshman year? In some creepy way that's kind of...sweet.

"There's no way you can remember what I was wearing."

"I do. It's imprinted in my brain." He taps his temple and grins. "It was one of the few times that I saw you smile, a real smile, while you were in school. Anyways, I thought you were one of the popular kids and I assumed I didn't have a chance. So, I went to the gym to work out instead. My brother said if I want to make friends and be noticed, I should try out for the football team. I could run and throw a ball and, well, everyone loves the jock. It worked well for him. The next day I tried out and made the team. John and Dan instantly became my friends and they took me under their wings. They showed me who I was allowed to hang out with and who not to. If I wanted anything and everything, I would listen to them. I was just their puppet." He sighs and rests his head on my shoulder as his hand dances aimlessly on my back.

"I was part of the not allowed to hang out group, huh?"

He nods. "I know it's hard to believe that I've been crushing on you since the first time I saw you. I wanted you, but I was selfish because I knew if I dated you—" He stops and buries his head in my neck.

He would lose his status as royalty among his peers.

Hunter Evans falls for nerd; his tragic story at eleven.

"I quickly got swept away in all the parties and everyone wanting to hang out with me. I had self-esteem again. For the first time, I felt like I was living, and I wasn't depressed. It felt good to be wanted. By sophomore year, I made varsity. I was winning games left and right and it became Dan and John who were looking to me, yet they still had this weird control over me. Kara was their ringleader, and like the bitch she is, it was her way or no way. Dan and John have this odd attachment to her."

"Probably because she blows them all the time," I mutter, rolling my eyes. But Dan and John have been following around Kara since middle school. Their noses are brown from being so far up her ass. Especially, John's. I know they used to date for a minute, and he's like her puppy dog.

"More than likely." He sighs deeply and when I look into his eyes, I can see that this all weighs heavily on his mind, a mix of guilt and shame blending in his green orbs. "I would see the things they would do to other people, what they would do to you and Riley, and I did nothing because I didn't want to be shunned. According to John, it was them or be a nobody. If I went against them, well they promised to ruin me, and I didn't want to go back to what life was like before I moved here. You understand that life, you know it sucks. I saw for years on and off how it affected you. And I knew those dickheads would have stopped at *nothing* to make sure they separated us." He shakes his head, regretfully.

"Why would you want me? I'm," I wave my hand up my body, "nothing special. Average. You have Kara. I hate her, despise her, but I can admit she's very pretty. More your type."

"You are my type. I know you don't believe me when I say you're hot, but you're hot. And it's time for you to start seeing and believing that for yourself. Kara is a vile bitch and there's nothing about her that is hot or cute. I've never once thought of her that way."

As much as I want to believe it, at this moment, they're just words. I'm too busy trying to absorb everything he's telling me and understand it all.

"And what about all the other girls you've been with?"

"There's no other girls, Brooke."

"Heather Landen! I know for sure you dated, junior year."

He rolls his eyes and groans. "Thanks for the reminder. That really was nothing. She drove me insane.

We did nothing more than kiss. I've had a couple dates, but I've never been *with* anyone. I just led everyone to believe differently."

"There's no way in hell. Kara said you got around, screwed everything in a skirt, and you do sorta have a rep."

"You really believed Kara?" I can make out the hint of hurt in his voice, but what did he expect?

"I've heard things, and how am I not supposed to believe the person that you've hung out with the last four years. Plus, look at you, you're hot. You don't have to say you were a virgin to make me feel better."

"But I was. You were my first." He states proudly and brushes his hand down my face. "I was never ready for sex, until you."

We lost our virginities...*together*? I guess he did fumble around a little bit, but he was still good.

"I swear to god, if you're lying to me, I will string you up by your balls," I threaten jokingly, but I'm also quite serious. I will hurt him if I find out he's lying.

"I'm not lying. I can't say that I didn't want to with other girls. Trust me, I was offered, but I couldn't. They all seemed so easy and that's not what I was after. I watched my brother go through girl after girl. He got crabs his freshman year of college because he was at some party and banged two girls at once." He laughs, and I can't help but laugh with him.

"He admitted that to you?"

"Oh, no. I was hanging out with him and some girl called his phone, I picked up while he was in the bathroom. Some girl started cursing and yelling how he gave her crabs. I hung up and he was sorta forced to tell me his side. His words of wisdom. "Always wrap it before you tap it. Especially the ones willing to give it away for nothing, because it means they've been around a few blocks, and pick up everything along the way."

I scrunch my nose in disgust. "Lovely."

I tease Riley all the time for being easy, but I know for a straight fact she puts a raincoat on it, and most of the time she's with Billy Montgomery, a surprisingly hunky tuba player from Falling Waters High school.

"Yeah, that's kind of when I knew that I would wait till I knew who I was going to have sex with. I'm glad I did because you were exactly what I wanted. I know I was selfish and arrogant and should've shouted what we had from the rooftops. Saying fuck them all, but I liked our bubble, and I didn't want the chance of anyone trying to ruin us, because I knew they would try." He sighs and kisses my cheek. "But I almost let that happen today. No, I let it happen countless times, especially with Kara. I don't know if I could say sorry enough. I let you down. I hurt you when I promised I wouldn't"

"You swear you didn't tell them my house smelled like a barn? Because this is the time to come clean," I blurt, remembering the hurt of John's comment and needing to make sure everything is out in the open. I want zero surprises.

"No. I swear, Brooke," he says firmly and tightens his hold around me. "I would never do that! I told you that."

I nod. I do believe that. John and Kara were always the ones to rag on me, trying to get a reaction. I shake my head as I remember some of the things they used to say to me years ago

"Here comes farmer Fred and the smell that follows...Look, guys, the cow has arrived...Brooke, it's time to go back to the pig farm. It's the only place you fit in now...."

I guess I should have known it was a John-like insult. Hunter is the only one in the group that doesn't talk shit, though he doesn't stop them either. But now I understand that a little better.

"Even if we weren't dating, I wouldn't say anything, especially to the person that has vastly improved my English skills."

"I get it. It doesn't make me happy, but I get it." I pause and twist the sheet around my finger. "Would you have ever asked me out if I didn't end up tutoring you?"

Hunter blushes and I can only wonder what that is about. "Well, you see, I really didn't need a tutor. I was passing all my classes with B's. Even English mind you," he jests, knowing I was about to make a witty comeback. "I asked Mr. Marshall if he would possibly offer for you to tutor me. He knew I liked you. He yelled at me one day after class to stop drooling over you and pay attention. So let's just say he helped me out because I didn't have the guts to come out and say I liked you."

"So, our teacher hooked us up. That's *odd*." I shake my head with a chuckle, leaving me wondering how far a teacher's job is really supposed to go. I knew something was up when Mr. Marshall said that Hunter needed help to get into college when he already got into three schools. Oh, and *help* with French when he's speaks it perfectly.

"A little. Also, I wanted to improve. I told you I wasn't sure if football was the way I wanted to go. I have only a five percent chance to make it to the big leagues. Plus, it was something I never saw myself doing. I want more in life than busted knees, concussions, and bad backs."

"I don't doubt you will, Hunter. I really don't think you're a dumbass."

"That means a lot coming from you, Brooklyn." He runs his lips across my cheek, over my nose, to my lips. His tongue brushes against mine, sending me into a tailspin and I know it's something that I don't want to ever stop doing with him.

I pull away from him, his nose still touching mine. "Will you still be mine, Brooke?" he says ever so softly, his eyes closed in a prayer.

"As long as from here on out, I'm not your dirty little secret," I say, mustering up all my strength and conviction. "I won't go back to being hidden and ashamed of." If this relationship with Hunter has shown me anything, it's that I should be proud of who I am, and I shouldn't let some stupid label define me.

"No more hiding, Angel. I promise." He gently kisses me before moving to suck on the nape of my neck.

I brush my hand through his hair. "I'm sorry about your jacket. I shouldn't have done that. I knew the deal with us. I should've been clearer that I didn't want to hide anymore." I feel like crap now for taking that knife to his jacket before I gave him a chance to fully explain.

"It's okay, I'm actually glad it's all out now, maybe not with how it went down, but I needed that push. And it's just a jacket, you mean a hell of a lot more to me. Also, I'll know now to not make you mad, and if I do, make sure you're not around sharp objects and some of my prized possessions…mainly my balls. I would like to keep those attached. Please."

"No ball cutting, got it."

We sit curled around each other for I don't know how much longer without saying a word. Our hands caress each other's bare skin, doing all the talking for us.

"I really do need to get home now," I tell him and nuzzle my head into his shoulder. I remember that I have had my phone off this whole time and I have no idea if my parents have been looking for me. Although, it's still early so I doubt they called the police yet for the daughter that never misses her curfew. Ever.

"Let me drive you."

"You don't have to."

"Yes, I do. I want to make sure you get home safe. It's dark and it's my duty as your boyfriend to see you home."

147

I nod, not knowing what else to say. We get dressed and he lets me borrow the shirt he wore today. I pull the collar to my nose and revel in his scent that's now wrapped around my body.

We pile into his car and he drives me the few short miles to my house. He takes my hand before I'm able to reach for the handle and pulls me over the console.

"I love you, Brooklyn."

"I know," I murmur, and there's a small glimmer of hurt in his eyes, but it's gone in a flash. He grabs my chin and brings me to his lips and softly kisses me.

"I don't expect you to say it back right away. I'll wait for you, but know, I'll spend every day telling you, till you believe me, and every day after that once you do. I know how you truly feel about me, even if you can't say it out loud, and at this moment, that's all that matters for me."

"I believe you, it's just…" I bite my lip and look towards the carpet. So, maybe I don't 100% believe him, because I fear he'll still hurt me, but I so badly want to trust him, more than anything. There's a dead weight on my heart filled with everything that happened and what I just learned. It's too much all at once.

He lifts my chin and places a light kiss on my lips. "I know…it's okay."

With one final goodbye, I get out of the car and walk into my house. My parents are sitting on the couch watching some sitcom and I try to sneak by them, but I'm caught red-handed by the squeaky floorboards.

"We've been trying to call you, Brooke. Where have you been?" My mother stands and comes walking over to me.

"I've been with Hunter. My phone died. I'm sorry." I put on my big puppy eyes and a large pout to show her I'm sorry for worrying her.

"It's okay. Although, Riley has been blowing up the

house line looking for you. Along with some hang up calls. Is something going on?"

"Not that I know of," I say, unsure, wondering why Riley is trying to get a hold of me. I know if someone is hurt, she would've told my mom.

"I'll go call her."

"Alright, next time charge your phone. I'm sure Hunter has a charger you could use."

"I know. We got wrapped in a movie. I didn't even notice till I left." I lie smoothly, and she narrows her eyes at me with doubt. It might have something to do with the oversized '*Twenty-One Pilots*' shirt I'm wearing, that I'm sure they've seen Hunter wear a couple of times.

"Okay, well go call her back before she has a panic attack and get some rest, you look beat." I give my mom and dad a hug before heading to the safety of my room.

Once I get my phone turned back on, it beeps with a bunch of notifications. I ignore them and dial Riley's number.

"Where have you been? I've been trying to call you for hours!" she squeals the second she picks up, not even saying hello.

"I've been at Hunter's and had my phone off. What's the emergency?"

"Did he tell you what he did? The whole school has gone mad about your love affair. Kara is on the warpath."

Great. Because that's all I need right now.

"He told me he told off his friends, but nothing else really."

"Well, maybe he doesn't know. He stormed away after he went ballistic on their asses. I'll send you the video. It was epic, Brooke. It's like *West Side Story* at school now. And you two are the star-crossed lovers. Okay, no, you're maybe more like Sandy and Danny from *Grease*. Maybe you should come to school in leather...."

I laugh at her and now realize that we have spent way

too much time watching movies. "I don't think I could pull off a full leather outfit nor would my dad let me leave the house in it," I joke, then pull my hair, focusing back on the actual situation, "but back up, there's a video?"

"Mmm-Hmmm… It's the best thing I've seen all year…five stars." She hoots.

"God, Riley. What do I do now?" I groan and fall back on my bed, wanting to hide under the covers. I'm not ready to get tossed into the limelight.

"Walk into school tomorrow with your head held high, holding your man's hand as you walk through the halls. Most people are amazed he had the guts to stand up to them. They made everyone's life miserable, including some of the other populars. Kara made sure to keep her queen bee status and to do so she made many people hate her and fear her along the way. This is justice for everything she's ever done."

"Or we are outcasted and shunned. It wouldn't be any different for me, but for Hunter, it will be. And you know they'll retaliate." Kara won't go down without a fight. It's not her style.

"All you can do now is go for it. We're out of school in three months. Enjoy this, you're out in the open now. He's not perfect with what he did, but it's obvious he cares for you."

"He told me he loved me," I blurt out.

"I know. He told everyone he loved you," she giggles.

"But I didn't say it back," I tell her and her laughter stops.

"Oh. Yikes. How did he take that?"

"Fine, I guess. He said he is willing to wait for me to say it back, but he says he knows how I really feel." I shrug even though she can't see me on the other end.

"That you *loooooove* him…"

"Maybe, but I need to really *see* it. What happened

150

today still stings. I know that I went along with the idea of not telling anyone, and that's my fault as much as his. That's not so much the issue and I understand him a little better now, but it's like if he truly loved me, why didn't he defend me *while* I was there." It would have stopped me from playing with a butcher knife, that's for sure.

"Watch the video. Then maybe you'll believe a little more that he means it. But you don't have to rush. I don't blame you, but also, don't fight it. Like I said, come to school tomorrow and hold that head up high. I gotta run, but I'll see you tomorrow. And I expect you to walk through those double doors tomorrow holding that boy's hand proudly," she says sternly, and I know if she were standing in front of me she would be wagging her finger at me.

"Alright, alright, I get it. Good night, Riley."

"Mwah."

I hang up with my crazy best friend and a few minutes later my phone beeps with the video she sent me. My thumb hovers over the play button. I take a steady breath, knowing I have to watch the events that are going to change my high school life, again. Making it full screen, I hit play. It begins with me in the middle telling Kara and Hunter off. The camera follows me as I walk off and I can see the tears in my eyes. Off-screen, you can hear Hunter calling my name and the camera swings back to him. He started going after me, but Kara grabs his arm and pulls him back. "Let her go, the crybaby will be alright."

Hunter turns to her, his face is red, and I can see a vein in his neck pulsing. He's seething and looks ready to kill. "WHAT THE FUCK IS YOUR PROBLEM? WHY ARE YOU ALWAYS SUCH A FUCKING BITCH? AND GET YOUR FUCKING FILTHY PAWS OFF ME." His arm yanks from her hold and she goes stumbling back a couple feet.

I roll my eyes and wonder why he couldn't stand up to them before I walked away hurt. But I guess he needed that kick in the head that he was going to lose me if he didn't start standing up for himself. Kara's face is a picture—wide-eyed and I swear I see the sweat on her brow, as most of all his anger is aimed at her. The rest of them stand back, watching, confused by his sudden outburst.

"Don't tell me you've gone soft for the freak, Hunter." Kara laughs nervously as she looks at the crowd forming around her. Hunter clenches his fists at his sides and looks ready to punch her. I wish he would, but I know he wouldn't hit a girl, no matter if she deserves it. "What have I told you if you stick up for her?"

"Shut the fuck up," he growls menacingly, and I can see panic flash in Kara's eyes.

"Hunter, calm down, man." John grabs his shoulder and Hunter pushes him off.

"No, I'm so sick of her shit. Like where do you come off making up shit? To what? Embarrass her? What has she ever done to you fuckheads?"

"Why do you fucking care?" John snaps. His face is blood red and looks ready to fight. "She's a fucking nobody."

"Because I'm in love with her!" Hunter shouts and I swear Kara and Emma's jaws drop to the ground. "I've let you walk all over me for years, control who I can and cannot like. Why? Because they're different? You treat everyone that's not in our crap ass circle like shit. Including me and I let you. I stood back and let it happen for too long, all because I thought I needed you assholes to survive high school. Brooke is an amazing girl and has never done anything to any of you, but *what?* Be smarter than you? Hotter than you? Well, I hate to break it to you, most of the school is."

Laughter erupts from the crowd that's watching the

display unfold and from my own lips too.

"Hunter, you don't know what you're talking about babe." Kara approaches him, but I can see she's wary. "We made you. You need us. That helpless little bookworm isn't going to take you anywhere but down. You would've never been the football star you are or gotten into any of those colleges if it wasn't for us." She goes to put her hand on his chest and he slaps it away. *Hard.* I can hear it echo off the hallway walls. Kara grabs her hands and her eyes start to water as the crowd laughs louder, including the guy holding the camera. No one steps forward to help the wounded queen.

"I made the team on my own. It was my talent that got me scholarships. Unless you're telling me, your whore self, slept with all the deans of admission?"

Oh, snap. I'm whooping and giggling so loud I hope it doesn't bring my parents in here.

"She does like spreading those legs, man," a random guy shouts out from the crowd.

"I'm sick and tired of watching you guys make other people's lives hell. I'm just as much to blame for the shit you've done, especially when it came to my girlfriend. I couldn't show her off because I didn't want you skanks making her life harder than you already make it, and selfishly, I knew you would make me feel like crap for wanting to be with her. But it ends now, and so does this so-called friendship we had. I'd rather be an outcast then hang with a bunch of shitheads any longer. Now excuse me, I need to find my girlfriend."

"You walk away now, Hunter, I'll make sure everyone hates you and knows what a loser you are. I can still ruin you," Kara yells out. John and Dan appear to be in shock and Emma is opening and closing her mouth like a goldfish.

"I don't fucking care because Brooke is right, you're a dumbass bitch that will end up on a corner, trying to survive, because once high school is over, you'll be nothing. Shit, you couldn't even get into a lame college party because you spend so much time being a slutty bitch that you can't even do simple fucking math. Your dad had to pay the school just so you could graduate this year. You'll end up being a community college failure when nobody falls for your shitty superior attitude. You can't sleep with teachers for better grades, or have daddy pay them off for you there. And everyone will realize how much better they are than you and wonder why they thought you were so fucking special. All of you are nothing and soon to be no one. Actually..." he turns to address the crowd that has gotten bigger and bigger with each passing second. The bell had rung like five minutes ago.

I even see some teachers hanging around, muted, watching queen Kara getting taken down. "I think that you can all see now, that these four are really nothing and you shouldn't worry about what they think. Every single one of you will amount to more in your life than they ever will and, who knows, maybe one day be polishing your shoes. They haven't done shit for anyone but try to hurt everyone that is better than them. Bullies are only bullies because of jealousy. And trust me, they're jealous of all of you. Do something. Do better than me. Stand up to them because they don't have a leg to stand on anymore. Squish them down like the disgusting roaches they are."

The crowd is nodding their heads, and I hear some shit being called out to the nasty four, and balls of paper and maybe even food being thrown at them before Hunter storms away.

The guy with the camera turns it to himself. "Well, there you have it, folks, the real king of the school, Hunter Evans, has spoken," he laughs, "I think it's safe to say we stand with Evans. Finally, someone served Kara and her minions on a platter...she's only been making lives hell since middle school..."

"Who is Brooke?" I hear someone next to the guy ask.

"The hottie that stormed off earlier. Hunter better go get her before I do." He hoots and the video goes black.

I do have to say I am impressed with how he stood up to them. Tonight, I will sleep a little better knowing that he did stand up for me, even if he was a tiny bit late. Maybe I can accept that our relationship won't be expiring any time soon.

And I know it is because I do truly love him.

.

CHAPTER ELEVEN

"I want you to look at me. I want you to see me. This is who I am. This is what makes me, me. I might change on the outside, but you'll never change who I am on the inside. I'm strong willed. Determined. I might be a little bit troubled. Been hurt once or twice. But I'm perfect. See me for who I am."

Brooklyn

A new day has arrived and now I have to face the world. The video of Hunter *finally* sticking up for me, but mainly himself, has gone viral. Not just around our school, but it has twenty thousand hits on YouTube. There's even some crazy parody going around with a song called "The bitch waz told" being dubbed into the background. My Facebook page that I haven't touched in years, has blown up with comments of how awesome that someone brought Kara's group down and put them in their place. But the biggest response was Hunter's status change from single to in a relationship with Brooklyn Turner.

Along with the status update, he posted some pictures of us: our first date, where we ate chicken at the park, a selfie of us kissing, and one of me sitting out by the lake with the sun setting behind me. Underneath, it reads, *"The most beautiful, amazing girl in the world."* And I do have to admit, that I do look pretty hot in that picture.

I guess it isn't official until it's Facebook official. Now he has literally told the "world" he's a taken man.

I have no idea what this day will bring, but I'm taking Riley's advice, and going in with my head held high. I won't let anyone bring me down again.

When I called Hunter after I watched the video, telling him how I saw what he did. He was quite shocked there was a video, but happy that there was proof that he did it. He was worried I would never believe he had told them to fuck off.

I *had* believed him, but I wasn't expecting *everything* I saw.

My only hope is that my parents don't see the video. I don't want to explain any of it to them. Thankfully, they don't spend their days cruising YouTube searching for cat videos and car crashes.

I'm dressed in my maroon dress with buttons that go all the way down the front and a pair of black leggings. My hair is up in a ponytail, *just* because. I thought about wearing my glasses, but I hate those things now. I grab my backpack and head out the door to Riley's house since we walk in together every morning.

I'm stopped in my tracks when I see Hunter leaning against his silver convertible. I love his car: it's sleek, just like him, and it beats the beat-up Honda I have. I never drive unless I have to and when I do drive, I steal my mom's car.

"Hey, what are you doing here?" Un-freezing my steps to walk over to him.

"I wanted to give my girl a ride to school, and give her this." He reaches through the open window and pulls out a brown paper bag. He hands it to me and I look inside.

There's a bunch of little muffins inside, and it looks to be my favorites, double chocolate and blueberry.

"Thank you. I was quite hungry. Where did you get these from? They look good."

"I made them," he says with an innocent twinkle in his eye.

"*You* bake?"

"What? You don't think I can't figure how to put egg and flour in a bowl?"

"You just don't strike me as the Betty Crocker type."

"Well, maybe I am, now." He crosses his arms and gives me a fake pout. "Also, *maybe* my sister helped a little...but I totally mixed it all together."

"Thank you." I throw my arms around him and kiss him on the cheek. He wraps his arms around my waist and buries his head in my neck. I can't believe he baked for me, something so simple means so much right now.

"We should get going, I think we have an interesting day ahead of us."

I groan, not wanting to think about it. "Yeah, we can swing by and get Riley, right? We always walk in together."

"I know. I figured we would get her. I think I gave you enough muffins to share with Riley," he says as I walk to the passenger side of the car.

"Share? Pfft. I don't think so." I'm about to sit down and there are two peach and yellow roses, resting on the seat, with a folded piece of paper resting on top of them. I pick them up and put the roses to my nose before sitting down.

Hunter starts the car, and I unfold the note.

Brooklyn,

I've been a selfish jerk this last month for never showing how much you mean to

159

me. I cared more about myself then I did you. I wanted you to trust me and trust my feelings for you, that if we were at a point, united together, we could stand against it all. Although, when you finally let me in, I broke that trust in an instant. I should've stood up for you the second you came to me and never let any of them open their mouths. For that, I'm most sorry for, and I'll never let it happen again.

I thought I needed to protect you from the backlash of the ones that wouldn't want us together and even though that's partly true, it was more about me. I'm sorry I was such a coward to not give you everything you deserve and treat you like the Princess you are. You have a lot more backbone than I do.

It was always me who needed to change, not you. I'm glad you stayed true to yourself. Sure, you changed the way you looked on the outside, but everything inside you stayed the same, you just finally showed it off.

It's you who makes me stronger, and it's because of you I want to be a better person and stick up for what I want, instead of listening to the ones that never knew the real me. Besides my family, it's only you that knows who I really am, inside and out.

I love you, Brooke. From this moment on I'm going to stand by you and our relationship. No more secrets, no more hiding. I should've shown you off to the

world in the first place. I'm going to keep showing you every day how much you mean to me and it probably still won't make up for what an ass I've been, but I'm going to try.
Please know that everything we shared together, everything that I said and did, was real. Please never doubt that.
I love you.

-Hunter

Out of the corner of my eyes, I see Hunter eyeing me as we park in Riley's driveaway. I fling off my seatbelt and his eyes go wide startled by my action. His eyes flash between me and the door, probably thinking I'm going to bolt. Instead, I reach over the console, grabbing fistfuls of his hair, and kiss him with everything I have. He moans against my lips, and his arms slide around my back.

I pull away from him and run my hand down his face. "I don't think you're a coward, Hunter. A little scared and selfish, yes, but I went along with it as well. I could have stopped it, but I didn't have the guts to say no either. In the beginning, I thought it was a sick game, but as time went on you were right about them going after me. Kara proved that a couple times she would make my life hell. And our bubble was nice. Sometimes it didn't matter, I was happy, then sometimes I hated it. We both messed up, but it's over now, right?"

"Yes, it's over. You're mine and I want everyone to know."

"I think they already do." I smirk, leaning over to kiss him, but our lips are unable to meet when there's a knock on the passenger window. I turn to find Riley looking in, making goofy faces at us, and I roll down the window.

"You know when I came out here this morning, like I have almost every morning for years, never did I think that I would find two people sucking face in a car in my driveway. Turner, we've talked about your PDA. I'm all happy for you, but I don't want to see it." She rolls her eyes. "Anyways, we're taking wheels this morning, I'm guessing?"

"Yeah, hop in. Hunter made me mini muffins and I *guess* I can share with you."

Riley jumps into the backseat. "Mini muffins? Impressive, Evans." I take two muffins out and pass the bag to Riley.

I pop one in my mouth and chew. And hell, these are delicious; much better than the packaged ones I get all the time. "These are actually really good." I moan and pop another one into my mouth.

"Ye, of little faith. Brooklyn, I'm hurt." He gasps and places his hand over his heart.

"Well, I'm sorry. It's not every day you find out the star running back can actually bake, and it tastes good too. But now that I know, I expect these every morning."

"I'll let my sister know." He grins over at me, and I smack him in the arm.

When we arrive at the school we pile out of Hunter's car and I stand still staring at the front doors, watching other students make their way in.

Riley comes next to me and puts her arm around my shoulder. "Remember, head up Brookey. You got this. 98% of the school is on your side."

"How do you know that?" I look at her like she's lost her mind.

"YouTube and Facebook comments don't lie, my dear. Plus, thanks to Hunter, nobody is afraid of them anymore. They've been humiliated to the extreme. Not just here, but all over the internet. Hunter was the popular one, the most liked out of the hateful five. You know because he was the only nice one."

"Hateful five? That's what we were called?" Hunter asks confused and maybe even slightly hurt. I've never heard them called that before.

"It was made up by someone and it's kind of stuck. I guess it would be hateful four now since you're out of the group. I thought you were on top of this stuff. Shit, there's also memes, hashtags, and even people giving up their stories of how they made their lives suck. They're hated. And after all the shit Kara has done to us, I'm thankful for it myself. Maybe this was supposed to happen this way. Payback at its fullest." Riley shrugs and looks over at us and smiles. "You know that old sayin' *everything happens for a reason…*"

"You're right, Riley. Somewhere in all that babble, you are right." I giggle and shove her shoulder.

"Shut up!" She nudges me back. "Of course, I'm right. Now, let's get inside. Hunter, take your girl's hand and let's show them all how amazing Brooke Turner is."

As we walk through the halls, there's a sudden hush among everyone, and they're all looking at us. It's like the movies and all we need is some music playing behind us to fill the scene. Hunter's hand is around mine and we stand shoulder to shoulder. He appears unaffected by the looks, but I guess he's used to them.

Riley is on the other side of me and she's eating up the attention and flinging her blonde hair around. The girl always knows how to make a laugh out of an awkward situation. She smiles over at Hunter and me. "I gotta soak up this attention. I've never been around an "it" couple before."

'It' couple? Are we really an *'it'* couple now?

We make it to our lockers and Hunter and I just stare at each other, not saying a word. He bends down and kisses me gently, then runs his finger down my face. "Beautiful."

And cue my furious blush.

"Okay, if this is what the two of you are going to be like *alllll* the time now, I'm gonna need a barf bag." Riley twists her nose and then giggles. "I'll see you two later.

Riley bounces off to class and it's now me and Hunter all alone. Well, along with our passing classmates, staring at us on their way to class.

Hunter grabs my ponytail and wraps it around his wrist. "Remember when I said I liked you better with your hair down?" His mouth parts and he's looking at me intently, his green eyes darkening. His bedroom eyes. The eyes that scream out how much he wants me.

"Yeah?" I gulp, his actions sending tingles all the way down to my core. All I can think about is finding an abandoned janitor's closet.

"I changed my mind. I like it up, so I can do this." He pulls me toward him, using my ponytail, and crashes his lips on mine, pressing me against the lockers.

"Damn, Evans. Come up for air." Someone hollers out to us. Hunter breaks away and looks to the person who interrupted our moment.

"Shut up, Mackie," he yells out, and a smile crosses his face. He turns back to me and places a light kiss on my lips. "It's a good thing he stopped us, I might have taken you right here."

"I wouldn't have minded," I pant, needy and turned on.

What better way could there be to lay claim to a man?

"Me either, but we should get to class. I'll wait for you outside your third period and we can walk to French together. I love you, angel." He gives me a kiss on the cheek, before rushing away. And I'm sure his quick getaway is so he can't be disappointed that I didn't say the words back.

My eyes follow him down the hall and I admire his

firm ass till it disappears. I gather what I need for my next two classes and start heading towards my first period. As I climb the stairs, people greet me, like we've been old friends. I smile politely back, and I'm amazed by the sudden thrust into popularity.

If I'm honest, I had hoped this might have happened when I changed my appearance, but all I got were a few passing looks. Nobody had genuinely reached out to try to acknowledge me or try to become my friend, maybe a handful at most. I guess that only happens in the movies, but now because of Hunter's public display and taking down the most feared bullies, it's like everyone is going to try and be my friend.

"Hey, Brooke," Ian greets me as we walk into class. Ian had been someone I would consider a friend, even if we don't really hang out outside school except on rare occasions. However, after he asked me out, and I'd simply told him no, he stopped talking to me. Hell, he wouldn't even look in my direction.

"What's up, Ian?"

"So, you and Hunter Evans," he says as a statement and not a question.

"Yeah?"

"You sure that's what you want? He's a giant prick. I bet he didn't tell you what he said to me after I asked you out?"

Huh?

"No? What did he say?" My curiosity spikes wondering what in the world he's talking about. When I told Hunter about Ian asking me out, I saw jealousy written all over his face and steam coming out of his ears. Part of me had hoped it would be a push to Hunter to say something about us, but it hadn't worked. Once the steam settled, he said that he trusted me and he knew I was his, and he was mine.

"He cornered me after school and told me to stay

away from you because you were his girl. That basically, I wasn't allowed to look at you or talk to you or even say your name." He scoffs, disgusted. "He threatened to beat the shit out of me if I did. We've all seen the videos, Brooke. What kind of guy wouldn't want to show you off? Don't you want someone that would have always been proud to have you on their arm?"

"You mean someone like you?" I bite out bitterly.

"Exactly," A large grin spreads over his face and he steps closer to me. "You two don't belong together. You're so *different*…from him. Me and you would be perfect together." He reaches out to grab my hand and I yank it away before he can take it. Is this him trying to *impress* me?

"Different?" I snort, taking a step back. "See, I think that's where you're wrong. Even *if* we were so *different* from each other, don't they say opposites attract? But also, you know nothing about our relationship. We have a lot more in common than you think."

"Like what?"

"Well, that's only for me to know, Ian, and if I wanted to date you, I would have said yes. But I don't. Now, maybe Hunter had his reasons for what he did. Sounds like to me, he got jealous and wanted you to know I was his. And I have to say, I kind of like that side of him and it shows he was proud of me, even if everyone didn't know about us yet. So do me a favor, don't come to me and try to undermine our relationship. And it might be a good idea to listen to him and stay away from me if you're going to do all that." With a flick of my ponytail, I walk into the classroom

.

Stronger

I come out of third period, and like promised, Hunter's waiting for me outside of class. I skip over to him, a smile on my face and it feels so freeing not to have to worry about being seen. "Hey."

"Hey. How was class?" He drapes his arm around my waist and we take a short stroll to his locker.

"First period was informative. Ian came up to me today and told me something interesting." His body tenses and I see a guilty look cross his face as he opens his locker.

"Oh? What was that?" He shoves a book into his locker, not able to look at me. I want to laugh at how nervous he's acting. I figure I should have a little fun with it.

"I'd rather hear what you have to say."

He sighs, closing his locker and leans back against it, resigning himself that he has to confess to me. "After you told me he asked you out, I did my best to let it go. It was really hard, and I was also dealing with some bullshit with John and Kara on top of it. I spent an hour in the gym after school because I was so worked up. I was mad at myself that I couldn't call you mine, but still coward enough to not do anything about it. After I beat the hell out of the bag, I didn't feel any better. If anything, I hated myself more."

I remember that day. He came to my house, a disheveled, stressed out mess. I'd tried to ask him what was wrong; the Ian thing didn't even register to me because he shook it off so easy. He told me it was nothing and just needed to see me. We ended up having an intense

167

make-out session on the couch. He kept saying all these sweet things to me, like how much he cared about me, how I was his, and how wonderful I was. Now that I think about it, it was easy to tell he might have loved me then.

"When I went into the locker room, I heard him talking to his buddy about all the things he was going to do to you after your so-called date. Disgraceful things. Well, after his friend left, I set him straight. Told him you were my girl and if I heard him utter your name again, I would pound him." He shrugs.

"And you weren't worried about him saying something to anyone?"

Ian was a lot like me and his voice wouldn't go far in this school. Starting a *rumor* against the most popular kid in school would have only made it as far as his couple of friends.

"No, I knew he wouldn't because I told him not to say your name. You can't go running your mouth if you can't explain who you're talking about…" he trails off with a shrug.

"Okay." I smile and reach on my tippy toes to kiss his cheek. Maybe I should have tried the jealousy angle harder. The thought makes me giggle to myself.

"What's so funny?"

"Nothing, but it's nice to hear that you still had my back. Well, *kind of*. But I'll take it." I grab his hand and pull him down the hall, but he yanks me back to his chest.

"You're not mad? It makes me no better than the other four."

"Nope because I believe you were defending me. I also told him that maybe he should listen to you and stay away. I guess he was always kind of a creep. Anyways, it's no big deal and kind of good to know."

"I can't believe he told you. I guess I wasn't clear enough."

"He thought since we were public now, that he could

try to sell you down the river and I would dump you for him."

"I should punch his face in," Hunter growls. His possessiveness is cute, and I find myself grinning like a loon at him.

"Nah, you don't want to go back to being one of the hateful five now." I tease, and he slings his arm around my shoulder again as we move back down the hallway to class.

"No, I wouldn't want that."

We're halfway to French, all eyes on us as we pass everyone, and that's when something occurs to me: Where are Kara, Emma, John, and Dan? I would have sworn I would have seen them already. They wouldn't go down this easy. A chill runs down my spine that something is wrong; it's like the air shifted. I try to shake it off and figure I'm overthinking. The fact that they haven't even run through my mind till now is sort of shocking.

"I'm surprised I haven't seen Kara or any of them today. I expected, I don't know, something from them." I address my ponderings to Hunter.

"None of them came to school today. Hopefully, they were humiliated enough with the video and stay away." We're outside Mr. Marshall's classroom and Hunter grabs my waist and kisses my forehead. "If you have any problems, tell me right away, understand?" Concern swims in his eyes but so does his love for me, which makes my heart thump wildly in my chest, and those damn unicorns and rainbows are back. How can I not love him? How can I not tell him right here, even if the timing isn't perfect?

"I will. I promise" I reach up and touch the light stubble on his face and steady myself to let the next words flow out without more hesitation. "Hunter...Je t'aime" *I love you.*

A large smile crosses his face and his eyes shine bright. "You mean that?"

"I do. I know your feelings are real for me and I shouldn't deny it anymore to you."

"Oh, Brooke. Je t'aime." He bends down to kiss me, and tugs on my hair as my hand's grip around his neck. Around us, I can hear the hoots and hollers of the other students, but I don't care. I've been waiting for this moment for so long to show everyone he is mine.

We are interrupted by a rough clearing of the throat. We separate and come face to face with Mr. Marshall. "As thrilled as I am for the both of you, it's time for class."

My cheeks heat up and now I want to go hide somewhere. "Sorry, Mr. Marshall," I mutter, and Hunter laughs, taking my hand to walk me to my desk.

"I have something special planned for us this afternoon. I think you're going to like it," he gives me a wolfish grin.

"I look forward to it." I give him one last swift kiss on the cheek, before taking my seat.

"Say it one more time." He leans on my desk, and his nose touches mine.

"Take your seat, Mr. Evans." Mr. Marshall claps his shoulder, making him stand and move away from my desk.

The class laughs behind us, when Hunter raises his hands, defensively. "Alright, alright. Was just testing out the language of love on my lady," he chuckles and takes his seat.

"Alright, settle down class. Let's get started."

As per usual, Hunter stares at me while Mr. Marshall writes on the whiteboard. I can tell there are several extra eyes on me as well. I ignore them and draw my attention to Hunter.

'I love you,' I mouth to him.

He blows me a kiss and mouths back the same words

to me.

The final bell rang ten minutes ago and I'm waiting by Hunter's car, wondering what the holdup is. One of his teammates, Daryl, stopped him in the hall on the way out, saying the coach needed to talk to them about their final game. Almost everyone is gone for the day and I debate texting him to tell him I'll walk home and he can meet me there.

I pull my phone out of my backpack when a car, screeching its tires pulls into the parking lot. The beat up Cavalier hits its brakes behind Hunter's car. Two people fly out of the car, my panic rises, and I drop my backpack and run.

Kara and John are coming at me, and their faces are murderous.

CHAPTER TWELVE

"In the face of danger, you need to be brave to survive. There's always someone that's going to try and bring you down, and if you're going to go down, go down swinging. But know you will be able to get up again because you're strong enough to do so. Don't let anybody destroy the courage that you have built for yourself."

Brooklyn

I'm running across the parking lot with John hot on my heels. I know there's no way I'm going to be able to outrun him, but I have to try. The evil in their eyes is terrifying and if they get a hold of me, I have no idea what they're going to do with me. I do know it won't be good.

I scream for help, but it's useless, nobody is around. Nobody ever is when you need them the most.

"Where the fuck do you think you're going, bitch?" Kara cackles behind me.

"Gotcha." Strong arms grab me across my stomach, lifting me off the ground. I'm caught.

"No! Get off me!" I kick and scream, fighting against my captor. But it's no use, John holds me tighter, making my ribs ache, as he carries me back to the car. My phone—my lifeline—slips from my hand to the grass below. I kick at John again, "Let me go."

Please. Let me go.

"Shut up, bitch." Kara sneers and knocks me in the head with her fist.

John throws me in the back of the car and slams the door behind me. Dan is in the front, holding his phone up, I'm sure recording everything. Emma is on my left. John rushes to the driver side and I try to open the door, but its child locked.

Emma is laughing like a crazy person. "What's wrong, Brooklyn?" The side door opens and Kara pushes Emma aside.

"Go!" she yells and the car lurches forwards, screeching tires along the way.

"What the hell are you doing? Let me go!" I scream and kick the back of Dan's seat.

"Say cheese," Dan says, recording my humiliation.

"You're so fucking whiny, Brooklyn. Shut the hell up and enjoy the ride," Kara hisses, hitting me in the head again, this time with a harder object. My ears start to ring from the blow and I'm mildly woozy.

"You're psychotic, Kara," I croak through my tears. Tears I'm trying so hard not to release. But the pain lancing through me makes it impossible.

"Maybe…" She smirks and flips her damn hair as if she's proud of the assessment. "I told you to stay away from Hunter and from us, but you didn't listen. Now payback has been issued for what you did to us."

Emma grabs a fistful of my hair, pulling so hard, my scalp aches, and I fear I might go bald. Kara reaches to the floor, and I manage to give her a good punch to the face. Too bad I missed her nose.

"Fucking bitch," she growls, grabbing her cheek. Emma pulls harder on my hair, so now I'm looking at the roof. I lift my legs to kick at Kara and jab my elbows trying to get Emma off me. I think I hit Kara a few times before she yells for Dan to grab my legs. Kara reaches for my hands and I'm able to scratch her face with my nails.

"Emma choke the bitch till I get her wrapped up." Emma releases my hair, and I elbow her in the chin. It only serves to piss her off and grab my hair again before she puts her arm around my neck. She squeezes hard, leaving me dazed, and giving Kara the ability to tie my hands together.

"I didn't do anything. You just got called out for the assholes you are. Sorry to tell you everyone already had that information," I snarl, even though my vocal cords are squished.

Kara's fist comes flying at my face and hits me hard in the cheek. My teeth rattle and I know my cheek is going to bruise. "Bitch, just shut your face. This isn't going to end well for you no matter how hard you fight." Kara threatens and lays another closed fist to my head.

My eyes close, the dizziness getting overwhelming. My face is throbbing, and a steel drum band is playing right on my brain.

I decide it's better not to fight or talk on the way to wherever we're going and hope their adrenaline of attacking me wears off. Plus, Emma is still holding me around the neck, but her grip has loosened.

"Where are we going?" Dan asks, sounding confused and it makes me peel open my eyes. "I thought we were going to your house, Kara."

"Change of plans. I figured the further out we are the better that way when she bleeds, I don't have to explain the bloodstains to my parents. Plus, it'll make her journey back longer." She laughs like a crazed hyena. "Don't worry about it. John and I have it under control." She waves him off and nobody else talks the rest of the journey

We pull up to a large house and pull into the garage. I know we are at least fifteen to twenty minutes outside of

Fairview. The back door flies open and Emma yanks my hair and pulls me out of the car. I kick my legs up and I manage a few kicks into Kara's side.

I'm thrown to the hard concrete of the garage and several kicks are delivered to my gut. All served by Kara. The boys are laughing at my misery.

I can't believe Hunter ever considered these people friends and it makes me wonder if they've done this to someone else—and was Hunter a part of it if they did?

I automatically know he wasn't. He might have been stupid to think these people were human enough to be friends, but he's nowhere evil enough to do this stuff to another human being. I have a feeling he would have stood against this shit.

And more than likely, I'm the first victim.

"Get up. At least try to fight back," Kara yells, still laying blow after blow into me.

How does she want me to fight back with my hands tied? Then I think, that's probably her point.

"I should've done this shit to you after you broke my nose in eighth because it's obvious I didn't make myself clear for you to keep your damn head down." She kicks me once more in the ribs and the tears fall freely down my face. I swear I heard something crack, and the pain is intense.

"The fucking dork is crying…" I think that was John taunting, but everything sounds so far away.

I'm glad they feel proud, being able to make someone cry who is unable to fight back. I close my eyes, the tears burn my skin as they hit open wounds. I feel like I might vomit from the last kick to my stomach. My only hope is that Hunter sees my stuff and knows something is wrong.

"Pick this bitch up, John," Kara demands.

I'm lifted off the ground, but I let my legs stay like jello, so I don't stand. "Stand up, you stupid whore," John yells into my ear intensifying the pounding in my head.

I lift my foot backward, aiming for John's nuts. I know I miss when he sends me flying into the car. "I don't think so, you stupid bitch."

"Hey, don't hurt the car, man," Dan chuckles. "It's an innocent."

Kara comes after me and begins swinging again. I put my arms up in defense, hoping to stop some of her hits. I'm knocked around a couple more times before she moves away. My head is pounding so hard, and all I want to do now is sleep. They have so much hatred for me, mainly Kara, that I don't understand. How can someone hate someone so much for liking a boy, or just being different?

My arms drop and Kara is still in front of me, her brown eyes glowing in her fury and her hatred. "You're going to pay and wish for your death." She hits me again in the face before I can get my hands back up. Her words shake me, and I wonder if she wants to kill me. Right now, it wouldn't be such a surprise if she did.

"Get her inside. I think it's time to check out why Hunter fell for the damn nerd. Maybe we should make her over some more so she's not so easy on his eyes."

Hunter

"Daryl, I need to go…" I'm in the locker room, losing my patience waiting for Coach Anders to show up. Nobody else from the team is here, so I don't know what he could possibly want to talk to me about. I look over at Daryl, he looks twitchy, which just adds to my confusion.

"Just give him another minute, maybe he got tied up or something."

I need to get out of here. I have a hundred things planned for this afternoon with Brooke. I want to take her on a bunch of dates that I should've taken her on before. I have simple things in mind like bowling and a movie then my mom and sister are helping me set up a romantic dinner. I want to give her all the things she should've gotten in the beginning.

She said she loved me, and I've been on some kind of high since. I'm trying to stay focused on the tasks I want to do first with her to win her over and show her what she means to me, then finding somewhere that I can have my way with her.

Movie theaters are dark, I'm sure we can find a way to fool around a little.

Daryl's phone beeps and when he looks at it, his eyes go wide. "What the hell?" he says below a whisper, before shoving it back in his pocket. Now Daryl looks even more nervous and twitchy then he was a moment ago. But he's the least of my worries right now.

"To hell with this. I have things to do." I don't even wait for him to say anything and turn to leave. I push open the locker room door and come face to face with Coach Anders.

"What are you doing here, Evans?" he asks me, looking me over and then behind me where Daryl is.

"There's no practice today, but I can admire your eagerness," he jokes, but I'm not laughing.

"Daryl said you needed to talk to me?"

"No, I didn't."

I turn back to Daryl and sweat forms on his brow as he looks away from me. Something is up. I stomp over to him, anger seeping out of my pores. "What the hell is going on, Daryl?"

"I'm sorry, man," he mumbles, still avoiding eye contact. "I um—"

"Sorry about what?" I hiss, inching closer so I'm right in his face.

"They told me it was just going to be a little prank and I was to distract you for a few minutes. I thought it meant like throwing eggs at her or something. I didn't know they were taking her," he stutters, not making much sense. But hearing him say 'take her,' I know he's talking about Brooke.

"Who?" I roar and grab his collar, pushing him hard to the lockers. If Brooke has one hair out of place when I get back to her, I'm going to kill whoever touched her.

"Hunter!" Coach Anders yells and pushes us apart. "Daryl, what is going on?"

"Kara and John, they told me to distract you. They said they were going to play a harmless prank on Brooke, embarrass her to make up for the video of them that went viral. I didn't know they were taking her anywhere or going to physically hurt her. They just sent me a picture. I'm sorry…" I go to punch him, but Coach catches my flying fist.

"Settle, Hunter," he barks and pulls me away from Daryl. "I understand you're mad, but you're not going to get anywhere knocking him out." Coach places his hand on my chest to keep me at bay and turns back to the squirmy fucker. "Now Daryl, do you know where they're taking her?"

179

"No, they just sent me this." Daryl pulls at his phone and opens his Snapchat. It's a picture of Brooke with Emma and Kara. She looks panicked, and her bottom lip has been sliced open. Under the picture, it says "payback in motion, going to fuck up a bitch, and show her not to mess with us ever again." It was sent from Dan's account.

I want to punch him, I want to throw his phone, I want to destroy everything in my path, but I need to find her. "I need to go find her. And you better hope she's okay or you're going to be a dead man."

My heart is racing as I dart out of the locker room. I'm well aware that Coach Anders and Daryl are behind me, but my focus is on getting to Brooke. There's a part of me praying that this is a sick joke, and I'm going to find her just fine standing at my car.

Coach is yelling at me, but I'm not making out the words as I make it outside and race to the parking lot. There are only a few cars left and my heart breaks when I don't see her by my car. "FUCK!!"

I notice a lump of something blue in front of the passenger side of my car and rush to see what it is. When I get there, it's her backpack. I look around the area trying to play detective and I see fresh skid marks on the road. Coach is on his phone talking to someone, it might be school security, and Daryl is walking around lost. I take out my phone and try to call her. Maybe she will answer. Maybe *they* will answer. But then I hear my ringtone coming from the grassy area of the parking lot, and I know that hope is lost. Daryl bends down and picks up her phone.

"They didn't say anything about where they were taking her?" I snarl at Daryl snatching the phone out of his hands.

"No, I swear." Daryl's voice shakes. At least he looks legit worried about what is going on.

It's as if I can feel the world slip beneath my feet and

it's all my fault. She wouldn't be in this predicament if it wasn't for me. If I just told them straight out how I felt, Brooke wouldn't be in danger. I never expected them to go this far to get even. I have no idea what they are willing to do to her and how far they will go. All I know is she needs to be found.

"I'm calling the cops. Then somehow find a way to tell her parents," I mutter, and I keep praying that she's alright.

Please, God, let her be alright.

Brooklyn

I was brought down to the basement and they tied me up to a chair, like the hostage that I am. "I want a moment alone with the vermin," Kara barks at the other three. "Then we can move on with our plan." Everything is fuzzy, but I make out Emma and Dan going up the stairs. John whispers something in Kara's ear, and even though it's blurry, John looks at me with a devious grin that chills me. She gives him a kiss on the cheek telling him she'll handle me.

Once John leaves, Kara comes and stands in front of me. My eyes droop, the pain ringing through my head is becoming too much to bear. My stomach is killing me, my face is throbbing, and I have sharp pains shooting through my back. I just want to close my eyes now. Kara grabs my chin, and her lips twitch as she growls, "Look at me…"

It's the last thing I want to do, but I don't think I could handle any more hits. I look at her and there's something scary in her eyes. I can't help but wonder if that crazed look had always been there. Looking Kara in the eyes wasn't something I ever did, and I hope after this if I make it out, I never will again. Though I can't help feeling good when I see my nail marks in her cheek and a purple circle appearing around them. At least I got something in.

"I've spent years trying to get Hunter's attention. I didn't understand why he wouldn't want to be with me. It was bad enough when he dated Heather. I could tell he wasn't that into her. I was happy when he dumped her, but she kept getting in the way to try and get him back. Even after they broke up he paid more attention to her than me. So, what did I do… I got rid of the bitch." She cackles like the evil witch bitch she is, but her laughing makes my head hurt more. I only wonder what she would do, if I barfed all over her right now.

And what did she do to Heather? She did leave school suddenly. Then I remember, she was an army brat, and her dad got stationed in Japan. Pretending to do away with Heather, I guess is her lame scare tactic. I guess she forgets I'm smart enough not to fall for it. Even with an achy throbbing, ready to explode head.

"Even after she was gone… he still didn't—he always told me no, he didn't like me that way. *Me.* Who *doesn't* like me that way?" she screams and let's go of my face. She paces the floor before coming back over to me. She grabs my chin once again, her nails leaving indentations in my skin. "Then you came along. He spent all his time with you and was always staring at your ·disgusting face. The bastard even admitted that he liked you. YOU! I was livid, but I had hoped after my threat he would stay away. *BUT* then what does he do? He tells the whole fucking school he was in fucking love with you! All my hard work to make you nothing and somehow you still managed to get his attention. How'd you do it, Brooke? Huh?" She hits me in the face again. Tears well in my eyes, from the pain and maybe from fear. "You're so fucking ugly…nothing special"

"Sticks and stones might break my bones, but words will never hurt me," I mutter the famous saying that you're taught as a kid. A painful smirk crosses my face.

Surprisingly, in the situation, it's perfect. Her words do mean nothing. They should have always meant nothing. She's a jealous cow.

It's amazing how life comes into perspective when you have to fight for it.

"Shut up, you stupid whore." She slaps me open-handed, and the ringing in my ears gets louder. "You're going to fucking pay and so is he. I will never let you be better than me. When I first met you, you had everything, all the attention. I hated you. It wasn't fair how guys wanted you and you had all these stupid two-bit friends. You don't know how good it felt to destroy you. It was so fucking easy, and I had so much fun. I never wanted to stop ruining anybody that got in my way. I became the queen when I took you and the other bitches down. Because you see now, I'm what all the guys want, everyone wants to be me, and there's no way I'm going to let you take that away from me, again. And when I'm done with you, he won't even be able to look at you anymore. No guy will. Well, that's if there's anything left of you."

Kara storms away to go upstairs. She's unstable and I'm the one that's going to pay when she finishes cracking all the way.

The overwhelming pain in my head and in my stomach is too much, and I end up vomiting. Thankfully,

I could move my head enough that it landed mostly next to my side and not on my lap. I'm sure they would've loved that.

What feels like hours later, I hear the basement door creak open again. I've tried working my hands out of the ropes, but it appears someone knows their sailor knots. My foggy mind drifts to Hunter and I keep hoping he's figured out something is wrong and comes to find me.

The thought of Hunter and knowing he loves me is all I want to think of right now. A happy place. I think back to this morning with his note, the mini muffins, the flowers, the kisses, his I love you's.

I need to fight. I can't let them break me. I know that's what they want. They want me to feel like nothing, be nothing, so it seems like they win. No matter the beating they give me, I'm not going to let that happen. Not again. They've won for so many years. I'm now back to the person I was before they tore me apart, and they can't have that part of me again.

The hateful four gather in front of me. Dan still with his damn phone pointed at me. They make fun of me throwing up, call me names, try to get a rise out of me, but I ignore it. Kara comes up to me and grabs at the collar of my dress. "Now let's see what has Hunter so impressed with you."

She rips open my maroon dress and buttons go flying in all directions. I look down and notice bruises forming on my stomach. "I don't get what Hunter would see in you? You're disgusting" Kara spits.

No, you are, you, stupid bitch.

"She does have a nice rack though," Dan comments, snickering.

"Shut up, you idiot," Kara growls at him and Emma smacks him in the head. I notice Dan roll his eyes in response.

"All I'm saying is I would do her," he smirks, trying

to make it into a joke.

"Just send the damn video douchebag. Let Hunter know we have his little *angel*. And soon, there won't be any reason for anybody to ever think she's hot again."

"Kara? What the fuck? We're just supposed to rough her up and leave her somewhere to walk home. I know you're pissed, but I have a scholarship to Jamestown. If anyone finds out I'm involved, I'll be screwed," Dan tries to reason, but it falls on deaf ears.

"You're already involved you dumbass. NOW SEND IT!" Kara marches to him and smacks him in the head.

I can truly feel all the love these four have for each other.

"John, come on," Dan pleads, turning to his friend in hopes he'll save him.

"Just do it, Dan. Hunter will remember his loyalty. No pussy is that good to turn on his friends." If I had the energy to roll my eyes, I would.

"We beat up his girlfriend. If we send him that video, he'll have proof. I'm not doing it. And I think we should let her go. She's had enough, and she doesn't look good. She's going to need medical help."

I wonder where Dan's conscience came from suddenly, but I'm thankful for it. He's the only one who hasn't laid a hand on me but to hold me or carry me around.

"You're such a fucking wuss." Kara shoves his chest. "Give me the damn phone motherfucker." She goes reaching for the phone and he holds it above his head.

"Fuck off Kara! I'm done."

"John," Kara whines, and I flinch when John lays a heavy punch into Dan's head. I look over at Emma and see she's shaking and starting to get nervous about all the changes in the plan. She pales as she stares down at Dan who is laid out on the ground, unmoving.

185

John takes the phone and hands it to Kara. She kisses him on the cheek and walks over to me. "Maybe I'll send him a little message instead, for him to come and join us." She points the phone at herself and flips her damn hair, "Oh, Hunter boy. Look who we have." She aims the camera to me, then back to her, "She's just so pretty now, isn't she? To think if you had just gone out with me, your little Brooke wouldn't be here, bleeding, and choking on her own vomit. You did this to her. Should've stayed away like I told you. Now, this stupid whore will get what has always been coming to her, and you'll get to watch her suffer." She points the camera back to me. "You're on, bitch. Say hi to Hunter."

In my sad, pathetic state, there's only one thing I want to say to him. "Hunter... I love you..."

Hunter

I'm sitting in the Turner's house—waiting for any kind of news on Brooke. Cops have been in and out since I called them about an hour ago. They've been to all their houses, but there's no sign of anyone inside. John's parents were home though, and they mentioned how they haven't seen him since yesterday. They even checked all the places I know they frequent and nothing. I have no idea where they are, and I would be the one that should know. Daryl was questioned, but he lacked any new information.

I called Max seconds after I got off the phone with the cops. It was the hardest call I've ever made, to tell him his daughter has been taken by people I thought were my friends. When I got to the house, Terri and Max were there, and I broke down, telling them everything. About how I kept our relationship hidden and my reasons why. To the confession of my love to her that landed on YouTube and ended up exiling the people that took her.

I thought they were both going to kill me, but my greatest surprise was when Terri wrapped me in her arms. She tried to tell me that everything would be okay, that we would find her. Max, on the other hand, remained quiet.

I know we will find her. I just don't know what state she's going to be in when we do. If I wasn't friends with them, if I'd showed her off from the beginning, if I'd said hi to her freshman year, this might have not happened.

I should've said hi to her Freshman year.

Fucking coward.

I pull on my hair, wanting to yell. She just told me she loved me and now I might lose her because I don't see how she could ever want me again after this. They've hurt her. They hurt her because of me. She doesn't deserve their anger and their torment.

She's going to hate me. I hate me.

A hand grasps my shoulder and I turn to my mom. My mother and father didn't waste a second to come over and be here. They know how crazy I am about Brooke, and they already adore her after one meeting.

I should've brought her around more.

My dad quickly jumped into action; being a lawyer can make things happen quicker if need to be. My mother has been talking with Terri and Max, giving her best moral support. It sucks that the first time my parents meet hers, it's in this situation.

"I know it's hard, but you need to try and relax. Deep breaths. You're not doing her any good ripping your hair out."

"I keep trying to figure out where they would have taken her. Why would they do this? I showed you what they already did to her, and that was only after maybe a couple minutes." My voice cracks, all my agony, the unshed tears lumping in my throat.

My mom pulls me into a hug. She doesn't say anything and tries her best to comfort me. My dad has been on the phone trying to get in contact with Dan, Emma, and Kara's parents. He thought it would be quicker than the cops trying to get any information out of them as to where their children would have gone. Riley and her folks are here as well. Riley came up to me shortly after my break down with Max and Terri and hugged me for dear life. I'm thankful Brooke has someone like Riley in her life. I must have told her I was sorry a million times before she slapped me in the chest and told me to shut up. It helped for about a second to snap me out my self-loathing. She reminded me how strong our girl was, and if anyone comes out of this on top, it'll be Brooke.

She is so much stronger than anyone else I know, especially me.

Max comes and sits on my other side and I feel him clamp my shoulder. I pull myself away from my mother and look at him. "You didn't do this, Hunter," he says, the first words he's said to me since I told him everything going on.

"Didn't I?" My voice shakes.

"No. You didn't. They did. You didn't make them take her, you didn't make them hit her. Just because you kept this away from them doesn't make you the aggressor. We all make mistakes, make poor judgments, but it's about what you do after your mistakes. You're here now, helping to find her. You called the cops, you called us, you're doing all you can do. And when we get her back, after me and her mom have stopped hugging her," he gives a light chuckle, "you're going to hug her, and you're going to need to be strong because she's going to need you. Hopefully, we will be lucky, and they haven't done anything else. Now buck up, son." He slaps my back and goes to stand.

Time is as if it's at a standstill; minutes feel like hours, and I feel like I need to be doing more. I just don't know what. Terri sits next to me and hands me a bottle of water.

"You need to drink something…" she says softly.

"Thank you." I look up at the distraught woman. She's been trying so hard to keep herself from breaking down, but she has silent tears rolling down her face. There's a part of me that wants to reach out and hug her. In just the short time, I've grown close to this family. They accepted me with open arms. They didn't kill me when I told them some dipshits took their daughter because of how I treated her at the beginning of our relationship.

My phone pings in my pocket and I reach for it, hoping maybe one of them would try to reach out to me. When I pull it out it's a text from Kara.

"I got a text message," I tell Terri, holding my phone open so she can see. She waves one of the cops over.

Once two cops and Max are hovering over me to look, I open the message and it's a video. Instantly, I feel sick when Kara's face fills the screen. Her vile words make my stomach turn.

Then when Brooke's beaten body fills the screen, Terri breaks down into heavy sobs.

Brooke's dress is ripped open, she's black and blue and bleeding. Her cheeks and lips are swollen. Her stomach is also covered in bruises, a large one on her right side. She's got cuts everywhere and appears to be bleeding from her chin. My stomach turns, and I get queasy thinking about all the things they must have done to her to be in such a state. I want to hope this is all a dream, that I will wake up, and she'll be in my arms, in one piece.

"My baby," Terri cries out and Max engulfs her in a hug, trying to comfort her. I can tell Max is doing his best to keep his emotions together. I wasn't even aware that everyone else had moved around me to watch until Riley started cursing quietly as she cried for her best friend.

"You're on, bitch. Say hi to Hunter."

Brooke looks up at the camera, and even in her state, I can make out how beautiful she is. Her honey eyes are glassy from her tears and all I want to do is reach out and grab her. Take her away from the horrors she's living.

"Hunter… I love you…"

I choke back the lump in my throat. She still says she loves me even after everything they've done to her.

"BITCH!" Kara's foot lifts to kick Brooke in the stomach before the video cuts off.

The cop asks for my phone to see if they can get a possible trace on where the message came from. I ask them to forward the video to someone else's phone. "I have this odd feeling I've seen this place before."

I'm determined more than ever to find her. The video gave little away to the exterior, but there's something familiar about it. They agree and send it to another phone. Max and Terri leave to let me watch. My mom sits by me again, rubbing my back as I experience heartbreaking torture over and over again.

As much as I hate it, I study the video what feels like a hundred times. Watching my girl in pain is like a stab into my heart every time I see it.

Then I spot the picture behind Brooke, and her whereabouts hit me like a ton of bricks.

"I know where she is!"

CHAPTER THIRTEEN

"I'm going to look down at the face of fear and laugh. No matter my pain, my aches, I will not let fear win me over. There will be good with the bad, but I only have one life to live, and I won't let fear or evil take me over because I can't let them win more than they already have once."

Hunter

"I know where she is!" I announce to everyone as I jump to my feet. Two cops and Max come rushing over to me. "She's at Kara's Uncle Larry's house…he lives over in Wellsbrook. I remember the painting on the wall." Behind Brooke is a hideous painting of a naked lady, with a full arm sleeve tattoo. I remember asking Kara about it because it was odd, something about a girl that got away from her uncle. "I've only been there once for a party, but that's his house. I know it is."

"Do you remember where?"

Fuck. The directions are vague. It was six months ago.

"Maybe if I had a map."

"I'm already on it," my father yells with his cell phone pressed to his ear. "I have Kara's dad on the line. His brother is out of town on business and Kara goes over there a lot." My dad writes down the address on a sheet of paper and hands it to the lead officer. I tell my mother wordlessly that I'm going. She tells me she'll stay here, and I don't wait for the rest of what she says as everyone goes flying out the door, and I'm on the heels of Max and Terri.

"Can I come with you?" I ask Max as he flings open his car door. He nods and tells me to get in the backseat. Seconds later, we are peeling out of the driveway of the house.

The drive seems to take forever, even following behind our police escort and going through every red light. My heart is racing, I'm sweating in places I didn't know I could because of my panic, hoping that I'm right. I know I'm right. That hideous ass painting scarred me for life.

We arrive at the house and I'm relieved to see an ambulance is already out front. There are at least twenty cop cars out here and yellow tape is being spun out around the house. Some of the officers are scoping out the place and surrounding it with their guns drawn. I'm sure Kara and the rest have to be aware of the activity outside. I just hope it doesn't make them do anything more drastic to Brooke then they already have.

Watching this unfold is like watching a scene from a movie. Except this movie is live action, the sounds of sirens, and the yelling over the radios is real. There's no pause button and no rewind to go back and fix it—and no fast forward to get through the pain.

We're told to stay back as officers' rush into the house. Minutes later they're dragging Kara and John out in handcuffs. EMTs rush in with stretchers and medical bags.

When I look over at the two, all I feel is uncontrollable rage and anger. I make a move towards them and Max grabs my shoulder. "Steady. Stay here. I'm going to talk to the officers. Don't do anything stupid. You don't need to end up in the back of the police car with them." He leaves me and goes to talk to one of the officers. He's right, but damn it, it would make me feel better.

I glance over at Terri and she's shaking like a leaf. I move over to her, not sure how to comfort her. "It's going to be okay. She's going to be okay," I try to state firmly, but it comes out more like a question. She looks over at me and grabs my forearm as we turn to stare at the front door, waiting. Max walks back over just as they pull the stretcher out of the house. Brooke's red curls hang from the gurney and she's wearing an oxygen mask. The three of us run over to her and when we get a glimpse of her, Terri breaks down, and I'm close behind. I saw the video but seeing it in person is ten times worse.

My beautiful girl.

My angel.

How could they have done this to her? Why would they go this far? All because their egos have been stepped all over?

She's never done a single thing to hurt anyone before. She didn't deserve this. It should've been me at the brunt of their attacks. It was me that humiliated them and got them all over YouTube, not her. All we did was love each other and this is where it got us.

"She lost consciousness when she saw us, her blood pressure is dangerously low, but her pulse is in the normal range. We're taking her to Wellsbrook Methodist. Only one person can ride with us."

"Terri, go, we'll meet you there," Max tells his wife and she wastes no time hopping in the back of the ambulance with Brooke.

Max and I run back to his car to follow the ambulance. On my way, I see Kara and John in the back of the police cruisers. They both look full of angst, but

Kara still manages to sneer when she sees me. I want to go over there and return the favor, but I need to get to Brooke more. I bet this is not how they expected today to end. The assholes probably thought they would get away with this. I'm going to make sure they pay for everything they did to Brooke. There's no way Mommy and Daddy are going to get them out of this one.

I call Riley and my parents to tell them the news and what hospital they are sending Brooke to. Other than that, the car ride is hushed as Max follows closely behind the ambulance.

We arrive at the hospital in under five minutes when it should have taken ten. They wheel Brooke through the ER entrance to the back and once we get to the double doors, a nurse tells us we have to wait so they can evaluate her.

They run through Brooke's medical history, checking for allergies, her medications, prior surgeries and so on. After all the questions are answered, they leave us to wait on stiff plastic chairs. Max is holding onto Terri for dear life. No parent should ever have to see their child in such a way. I can't even imagine the thoughts they have running through their heads.

I was beaten up tons of times, put in the hospital, but this—*this* is extreme. It's as if they were trying to kill her. I can't wrap my mind around the evil of it. Never in a million years did I see it going this far. Was I that blind or was I the thing that broke the camel's back?

It feels as if an eternity goes by while we wait for news. Doctors and nurses have come in and out of the triage room, but no one has stopped to talk to us. My parents and Riley are in a separate waiting room since they couldn't come back to the ER. If I know my dad, he's doing his best to work up a case against these assholes.

"Mr. and Mrs. Turner?" A doctor in dark blue scrubs stands in front of us. The three of us rush to our feet.

"Yes, how's my daughter?"

"We need to take her for a CT and have a closer look. It appears she has a concussion. The EMT told us she threw up on the scene, so we need to check for any brain damage. Also, with the number of bruises on her abdomen, we need to check for any internal bleeding. She has blood in her urine, so we're worried about her kidneys. She also has two broken ribs on her right side. She's still unconscious, but otherwise, she's stable. After we run the tests, we are going to put her up in the ICU for further observation. She needed five stitches above her eye and twenty on the side of her head above the ear. The other cuts are superficial. I'll be back soon to discuss more and answer any questions you have."

"Thank you, doctor," Max says, his voice cracking.

"A nurse will bring you upstairs to the other waiting room."

God, please let her be okay.

We've been in the ICU waiting room for about a half hour. Riley, her parents, and my mom have joined us in our pacing and watching the clock tick by.

My father and an officer enter the room causing Max to jump to his feet.

"What's going on?"

"I realize this might not be a good time, but I was wondering if you would like to know what is going on with the perpetrators?" Officer Michaels flips open his notebook and pulls out a pen.

"Yes, please. I only got a small amount of

information earlier," Max says, his hand holding tightly to Terri's.

"And you're okay with everyone in this room being privy to the information, Mr. Turner?"

"Yes, please."

"When we arrived on the scene, it appears three out of the four subjects were fighting with each other. Miss Turner was tied to a chair but was conscious at the time. The subjects were quickly arrested, except Dan Rockland, he was unconscious at the scene. We then untied your daughter and laid her down till the medics arrived. It was when they came in the door, she muttered something and passed out.

"Emma Williams was hysterical before we took her out. We had her wait inside with an officer while they got Miss Turner and Mr. Rockland tended to and out of the house. Miss Williams started talking right away. She confessed that the four of them made a plan yesterday evening to take Miss Turner and rough her up, film it for everyone to see, then leave her somewhere to walk home, possibly naked. They wanted to embarrass her, like she did them, while also getting even with Hunter Evans. She said, I quote, "so he could see how ugly she really is." Officer Michaels looks over at me and my head falls into my hands.

It is my fault.

Terri gasps and I hear Riley mumble 'mother fuckers' under her breath. As for me, I'm in shock hearing their plan, and I want to know how hurting her helped them. Brooke would have said something, I'm sure. But I guess it shows how confident they thought they were, by thinking they could get away with it. And what they didn't know was that never in a million years would I see Brooke as ugly, no matter what cowardly, vicious things they did to her. No matter what marks they left on her, she will always be stunning to me. Everything about her inside and out is beautiful, and I'm in love with her because of who she is.

"Miss Williams has stated that the plan changed when they got to Larry Addams' house," the officer continues. "They were only supposed to go to Miss Addams' residence. Kara beat her up, while Mr. Rockland videotaped on his phone. We have the phone and the videos that support the abuse Miss Turner encountered and it is in evidence to be used against them. Afterward, Miss Williams said they took Miss Turner to the basement and tied her to a chair. At one point, Kara Addams was alone with her for at least twenty minutes. Miss Williams thought when Miss Addams came back from talking to Miss Turner, she seemed out of sorts."

"What do you mean out of sorts? What did she do to Brooke?" I ask in a panic, digging my nails into my scalp and yanking my hair. Max grabs my shoulder as a way to help calm me. Something he's been doing all day when it should be the other way around.

"I'm unaware of what happened between the two at that time. She said Miss Addams came back in a fit, angered, more so than before. Miss Addams and Mr. Hester are refusing to talk and waiting for lawyers. Also, I'm sure Miss Turner can give a better account."

Kara and John better hope I never run into them again, because I'm going to have to have my dad get me out of murder charges. Emma and Dan, I might just return the favor of what they did to Brooke.

"Were those videos shared or uploaded anywhere?" Max asks.

"The videos found on Mr. Rocklands and Miss Addams phone have not been uploaded. However, there was an image sent of Miss Turner beaten and tied to a chair via Snapchat to a large number of recipients."

"These freakin' kids—" Max grumbles and balls his hand into a fist. I'm right there with him in his anger and gripping the arm of this plastic chair, where I can hear it cracking. I'm glad no one saw the videos, but a picture is bad enough.

"Yes, but some of them did call 911 when they received the image to report it. There was an open chat amongst the recipients, but so far none have seemed pleased. The ones who had screenshot and saved the images have been identified. Mr. Evans here said he will help you handle them if need be. But so far, there's nothing floating around that we can see. If that changes, we will let you know."

I wonder how easy it would get these asswipes just to plea out for a life sentence, so no one is subjected to them ever again.

Officer Michael flips through his book and reads a couple of words before looking back to us. "Now, back on the scene, according to Miss Williams, when they all got back in the room, Miss Addams wanted to send a video to Mr. Evans," Officer Michaels continues, getting back to the events of what happened at the house. "Mr. Rockland went against it and Mr. Hester knocked him out. Soon after that event, we arrived and arrested them. They have been charged with kidnapping and assault and battery. Now, when Miss Turner is awake and ready, we will need to talk to her and get her account of the whole ordeal. You have my card if you need anything. I hope that Brooke makes a speedy recovery."

"Thank you, officer." Max stands up and shakes his hand.

My dad quickly offers his services pro bono and whatever Brooke and the Turner's will need, to help make sure that all four are locked away for as long as possible. He knows there will be no problems charging them with felony kidnapping and charging Kara and John as adults, since they're eighteen, and he will also push for the other two.

Stronger

He went on to tell us about a case in Florida, somewhat similar to this, where the assailants got off easy, walked away with nothing more than probation and letters of apology. That case, along with all the school shootings has been an eye-opener for the system. The more this type of violence keeps happening, people are starting to realize there needs to be heavier punishments for these crimes, and not just excusing them because they're *kids*. My dad said and I quote, '*you're never going to stop a generation from acting like punks, if you're only giving out slaps on the wrist.*' DA's are now more likely to try them as an adult and charge them with the correct crimes that match the act. I've never been more grateful for my father being a lawyer then I am in this moment. And a powerful one to boot.

After that, my dad's lawyer hat came off, and he asked if they would need anything for the night. The Turner's happily accepted his offer to pick them up some clothes and other essentials from home, since there was no way they were leaving.

We continue to wait even after my parents leave. We continue to pace the floors as our worries grow. I'm starting to believe doctors might be snails. I mean how long does it take to do a CT? Riley's parents gathered us some food and drinks, even though no one feels like eating. I've sent countless prayers for her to be alright, physically and most important, emotionally. I need to be strong for her, support her, but it's so hard to do when I feel as if I failed her. I was unable to protect her because I was a selfish prick.

And I swear that damn minute hand on that annoying, ticking, tocking, clock is going backward. All I want to do is rip it down from the wall and send it flying out the window.

We all just need to see her. Our girl needs to be okay.

We are half-heartedly watching the news when we

see that the media has gotten wind of what happened to Brooke. The story they are running simply states, teen kidnapped by school bullies and beaten. They give a little insight to where it happened and how four teens were arrested. Thankfully, Brooke's name isn't released since she's underage. But I know it's only a matter of time before *everyone* at school finds out. After that, Max changes the channel to the cartoon network to keep the background noise. Figures, it would be Brooke's favorite, "Scooby Doo," that is playing.

I have to chuckle inwardly and remember her telling me how even when she was younger, she always felt like Velma and Fred belonged together. Then she looked at me, and told me, "*the nerd always ends up with the hottie in the end. Because the hottie figures out not only does she have brains, but she's sexy under those glasses and the revolting orange sweater. And it would only be a matter of time before the bimbo will end up dying because hottie is always tired of saving her damn ass.*"

If there wasn't a truer statement.

"Turner Family," the same doctor from earlier addresses us and walks into the waiting room. We all stand and gather around the doctor eagerly.

"How is she?" I blurt out at the same time Terri does.

"She's doing alright, considering. She's a trooper that's for sure. While we were running Brooke's CT, she woke up for a bit. She's was groggy and in a lot of pain. She talked and knew where she was and could name her loved ones. We kept her awake while we ran her test. She does have a mild concussion, but no signs of brain injury. We will be keeping an eye on that, and run another test tomorrow to make sure it's still clear.

"The CT did show that Brooke has mild kidney bruising. We will need to keep that under observation for any signs of failure. Most of the time it will heal on its own in about a week with rest, and we will limit her fluid intake. But all her other organs are fine. We wrapped her broken ribs. Once we finished everything, she was still in a clear amount of pain, so we gave her pain meds and a sedative. Since there was no sign of brain injury and she appeared to be aware of her surroundings, we want her to be comfortable and get some sleep. Her body is exhausted from the trauma and we think the reason she passed out at the scene might have been from the adrenaline crash."

"My baby," Terri whispers, as tears stream down her face again.

"How long do you expect her recovery to take?" Max asks, pulling his wife tighter to him. "Will there be any side effects, anything we need to worry about?"

"She will need to stay in the hospital for a week or two for her kidney to heal. Once she wakes and we do another CT we can move her to a regular room for the rest of her stay. Fair warning, even with the light sedative she might sleep for a long while. Like I said before, her body is exhausted and she needs rest, lots of it. It's her body's way of healing. She also might wake up and go right back to sleep. It's important to let her sleep and don't be in a rush to wake her. But Brooke will be okay."

My shoulders sag in relief and I do believe I see the tension roll off Terri and Max's shoulders as well.

"I don't think she will have any long-lasting issues. Now her pressure is still low which is normal, she's breathing good, and her heart rate is steady. While she was awake, she never panicked and seems to be handling the ordeal well, but we will know more about her emotional state once she wakes fully."

"Can we go see her now?" Terri pleads.

"Yes, two at a time please."

Terri and Max enter her room first, while Riley and I stand in the hall, looking through the large glass windows.

I'm not leaving this place anytime soon and I don't

think Riley wants to either. I know my parents will understand that there's no way I'm not going to be under the same roof as my girl. I only wish I could hold her in my arms and tell her how much I love her.

Max comes out of the room first and walks over to us. You can see every ounce of pain and sorrow he's carrying reflected in his eyes. He has the weight of the world on his shoulders and appears to have aged in the last hours. He's emotionally destroyed. "Be prepared. I know you guys saw the video and you saw her on the scene Hunter, but it's still hard." He chokes out. He's been holding it in all day, I'm sure trying to be strong for his wife and everyone else. Now, this large man I've come to admire, is, in fact, crying and shedding his pain. His child was beaten and injured, lying in a hospital bed, and I think that would be too much for any parent.

I know it is for me. And it kills me to know I'm partly to blame for putting this father through this.

"I talked to the nurse and she doesn't have any problems with all of us being in with her. Come."

We follow Max into the room. Terri is standing on one side of the bed, holding Brooke's limp hand. Riley gasps loudly and starts to cry. "How could they?"

Max folds her in his arms to comfort her. I walk to the opposite side of the bed and take Brooke's other hand.

She has an IV just below her knuckles, a bunch of wires hooked up to her, and is surrounded by beeping machines. Her face is puffy and purple, with cuts and scrapes. Her neck is also tinted in hues of blue. She has bruises around her wrist and arms from when they tied her up and maybe from defending herself. She looks so frail and tiny. But I know my beautiful girl is under there. My cheeks are wet and the pain in my heart is heavy. I bend down to kiss her forehead and the corner of her lips.

"I'm here, Angel. I'm never going anywhere. I'm so sorry...I love you."

Stronger

I'm pacing the waiting room of the ICU, waiting for my turn with Brooke. It's been twenty-two hours since I've seen her awake, since I've seen her smile, and since she's kissed me back. The hospital has a strict policy of two in the room, well, depending who the nurse is. The night nurses let us all four stay, while the day nurse, kicked Riley and me out. Our parents went home, but not before my mom gave me a stern lecture to eat something and try to rest. I told her I would, but I know that's not going to happen till I see Brooke's eyes open again. Thankfully, they also informed the school that we wouldn't be in for at least a week. One less thing to worry about.

Riley is asleep, slumped over in one of the chairs. None of us slept well last night. Every beep, every sound, and every time a nurse came in, we were on our toes hoping she had woken up.

"You need to sit down, Hunter," Riley mumbles, "and try to rest. You're making me dizzy."

"I thought you were sleeping?" I chuckle softly and move to sit down next to her.

"No. I don't think I'll be able to till she wakes up. But I know pacing and driving myself to the nutty farm isn't going to help her wake up any quicker. You heard the doctor; she's going to be okay. She needs the rest to heal," she reminds me and rubs my shoulder.

"I know. But at least if I see her awake, even for a minute, I'll know she's okay. Seeing is believing. After everything I put her through, I need to see that she's alright. I still can't help but blame myself. It's all because of me she's here. If I stayed away, if I wasn't friends with them, or if I'd told in the first place, I don't know…" I toss my head back, hitting the wall and close my eyes. "All I know is I just wanted to be with her, and I put her at risk because she was with me. I love her…and I don't know what I would do if she hated me. She needs to be okay…it would kill me too if she went back into hiding, being scared because of all of this." I ramble, expelling the thoughts that keep plaguing me. No matter how many times I'm told it's not my fault, I can't stop thinking that way.

"You need to stop beating yourself up. You might have been friends with them, but I don't think you could have ever seen how deranged Kara and John were. Especially, Kara. Even from what the officer said, neither did Dan or Emma. We all knew she was a bitch, but I don't think anyone could have predicted how far her evil went. All of them really. But they will pay and Brooke, she will heal."

"I know, but…"

"No buts. She has her parents, our parents, me, and most of all you. She's in love with you. Sure, you were a dumbass, but overall, I get where you were coming from. Despite all that, you helped bring Brooke out again. She grew more confident because of you. She got out of those damn clothes she had no business wearing. She's always been good-looking, but you helped her shine and be able to accept who she is. You gave her that damn push she's been needing, someone to see who she was, and not the girl Kara made her go hide into. All you can do now is be there for her and keep loving her. Now, I'm going to get a damn candy bar and a Mt. Dew, I need all the sugar I can get to stay awake. You want anything?" She stands up from her chair and digs around in her purse for change.

"No thanks. But Riley?"

Stronger

She swings her head back to look at me, still making her way to the candy machine. "Yeah?"

"Thank you."

"No problem. Brooke has always been there for me, and I'm going to be there for her, and her flashy boy toy." She smirks before going back to stick her dollar in the machine.

I smile for the first time today. Riley is going to be the humor that Brooke needs right now and I'm thankful because I don't think I could do it.

Riley sits next to me chomping away on a Kit-Kat and slurping down her Mt. Dew when Max and Terri come into the waiting room. They're smiling.

"She's awake," Terri says, "and she's doing well. She's in pain, and they gave her some more meds through her IV, so she might end up going back to sleep, but she's awake."

"Can we go see her?" I ask jumping to my feet as soon as Terri said she was awake.

"Of course, now that I know she's been awake. I think I might be able to eat again. The nurse is going to talk to the doctor. Once they check her over again and make sure her kidney function is stable, they're going to move her to a private room. But go...I know she wants to see you both."

I nod, opening my arms to give Terri a hug. I'm so ecstatic that I'm going to see my girl again, I might hug everyone that passes me in the hallway.

"Oh, dear boy, she's going to be alright." She pats my shoulder, before stepping away. "Go, before the meds put her out again." She gives a light chuckle and I run out the door with Riley behind me.

I put my hand on the handle and I notice Riley step back. "Aren't you coming in?"

"I will...in a few...you go see her first. She'll never admit it, but she would want to see you more than me right now. Go in, but I'm only giving you five because I want to see her before she dozes off."

I give her a nod before going inside. When the door clicks behind me, Brooke's head turns to me. It still aches to see her so bruised and swollen. But she looks better today than she did yesterday.

She's wearing her glasses, something I only see her wear from time to time now, no matter how many times I tell her I do find her sexy in them. She's now addicted to her contacts. Her hair is a tangled mess, and she's wearing a blue hospital gown, yet she's the most gorgeous girl in the world.

"Hey you," her voice croaks, and my breath is taken away when she smiles at me. That's the smile that took over my heart.

My girl is still here.

And she's not hiding.

Brooklyn

When I woke up and saw the white walls, I knew I was in the hospital. My head was aching and my sides were killing me. I recalled everything that happened back in that house, which led to me lying in this bed with a bunch of machines hooked to me.

After Kara kicked me when I told Hunter I loved

him, Emma went nuts on Kara. She started swinging at Kara, yelling, and screaming. She was going on how she was being a selfish bitch again, and to let me go. She was also crying about Dan. Through my haze, I could tell he still hadn't moved. John must have suckered punched him good to cause the long-term effect of being knocked out.

John had ended up grabbing Emma who was kicking around, still going crazy. I was forgotten, and they started fighting with each other. At that point, I was ready to go to sleep because watching them made me twice as exhausted.

John then held Emma down and Kara started drawing on my stomach, labeling my areas of fat, then took pictures. She wanted everyone to know that I was an ugly beast. Then there was a lot of banging and yelling. The feeling of sweet relief washed over my achy body when I saw the cops rush in. I knew then that it was over. I saw the EMT's and Kara in handcuffs and that's the last thing I remember before waking inside a CT scanner.

Once my parents noticed I was awake, I don't think I've ever been hugged so much and yet so gently in my life. They were both a mess, and I was so happy to see them. They explained my injuries and a nurse came to look me over.

I have yet to look in a mirror, and I'd rather not see it until I have to. A part of me knows if I see the marks they left on me, it will all become real how those people hurt me for nothing. I just have to try and remember when I do look, the promise I made to myself when I was tied to that damn chair: *Let this be what makes me stronger, not weaker.*

My mom and dad left to let Hunter and Riley in. Supposedly, the day nurse doesn't let more in than two at a time. My mom wasn't too happy about that. "People heal better surrounded by loved ones," she said. Which I can believe. I'm grateful the other two most important people in my life are here for me.

I hear the door open and I take a good look at the man that just walked through. I think he might look worse than I do.

Okay, maybe not. The bastard is still hot.

His hair is standing at all ends, his clothes are a wrinkled mess, he's pale, and looks exhausted with dark worry circles under his eyes.

"Hey, you." I give him a smile even though it hurts. I want to convey that no matter what, they didn't break me, and they didn't break us. My mom and dad told me what a disaster he was when he found out the hateful four took me. They also said that Hunter told them everything about the beginning of our relationship that led to why the four did what they did to me. So, I know he's spending this time blaming himself. I don't want that.

"Brooke, Brooke, Brooke..." he says my name repeatedly like a prayer. He walks over to me and grabs my hand and sits on the edge of my bed. "You have no idea how good it is to see you awake. How are you? Do you need anything?" Hunter brushes my hair back and kisses me on the forehead.

"I'm in a bit of pain, but they gave me some good stuff. And it's good to see you too, Hunter." I run my hands through his hair and pull him down to kiss me. He doesn't hesitate, but when his lips touch mine, I hiss. I wasn't expecting for my lips to hurt too, on top of everything else.

Maybe I should look in the damn mirror.

Hunter's face turns anxious and he shakes his head, his fingers ever so lightly brush my cheek. "I can't...I can't wrap my head around it all. That they could do this to you, or how anyone could do this to anyone." Tears well up in his eyes, but he wipes them away. "You haven't done anything to anyone and here you are and it's all because of me. I want to take this pain from you. It's not fair, it should be me, not you. Angel...I'm so sorry."

"Hunter," I wrap my arms around his neck and pull him to me. He's mindful of my sides, as he buries himself into my neck

"I'm so sorry, baby. I'm so sorry." My jock has broken down. I feel the wetness of his tears on my neck and all I can do is brush back his hair.

"Please don't hate me. Please…"

I hold him in my arms, savoring the way it feels to be close to him again. His guilt, pain, hurt, the fact that he's here, all but proves his love for me. I suffered the physical pain and he's suffering the emotional. This is what I'm sure they wanted in a way.

No more letting them win. No letting them break us.

I lift his face for him to look at me. "Hunter, I don't hate you. You didn't do this. And I'm sure they would've done this or something like it if you did tell them sooner. Kara has been finding a reason to do this for years, I'm sure. Please, don't think I hate you. I love you."

"I love you, always, Angel." His nose rubs against mine and kisses my face so gently, and so sweetly. "I'm supposed to be the stronger one here and holding you, but yet again, you prove to me how much stronger and braver you really are." His eyes shine and I know I've won him back, even for a little bit. He kisses me again. "Hey, I haven't told you how amazing you are today."

"No. But you have now."

I know, in this moment, nothing will tear us apart because we have each other. We can't let it, because then evil wins, and I was taught evil never wins. Today is about starting over and prevailing.

CHAPTER FOURTEEN

"If a couple can come out stronger and better through all the things life throws at them—they were the ones who were always meant to be together. Because no matter how bad things get or what is thrown at them, they'll always have each other to help pick up the pieces, rebuild, and grow from the mistakes."

Brooklyn

One Week Later

It's hard to believe that this boy lying next to me in my hospital bed, watching a rerun of *The Simpsons,* might be my happily ever after. I know I'm only seventeen and I've been through the gates of hell, but I think sometimes you know where your forever lies.

And mine is with Hunter Evans

We're stronger and better together.

My parents have gone home for the night. I *had* to make them go home. They need sleep in their own bed and if my mom fluffs my pillow one more time, well, I might lose my mind.

I'm doing very well according to the doctor. I still have some minor kidney bleeding, but they are keeping

me monitored closely. All I do is lie in this bed. *Fun times.*
Hopefully, by the end of the week, they'll let me up.

I finally looked at myself in the mirror the morning
after I woke up and ended up having my first break down
since I arrived.

*"Are you sure you want to do this?" Hunter asks
holding a portable mirror the nurse gave him*

*"Yes, I need to know." I wiggle my hand at him
wanting the mirror. I don't really want to, but I can feel
that my face is jacked up. I thought I could ignore it, but
once the meds wore off, I couldn't anymore.*

*He sighs and hands me the mirror. I brace myself,
prepared for the worst, but when I come face to face with
my reflection. I lose it.*

*It's worse than I ever pictured. My face is swollen
like a balloon, I have a hundred different shades of
purples and greens across my cheekbones, my nose, my
eyes, and my mouth. and there are stitches above my eye
and ear making me look like the undead.*

*"I'm a monster," I sob. I'm hideous and disgusting. I
throw the mirror to the floor and it cracks on impact. I'm
surprised it didn't break when my ugly mug appeared in
the glass.*

*Hunter wraps his arms carefully around me, and his
lips rest on my temple. "You're not a monster, you're
beautiful, stunning…"*

*"Are you blind?" I screech out, pushing him away.
"I'm like my own horror movie. I could easily scare away
animals and children." Big thick tears fall down my
monstrous face. I pull up my gown and start to undo my
wrap. I need to see everything.*

*"Brooke…" Hunter tries to stop me, but I glare at
him.*

*"I need to know." He doesn't get it. Why would he?
He's still perfect. "I feel it every time I move. I need to*

see."

I pull the wrap open and look down. I choke back more tears and snot when I see Kara's footprint on my ribcage. Along with other large bruises where she kicked me. She marked me with her hate.

"Okay, that's enough." Hunter grabs the wrap and puts it back around me. I allow him as I keep crying. And god damn, crying hurts, physically and emotionally.

"They ruined me, that's what they wanted." I hate them. I'm not even sure how I'm gonna get past this. Hunter wraps me in his arms and I bury myself into his neck. "They ruined me." He's rubbing my back and leaving light kisses on my head. My breath shakes as I'm comforted by his arms. I have to remind myself that he's here and hasn't run for the hills.

"Baby, that's not true. These bruises will heal and be nothing but a distant memory. They don't make you who you are, and I still see you. You'll always be beautiful. This doesn't change anything. You are still you, and I love you."

"I love you." I hiccup. My breathing starts to calm, and I embrace the fact that I'm in the arms of the person I need the most. He does make me feel better, he wants me, bruised or not. I can't let this shake me, and he's right, what I look like doesn't change anything. I'm still me. What they did to me won't ruin who I am. I just need to be stronger than their hate.

My mom, dad, and Riley caught us in that moment, and I was soon engulfed in a group hug. Being wrapped up in all of them, I remembered that the people that matter, aren't going to care about some little marks after it's all said and done. They love me. If anything, the crying ended up being therapeutic. No matter how strong I want to be, what I went through was traumatic. I just need to learn to process it.

After that event, I had to talk to a psychologist to evaluate my well-being. The psychologist thought I was doing amazingly well, but thought it would be good for me to see her for a bit, as I work through everything. I know I have to be realistic; I will have bad days with the good. But I'm lucky to have people to turn to when it's bad.

That same day I broke down I had to give my account to the police about everything that happened to me. I made sure when I recounted my story, I was alone to do so. My family and Hunter know what happened, for the most part, but I wanted to make it through the interview without someone gasping or crying.

Kara still isn't talking, but it looks like John is starting to. Dan and Emma have already begun telling their tale, but there have been some changes made from the original one, pointing more of the finger towards Kara. As for Dan, he didn't suffer any major injuries from John's punch. The only thanks I have for him is, if he didn't start saying no to sending the video, I wonder how much worse damage they would have done to me.

There was still one thing that weighed on my mind, and that was Heather. I knew she left the country, but maybe Kara did end up doing something to her before she left. I told the cops and they did manage to get in touch with her through Skype. She said the only problem she had with Kara was getting verbally harassed during and after dating Hunter, but never anything physical. Heather never told anyone about it, including Hunter.

Three days ago, they were all officially charged with their crimes at their initial hearing. Now we are awaiting their arraignment in a couple of days. James says the likelihood of Dan and Emma pleading guilty is good. The other two he said will be a little harder, so now it's just a waiting game. I was told Daryl was expelled from school, but not charged with anything.

Stronger

As I thought, there was no way to keep what happened to me from the ears of my fellow classmates. With the picture that was sent via Snapchat and the news reports, there was no way to deny it. I wasn't sure how anyone would react to it, so it was a surprise when Riley called me last night after I made her go home to get some beauty sleep, telling me there were all kinds of flowers, balloons, and cards outside my house. Also, this morning I received a couple bouquets of flowers from teachers, telling me to get well soon and they missed me around school.

As sweet as all that is, nothing beats Hunter's different color roses for the week. I'm starting to wonder if he has some deal with a floral shop for them to stay stocked in single roses. The roses always come with a note giving me his sweet words.

Today's was:

> *I love what I see on the outside: you're sexy, beautiful, and have the most amazing pair of eyes that I find myself getting lost in. But it's what's on the inside: your personality, your good heart and your strength—that makes you irresistible. You being you is why I love you...*

Can we say swoon?

He also got me a little pink elephant from the gift shop, I'm sure meant for a new baby girl, but I love it anyway.

I look over at Hunter who's lying on his side, one arm raised under his head, and the other laying over my hips. He's staring at me with a shy smile and leans over to gently kiss my cheek.

"How long before you get kicked out of my bed

tonight?" I grin and run my hands through his unruly hair.

"Well, your father is gone, so I think I have at least a couple hours before the nurse yells at me." He chuckles. It's always the second Hunter gets comfortable that someone is harping for him to get out of my bed. Surprisingly, my dad is more lenient than the nurses.

"You sure you want to spend another night here? I won't be upset if you want to go home."

"I know, but I want to enjoy as much time as I can with you. My parents are making me go back to school on Monday." He pushes out his bottom lip in a pout. "But I'll be here after school, and when you get out, I'll be at your side the second the bell rings. I might ask if I can just move into your house to be there as much as possible."

"Yeah, that's not going to happen." I giggle picturing that conversation. "But thank you." I kiss his lips lightly. After three days the swelling of my lips has died down, and it doesn't hurt too much to kiss him anymore.

"You're welcome, Angel."

The TV yells something about Saturday night entertainment, and I remember Hunter's final game was today. It was the championships and it had already been pushed back because of weather delays.

"Your game. You missed it."

He shrugs. "I don't care about a stupid football game. Nor do I really want to be around anyone at school right now."

"Hunter, you were looking forward to it."

"I was, until three of my teammates basically turned against me and involved themselves in hurting my girl. I don't know who I trust and, hell, I'd much rather be with you than some sweaty guys tackling me over a ball," he says matter-of-factly.

I reach over to rub my hand over his crotch. "Awww. That makes me want to play with your balls." I grin like a loon, such a simple thing of him always being hard when

216

he lays in bed with me is good for my self-esteem. He *wants* me even though I'm covered in hideous marks.

"Brooklyn," he growls, lifting my hand off the front of his pants, "you're not playing fair." He presses his lips to my knuckles.

"Sorry, I can't help myself," I tell him chewing on my bottom lip.

"Woman, stop your madness." He unhooks my lip from my teeth. "If you don't, I'm going to have to check myself into the fourth floor with those nice padded walls. Now, cut it out."

I watch as he adjusts himself and I break out into a fit of giggles. Yeah, it's no wonder daddy wanted to keep him out of my bed.

I grab my side, trying to ease my laughter. Fuck it hurts. But being able to laugh right now, it feels too good to stop. Hunter just rolls his eyes at me and kisses my forehead.

"Knock, knock," a male voice comes from the cracked door.

Hunter and I turn our heads as I yell to come in.

Mr. Marshall walks in the room carrying a large vase of lilies and daisies. Hunter sits up so damn fast when he sees him, you would have thought he had his hands in my pants.

"What are you doing here?" My voice croaks, feeling suddenly shy and wanting to hide my face in Hunter's chest.

I've been around my family, nurses, and doctors, but

not other people that knew what I looked like before. It's their reaction I worry about.

Deep breaths. He's harmless.

"I wanted to check on my favorite student. Well, all the teachers did, but I thought you might want to see your favorite teacher," he jokes with a toothy grin. "Well, Ms. Gaines offered—"

I cringe and Mr. Marshall laughs. "Aren't you glad I came now?" He places the vase of flowers down on the table along with the others. Mr. Marshall knows everyone in the school adores him. I think everyone has that one teacher they truly love. "How are you doing?" His tone grows serious.

I point to my face and shrug. "Besides this and having to stay in bed, I'm alright."

"You look well." He smiles, and I roll my eyes wondering if he's blind. "Hey, I'm a teacher, I don't lie. Sure, you have a couple bruises, but I can see that *you* are well."

"Told you." Hunter nudges me gently and brushes his lips to my temple. "She's been amazingly strong. I'm in awe of her," he tells Mr. Marshall while looking at me. I'm sure my purple cheeks have darkened with a red tint.

"I can tell. I actually have a couple of reasons why I'm here. Your teachers and Principal Marks and I had a conference to discuss how to handle your missed work while you recover."

"Oh god, I'm going to be buried in make-up work till I'm gray." I have no idea when I'm going back, and sometimes I wonder if I even want to go back. But I know I have to, for me, and as long as I have Hunter and Riley by my side, I can do it.

"I highly doubt you would have any issues, Miss Turner. However, since you're still on your way to be valedictorian, we weren't too worried about missing assignments and tests. We gave you an outline though, so you know where we are when you get back. You'll have to do some reading, and we gave you assignments to look over. But I know we won't have to worry about you falling behind, you could do it all in your sleep."

"That wouldn't include me too, would it?" Hunter perks up jokingly.

"No, Mr. Turner said you would be here, so I brought what you missed." He smirks, pulling a manila envelope out of his bag. "It's due, Friday."

"You're all heart, Mr. Marshall." Hunter takes the envelope from him, "at least I still have my tutor." He looks over at me and winks.

"There's something else I wanted to share with the both of you." He moves the chair closer to the bed, and Hunter takes my hand.

"What's going on?" My worry spikes. What more can he talk to us about other than school assignments?

"I had a couple of your fellow classmates approach the principal today."

"Why?" Hunter snaps, clearly annoyed, but my curiosity spikes further wondering what was said.

"It's not bad. I'm sure, as you know, word has gotten around about what happened. Believe me when I say people were shocked and outraged. I'll be blunt. There are always assholes that find it amusing, but the majority don't. So, some of the senior class wanted to find a way to keep this from happening again. Many of them victims themselves of the four. They brainstormed and came up with the idea of an anti-bullying program for the school. We have a zero-tolerance policy, but it's not enough. They want to do more, expand what has been started around some areas. Be able to give support to the student that's being bullied, especially to ones that might not have it. Make sure it's something safe that people can tell what's going on and work out a successful way to hopefully stop it. It's going to take lots of planning and trials, but if it works, well, there's a chance we could eventually get it to expand through the district, maybe the state."

"Really?" I'm baffled, amazed, and fascinated by all this.

People, my own classmates, coming together and helping. It sucks I had to be kidnapped and beaten first, but I guess sometimes you need a big moment to start seeing what's wrong with the world.

Hunter shakes his head and I push my hand through his hair. "Hunter, what's the matter? This is good."

He looks over to me, guilt once again forming in his eyes. I thought we moved past this. "It's great," he mumbles.

"But?" Come on Hunter, spill your guts to me.

"As he said, the people I considered friends made people's lives hell. I sat back and did nothing to try and stop it. I'm no better than them. Once in a while, they did it in front of me, and I did nothing."

I take his hand and press my lips to his palm. "You've got to stop blaming yourself for what they did. You made mistakes Hunter, everyone does. You felt you needed to protect yourself from them because that's how they dehumanized everyone. You knew if you showed weakness you would've been their next feeding. After what you told me, I can't blame you for not wanting to go down that road. It just took you some time to gather your strength, that backbone you were hiding, and do something. You did tell them off. It might have had some *consequences*, but they are not your fault."

I do think if Hunter told them he was with me in the first place, this would have happened anyways, or something like it. Hunter was something Kara couldn't have. Hunter was the claimed king of the school, even though he never knew his true power till much later, and for Kara to stay on top, she needed Hunter. Kara not

220

getting what she wants was like three-hundred two-year-olds throwing tantrums at the same time. When I was the one that ended up being the one that got him, I know it killed her. That time in the bathroom, when she first attacked me was because she saw something between Hunter and me. She felt threatened. Plus, she hated me. I would have been at the end of her rage, YouTube video, or not, once she knew Hunter was mine.

"I know it sucks because I do know how it feels and I let others feel the same."

"All you can do now is keep changing that. They're gone. Now, you can be better and who you want. We both can be what we want and who we are. Stronger together…"

"Better together," he says and smiles at me. "I still think we should come up with a handshake for that."

I roll my eyes. "No. Just no."

Mr. Marshall chuckles beside us and I already forgot he was here. "What you two have is good to see. Supporting one another and standing together. And I think that's something you both can maybe contribute to the program. Hunter, you're not the only one that did not interfere when it came to someone getting bullied. Many people don't stand up in fear of being ridiculed and bullied themselves. But as Brooke says, now all you can do is fix that. So, would you two be willing to help? Of course, when you're able to Brooke."

"Totally! Whatever I can do to help, I'll do it."

"Hunter?" Mr. Marshal asks, even though Hunter hasn't taken his eyes off me.

"Yeah, definitely," he says with conviction and a smile.

This all gives me better hope that maybe everything will be okay.

CHAPTER FIFTEEN

*"I'm free. I've come out of the shadows once
again to find myself. The person I thought would be
lost for good. Nobody will take me down again
because I faced the worst and came out stronger.
There might be steps backward, but I'll look at the
scars of the cruelest times and remember I'm better
then what they define."*

Brooklyn

It's been nine days of white walls, wires, beeps,
being poked, prodded, and treated like a lab rat. All I
wanna do is go home. They said there's a good chance
that I might be able to soon. The bleeding from my kidney
has stopped, and the last couple days they have let me
walk around a bit. It will all depend on what my tests say
when they come back from the lab.

Once Hunter started going home at night, I started
suffering from nightmares. I don't know if it has anything
to do with being alone in this room, or if all the shit that
happened to me has now gotten to me and it's starting to
haunt me, but I wish they would stop so I can move on
already.

The dreams are simple. It's Kara, and she's throwing
punches. Her snarling voice echoes in my ears, while the

other three laugh. I wake up screaming and covered in sweat. Then afterward, I'm left restless, and unable to sleep, where it makes me sick. One night, I awoke so violently, because I dreamed they pushed me off a dock into the water, the nurse had to come hold me till I calmed down.

Trauma be damned, falling dreams are the freaking worst. Then combined with the hateful four, well it sucks even more.

I talked to my new therapist, Dr. Fox, and she told me dreams were quite normal and can be part of the healing process. My brain is trying to work things out, get rid of the demons, but for that to work, my brain has to play out all my fears to be able to put them to rest. The hard part will be talking and working out the things my mind is trying to tell me. I want to be better, but sometimes all this feels like a step backward. It's hard to remember it is the only way to go forward.

My mom and dad are with me now because we are waiting for Hunter's dad to meet us with news on the hateful four.

"Do you have any idea what happened?" I ask my dad who talks with Mr. Evans often. I hope he knows, so I'm not left in suspense.

"All James would tell me is it's good, and I thought it would be better for us all to hear the news together," my dad tells me simply.

I take a breath, trying to relax.

Minutes later there's a quick rap on the door, before my boyfriend, James, and Riley come in. I get up and hug Riley first, before wrapping my arms tight around my man. He kisses me quickly on the lips, knowing we have an audience. Hunter takes my hand and sits on the edge of the bed with me.

"Do you know?" I whisper to Hunter, and he shakes his head. Riley comes to sit on my other side and takes

224

my other hand.

"You guys holding onto me is making me nervous. Mr. Evans?" My mom stares at James as anxiously as me. My dad looks relaxed, trusting the judicial system better than me, *or* he's plotting something if it fails. He does have a good poker face.

"Dan and Emma both pleaded guilty at their arraignment early this morning. Dan, as you know, was charged with a lesser crime of unlawful imprisonment."

I nod understanding. He's the only one that didn't touch me—well to physically hurt me.

"He's been very cooperative in questioning. He took the plea bargain of six months in prison with two years' probation. All of this is good since none have had any priors."

"Okay," I say softly. Next to me, I hear Hunter huff, but he doesn't say anything. I know he wants all of them locked up for life. But at least I know Dan's scholarship is out the window.

"Emma also pleaded guilty to second-degree kidnapping. She also has been cooperative in questioning. She said she knew nothing of the change of plans, but she went along with it because Kara threatened her otherwise. Now as you know, Kara and John were the ringleaders so the more evidence against them the better."

"Doesn't mean she doesn't deserve any less time," Hunter growls, and I grab his arm, telling him it's okay, though I agree with his assessment.

"I understand that, son, but you know how it is to be easily influenced. I had a long talk with her myself. She now knows what she did wrong, and I believe it as a lawyer. But also, remember the main person to hurt Brooklyn was Kara Addams."

"She's the one that needs to pay," I mumble and look around the room to the people I love. "I know they're all at fault, but it was Kara that did every hit. Emma might

225

have pulled my hair and choked me. John had been the one to grab me and tied me to the chair, but almost every single bruise and every injury was from Kara."

The tears spill down my face. It was her control, her jealousy, and her hatred that did this to me. I'm covered in bruises, kidney issues, concussions, and broken ribs because of *her*. She needs to pay. She hated me only because she wasn't me. I look around at my loved ones and know Kara didn't have anything close to what I have. I'm loved, and hopefully, she'll spend the rest of her life in jail.

Hunter wraps his arms around me and I curl into him. "Angel." He hushes me and smoothes my hair back. "It's okay." I didn't realize I was balling and had become a crumbled mess. I'm crying, hard, harder than when I first saw my injuries, but this is a different pain I feel. My soul aches deep inside, remembering the things Kara did to me. For the first time I ask, why me? Asking myself why I deserved this, and wondering why she hated me so much? I never did anything to her but breathe her air.

It hurts so bad that because I fell for a boy, it came this far. That one human could do this to another.

"Brooke?" I hear my dad, but I find myself unable to move from Hunter's arms.

I don't know how long I weep for. It feels like forever, but it's a sweet release. My dad rubs my back, Riley tells me it's okay, and Hunter kisses my head. However, it's Hunter's sweet smell that comforts me as I bury myself in his neck.

"I can come back…" James' concerned voice pierces my ears and my head shoots up.

"No!" I shout.

"Brooke, we can do this later." My mother rubs her hand down my cheek and wipes my tears away.

"No. I'm fine." I sniff, resting my head back on Hunter's shoulder. "I swear, I need to know. It's the only way I can have peace."

Peace. I need peace. Knowing that they're going to pay for their actions will be the only way I can start to have it.

James looks over to my dad and nods. "Go on."

"Well, Emma took the plea deal of four years with a chance of parole after two. She'll also have to pay a fine and probation after her sentencing."

Four years is good. No matter what, the best parts of her youth is spent in jail. "Alright, and the others?"

"John also pleaded guilty today to his charge of first-degree kidnapping with conspiracy to cause harm. He took the plea of twelve years and no chance of parole. Usually, cases like these aren't this easy. Most lawyers would have had them plead not guilty, to let them have their day in court and a chance at getting a lesser charge. But after talking with their parents, they knew that this was the best way to go. As egotistical as this might sound, it keeps their names from being in the media long term and will give the family some peace as well so they will be able to move on. All of them feel guilty for their children's actions, and they know they have to pay for their crimes. I have no doubt about that. But that being said, the vidco evidence we have is also very damaging to their case, which also makes it impossible not to show guilt."

James takes a deep breath. "Kara, as we thought would be our biggest problem. Even with the evidence stacked up against her, she planned to plead not guilty to first-degree kidnapping and first-degree assault tomorrow."

I roll my eyes. "I kind of figured she would do something like that." Hunter grips my hand tighter and presses his lips to my forehead.

"We did too, but we've been talking to her dad and lawyer. She's been reminded of the evidence against her.

Her own father wants her to plea out. He knows she's guilty and doesn't want to waste the court's time, nor do I believe he wants to pay for a lawyer. However, she didn't appear to care and thought she could fight it and win. John got wind of her not guilty plea and was pissed. He didn't want any chance of her getting a lesser charge than him. He started talking about what her actual plans were, that she was truly the mastermind behind it, and had the evidence to back it up." James' eyes drift to my dad's and he looks down to the ground, shaking his head.

Whatever the evidence is, I know it isn't good.

"It was more than just beating me up and dumping me, wasn't it?"

James nods grimly, "Kara's mother came forward with her journal...it..." James looks towards my dad again and then all heads turn to me. "Do you want to know, sweetie? The details aren't important."

I want to know. I don't know why, but I do. Plus, if we have to go to court, I would rather have time to process everything. Then I remember what Kara said to me when I was tied up.

"She was going to kill me, wasn't she?" My voice sounds so little to my ears, and I find myself shrinking. What if the cops didn't get there in time? Would she have—?

"I believe so, but it wasn't all 100% clear. There were lots of ramblings of revenge, but it did show intent to do serious harm to you. She also wrote part of the plan would have eventually involved Hunter. When they sent the video to Hunter, Kara was going to make him come get you, and then they would've jumped him too. I'll spare everyone the rest, but it shows clear premeditation before she even involved the other three. It seems Dan trying to stop it and Brooke saying she loved you, changed the direction of everything. Also, they didn't foresee you going to the cops either, son."

Stronger

I look over at Hunter and he's pale and green, if that's even possible. I wrap my arms around his waist and kiss the inside of his neck. "Hunter?"

He glances down and smiles at me weakly. We stare at each other conveying to one another that everything will be alright. That we can handle this together. Riley is rubbing my back giving me extra comfort.

"Are you saying Brooke is going to have to go to court and see that *girl*? And re-live it over again?" my mom asks, interrupting my moment with Hunter.

"Hopefully, not. The goal was to do everything we could do to avoid that. We are trying to tack on conspiracy to commit murder, but I don't know if that will go through. Unfortunately, we can't control what they decide to do. Kara was presented with the evidence we found, and according to her dad, she might be re-thinking a trial. She knows her choices, take the twenty-five years the DA will offer or the chance for sixty. There's no way she's going to be able to go to trial and come out not guilty. Even though she doesn't deserve it, if she's out in twenty-five she still has a chance at living her life. If she starts thinking straight, she'd take the plea," James says giving me hope. *I just want it to be over.*

"She'll barely have a life though at least," Riley murmurs, taking my hand. "She'll be what, forty or so when she gets out? Her looks will be gone, she'll probably get fat. No one will want to hire her, won't be around men, no friends, have no popularity. You know all that alone will be detrimental enough to her."

I laugh, picturing Kara in an orange jumpsuit, surrounded by a bunch of women wanting to make her their bitch. "God, you're right. I think that's pretty good justice if you ask me. And you know she'll easily become someone's bitch...probably some big butch lady with tattoos all over her face and ugly sores. Does questionable things to her—" I snap my mouth shut and look at my

229

parents and James. "Sorry..." My face scrunches, thinking I went too far, but they're all laughing with me.

"You're only stating the truth." Hunter kisses me and I join back in on the laughter.

We all share a good laugh. Something none of us have done in a while. So much weight lifted off our shoulders. I know even if we have to go to court for Kara, justice will be served. God knows her parents *won't* and *can't* buy her out of this.

Our laughs are broken up when my doctor comes in. "There appears to be a party going on in here." He smiles. "I think I'm about to give you something else to be excited about."

"I can go home?" I gleam.

"Yes. All your test came back with normal levels, so I don't see why we can't get you home tonight. I still want you to take it easy for a little while longer. Your ribs still need to heal, and since you said you were still getting headaches it would be even better to do so. They should ease hopefully in a few weeks. Light activity and I want you to still watch your liquid intake. If you have any severe dizziness, or blurred vision, or blood in your urine, I want you back to see me right away." The doctor takes another quick look at me and tells me a nurse will be back in a while to get my discharge papers ready.

I'm going home, and the ones that put me in this place, are going to be rotting in prison for a while.

Wet lips press against my cheek, across my eyelids, and over my nose, before they land gently on my lips. I also smell honeysuckle. I moan, knowing one of my favorite people is here with me now. I open my eyes and am met with Hunter's warm welcoming smile.

I spot the yellow honeysuckles laying on my nightstand and grin. "Hi, what time is it?" I reach up to touch his face.

"It's noon." He chuckles. "This bed must be very comfortable. I wasn't expecting you to still be asleep."

"Well, much better than that thin mat they were trying to pass off as a bed. I know you understand." I smirk, remembering all the nights he slept with me in the hospital. That's about the only thing I miss about that place.

Then I remember the nightmare I had that kept me awake for a while last night. But I won't tell him that right now. I don't need him to worry.

"Shouldn't you be at school?" I move to sit up against the headboard.

"Yeah, but I left early. I wanted to be the one to tell you the good news. I had to beg your parents to let me do it…" He chuckles. "But they think I've earned it to tell you." The large grin on his face is infectious. I know instantly what the news is.

"She pleaded guilty, didn't she?" My smile is now as big as his.

"She did. Twenty-five years. No parole. She's now permanently locked up in prison. Now it really is over."

For once, Kara did the right thing. I would have survived going to court, but the last thing I would want to do is deal with it longer then I had to.

"Thank god. It's over and they're gone." I pull him down, being mindful of my ribs, and kiss him with everything I have.

"Now for you to get all the way better, back to school, and normalcy." He chuckles.

"Normalcy? What the hell is that?" I joke, not ready

to think about going back to school or anything yet.

"Not sure, but…" he leans over and starts kissing me again all over my face, causing me to giggle, "this feels pretty normal to me. Why don't we practice our French kissing again, till your parents catch us and your dad throws me out of the house by the scruff of my neck." He wiggles his eyebrows.

"Sounds good to me…"

CHAPTER SIXTEEN

"Sometimes it takes a great tragedy to bring people together. To finally open the eyes that might have been blinded to the world around them. We quickly learn to work together and unite. Help the ones that are hurt and do what we can do to try to heal. It's never too late to make a difference. Because you never know whose soul you might mend back together if you never try."

Brooklyn

The smell of bacon and roses wakes me from my restless slumber. I blink open my eyes and I'm met with a bouquet of red, orange, and pink roses on my bed. I smile, knowing just who they're from. I've been out of the hospital for over a week and I'm starting to feel better. My kidney bruising has healed, but I still have to watch my intake of fluids. My ribs are still healing, my bruises are almost completely faded, and I look like me again, except the two light scars from where I had to get stitches. I'm still getting headaches, but overall, I feel better. Hunter has been by my side every second he can, which has helped in my recovery.

I put the roses to my nose and inhale their comforting smell. Although, it's the heavenly smell of bacon that gets me out of my bed. My stomach growls in anticipation of the greasy goodness that awaits me. I've been on a light diet for so long, it feels like I haven't had bacon in years.

I take the flowers with me and make my way to the kitchen. When I arrive, I'm stopped dead in my tracks when I see Hunter at the stove, shirtless.

This has to be a dream. Why is he in my kitchen without a shirt? And where are my parents?

I admire the way the muscles in his back flex and the way his ash brown hair bounces as he shakes his head at something. I've *missed* him. We haven't had sex since before the incident, and I feel like I'm going to explode if I don't have him soon. I want to reconnect with him again, in *that* way. The make out and cuddling sessions have been amazing, but I have needs. Needs I'm ready to have fulfilled again.

"I know you're behind me, Brooklyn."

I giggle, loving the fact that he can sense me around. "I'm just trying to figure out what you're doing and where your shirt went. Not that I mind." I'd much rather have him naked though.

He glances over his shoulder and gives me his winning smile. Turning off the burners, he moves the pan to the back and walks over to me. He stops right in front of me but doesn't touch me.

Touch me. I beg him with my eyes and a small smirk creases his lips. I know he's reading what I'm trying to tell him, but he still doesn't move. I let my eyes roam over his body and wet my lips, thinking about running my tongue over every inch of him.

"Thank you for the flowers, I love them," I purr and bat my eyes, trying to seduce him.

"You're welcome, Angel." He gives me a gentle kiss on the cheek. "I made us breakfast. Figured you would be hungry."

I shake my head, having to remind myself we are in

the middle of my kitchen because I'm seconds away from jumping his bones, and I have no idea where my parents are creeping around at.

"Yeah, I am, but um—where are my parents?"

"They needed to go handle something with your aunt last night. You had already passed out on me during the movie when she called. I guess she has some sort of minor crisis. They didn't want to go, but I offered to stay. I spent the night in the guest room. When I woke up, I decided to make us breakfast. They should be back this afternoon." He takes the flowers from my hands and places them on the counter.

"Doesn't explain why you're shirtless though. You risk getting burned this way." I raise my hand to run it down his chest over his taut abs. My lips land in the middle of his pecs and I inhale him.

"I was going to bring you breakfast in bed. I figured I'd give you something to look at while you eat. Thought maybe you would like the view."

"I do," I swoon. My hands work their way up his chest to around his neck. "Hunter, I want you."

"I want you too, angel, but we can't yet. You're still sore. I don't want to hurt you."

"But I'm much better, I swear. It's been three weeks."

"I know. But they said six weeks. I know your ribs are still sore, Brooke."

"Please…" I beg, playing with the hem of his sweatpants. "Can't we just try. The doctor said I could do light activity. I promise to tell you if it hurts, but I need you."

He grabs my hands and places them to his lips. I should've just shoved them in and grabbed, that would have gotten what I want. "Why don't we eat first. I wanted to talk to you also."

How the hell is this man's resolve stronger than

mine? He's a teenage boy. But no, he just has to be worried about my wellbeing.

Stupid, sweet bastard.

"You want to talk? Over sex?" I raise my eyebrow, not believing it for a second.

"Yes, because as much as I want to dive inside of you, we need to wait. I refuse to explain to your mom and dad, why all of a sudden, you're all sore again."

"You're no fun," I pout, crossing my arms over chest. He just laughs at me and spins me around, tapping my ass.

"Get back to bed and let me do what I had planned."

"Fine…" I groan, giving up—for now. I take two steps back toward my bedroom when he grabs my arm stopping me. "What?"

He doesn't say anything and steps in front of me. With a playful grin on his face, he wraps his arms around me and kisses me. It starts off slow but turns deep and feverish. His tongue flicks with mine and I can still taste the toothpaste on it. My hands find his hair as his find my ass. I think maybe I've convinced him for a romp in the sack, but I'm disappointed when he pushes me away.

"Why did you stop?" I whine, trying to pull his head back to me.

"You know why. I just wanted to let you know I do want you very much. Now, get in bed. I'll be there in a minute."

"Tease," I mumble and stomp my way back to my room, disappointed and hornier than before.

Five minutes later, Hunter comes back into my room carrying a tray full of the breakfast he made. He also put one of the roses in a skinny vase on the tray.

"I'm starting to wonder what classes you're taking at school. Do they offer 'how to wow your girl' or 'swoon 101' now?" I joke as he lays the tray over my legs. My mouth waters at the sight of the crispy bacon and cheesy scrambled eggs on my plate.

Hunter laughs and sits down next to me. "It just comes naturally, baby."

"Lucky me then." I pick up a piece of bacon and moan at the greasy, fatty goodness. I never thought I could miss bacon so much.

"I'm guessing it's good?"

"Mmm-hmm. It's the best thing I've had in my mouth in a long time." I eye his crotch and really want to wrap my lips around it.

He growls at me, having to adjust his junk. I'm determined to break down his resolve. I'm seconds away from stripping naked.

"You ready to get back to school next Monday?" The change in conversation instantly kills the mood.

He stabs some scrambled egg onto his fork and putting it to my lips to eat. I open up and chew. Shit, this is better than the bacon. The eggs are extra cheesy with a spice that I can't put my finger on.

How lucky did I get to find a man that can actually cook?

I swallow the fluffy cheesy deliciousness and shrug. I'm having mixed thoughts of going back. Even though it was my decision, a month was long enough for me to be out. "If I said yes, I would be lying…"

"What's going on? You're going back and forth on it. Your mom and dad said you didn't have to go back till you were ready."

"I know. I guess—" I twist the blanket in my hands, feeling anxious at the thought of walking those halls again. "I don't know, I keep thinking about everyone at school. How they will look at me, what they will say. I know they started this anti-bullying campaign because of what happened to me, but it doesn't mean everyone is on the same page. People might still be loyal to them like Daryl was."

Hunter moves the tray off my lap to the nightstand. He wraps me in his arms and moves me to his lap. I curl myself against him and rest my head on his shoulder.

"You had another nightmare last night." I frown. How does he know these things?

"Yeah. I hate that I keep having them. All I want to do is forget and move on. But my dreams keep taunting me. It's...annoying." I run my finger over his abs in order to try to distract myself.

Hunter plays with my hair and kisses the top of my head. His touch is comforting, and I let some of the tension roll off my shoulders. "It's okay to be scared, you know. I know you want to be strong and brush it all away, and you *have* been amazingly strong, angel. Don't think because you have these dreams makes you any less. They'll go away soon. I promise."

"I know. They're not as bad as they were in the beginning. I think Dr. Fox has helped a lot. And I guess going back to school is a stressor."

"You've seen the outreach to you. People care, and I don't think there's any way someone would even dare try to say something to you that would be rude or inappropriate. For one, they would have to deal with me and another they're going to have to deal with everyone else. Plus, you think Riley or I would let anything happen to you?" He stresses and cups my chin, forcing me to look him in his eyes.

"No," I whisper meekly. "It's been a lot of changes this year. I wish we could just graduate now?"

"I wish that too." His nose rubs mine before he pulls me into a kiss. I moan against his lips and tangle my hand in his hair. The boy either needs to stop kissing me or take me now. I'm so wound up. Hunter pulls away from me and runs his hand down my cheek. "Why do you keep stopping?"

He looks pensive and twists his lips together.

"Because I still have something to tell you…" He stops, I'm sure sensing the now worried look on my face. He lifts my chin and rubs his thumb over my lips. "It's good news. For the both of us."

My shoulders sag in relief. "Oh?"

"I got into Stanford and that's where I want to go." The words spill from his lips forcefully and determined.

Stanford? He got into Stanford? When the heck did this happen? When did he apply there? Why would he apply there when he had three different schools accept him in? Despite the hundred questions I have forming in my head, I can't help the jig I'm doing inside my head. We're going to college together.

"What about Duke? You can get an education there without football. I thought that's what you wanted."

"But they'll only take me if I play ball for them. Stanford was on my list way before we started dating, so was Harvard and Terry. Are you trying to tell me that you don't want me to be in the same place as you?" He frowns, and worry enters those sexy green orbs of his. I reach out and grab his hand.

"I didn't say that. I'm just surprised that's all. You never said that you applied to those schools. You didn't say anything." I should smack the crap out of him.

"I know. But I wanted to be sure there was a chance. I didn't want to get our hopes up."

"What did your parents say? They weren't upset about you giving up your scholarships?"

"No, they knew about my plans. Since I did so good on my SATs, my dad thought it would be a good idea and try to do more of what I wanted."

"You mean those Zach Morris scores you got? What 1502, 1520?"

"Who?"

"*Who*? *Who*? Saved by the bell. *'I'm so excited, I'm so excited?'*" I sing, and he shakes his head at me, looking

239

at me like I'm crazy. I roll my eyes, everyone should know such an iconic character and TV show. "Well, basically the good-looking popular kid did better than his very intelligent best friend on the SAT's. It's a TV show about high school students, that showed that popular kids and nerds can get along." He's still shaking his head at me confused, and I sigh, knowing I have a lot of work to conform this boy to the classics. "I guess while we are at Stanford, we will be catching you up on classic TV."

I'm still dancing inside knowing that we are going to college together. Forever almost feels certain now.

"As long as we're watching in your bed, I'll watch anything. But how did you find out? I never told anyone but my parents."

"A little birdie…" I giggle, knowing that his mom was the birdie that admitted it to me when I went over for dinner. She knew he had to like a girl because he didn't need a tutor with his scores and grades. "What I don't get is why you didn't tell me?"

"Well, I wanted you to keep thinking I was some dumb jock. Because I like the way you tutored me with your mouth and I wasn't giving that up:"

"Oh, you did, well maybe you should show me how well I tutored you then." He moves to kiss me on the lips and I shake my head. "I want my French kiss somewhere else today."

It's like the first day of school all over again and I'm the new kid. The anxiety, the nervousness, the butterflies in the stomach. I have no idea what's going to happen when I walk through those doors today. It's either going to suck or…

"It's going to be alright…" Hunter's voice pulls me out of my troubled musings. He gives me a kiss on my temple and holds on tight to my hand. I nod and stare at the pink tulip he gave me this morning with my special lunch. He's now started giving me different flowers for each day because he didn't want me to get bored with roses. I only hope that I show him in return how much it means to me.

"You're right. I'm trying." I sigh.

"I know you are. If you need me at any time, I have my phone on me. Buzz me and I'll come to wherever you are. Even in the middle of class. My teachers understand, I've already told them." He grins. *"I said 'you see me bolt, I've gone to get my girl.'"*

"And they were just okay with that?"

Hunter shrugs. "Sorta, but it doesn't matter because you know I will be there. Riley too. But I really think it will be alright. For the first time, I can trust nobody will do anything to hurt you or upset you."

I nod, trying to muster up all my courage I have buried under my bundle of nerves. "Let's do this thing." I clap my hands and do my best to sound cheerful.

We pile out of the car and before I can move a step towards the doors, Hunter has me pushed against his Mercedes. His tongue plunges into my mouth, and he's thoroughly sucking the life out of me with his kiss. My legs start to falter and I'm gripping his arms to keep upright. The last thing on my mind is what's behind those double doors, and it's a safe bet that's just what he wanted to accomplish. God, I love him.

Our lips part, and we're both breathless. He runs his hand down my face and rests his forehead to mine. "I wanted you to go there on a high note. I love you. I'm with you every step of the way."

241

Together we walk into the school. Once we cross over the entrance threshold, all the air leaves my lungs when I see the oversized banner. In bright blue and pink letters, it reads: "Welcome Back, Brooke."

"She's here…" I hear someone yell across the hall and people start clapping all around me. There are a couple people that I have talked to before, that I was always amicable with, come up and hug me. They all tell me how happy they are to see me, and that they're glad I'm okay.

Ian starts to approach me, and Hunter is shooting him a blazing glare that makes him and a couple others scatter. I smack Hunter on the chest to tell him to relax.

"That's not the welcome I thought I was going to get." My face burns at the sudden attention. I'm caught between being embarrassed and in awe. "Did you know about this?"

"Yeah, our class wanted you to feel welcome when you came back. I told you, they're on your side, baby. Surprisingly, there's a lot of good people around here. Unlike that buffoon you date," he jokes, but I know he's still fighting with his own insecurities with everything that happened and still blames himself. Even though, he doesn't always say it.

"But I happen to love that buffoon. No insulting my boyfriend or I'll kick your butt."

"I would like to see you try, Brooklyn…" He wiggles his eyebrows at me and scoops me carefully into his arms. I wrap my legs around his waist and before my lips can find his, our Principal is standing next to us, shaking his head.

Hunter places me down to the ground and I mutter my hello to Principal Marks. "Welcome back, Brooke. I guess it's safe to say you're doing well," he says with a straight face looking between Hunter and me.

"Yeah, I'm doing better than I could ever expect."

"That's good to hear, Brooke. You know my door is open if you need anything or have any troubles," he tells me sincerely.

"Thank you."

"I'm looking forward to seeing you both tomorrow night for the new program meeting. Also, keep the PDA off school grounds. I don't want to have to see you two in detention for something like that." He points to us and I instantly feel like an ordinary student now. Mr. Marks gives us one more look before walking back down the hall to remove a hat off Dean Franklin's head.

Principal Marks is pretty laid back and as far as principals go. He's respected among the students. I met with him last Friday, with my mom and dad. He apologized for what happened with Kara and the others, stating it was his job to be aware of the things that happened in his halls. He was visibly upset by it all. When the student body had approached him with the anti-bullying program idea, he'd had no idea how far the hateful four's reign of terror went. Kara and John really had put the fear of God in people so they wouldn't speak against them. Now, with the new program, he's hoping to come up with more efficient policies and anonymous ways to stop any abuse.

"He's gone," Hunter mutters and pushes me into the lockers, gently, to kiss me. I giggle against his lips and push him back. "What?"

"Alright, you buffoon, I need to head to class."

"I'll walk you." He winks and grabs a handful of my ass and pushes his tongue between my parted lips again.

"PDA, EVANS," Principal Mark yells from somewhere. "Last warning…."

Hunter and I start to crack up and jog down the hall. I'm wondering if this is the 'normal' Hunter was talking about.

I'm sitting at the lunch table with Riley, picking at the meal I was served from the cafeteria and wishing I had food from the hospital. "Why couldn't they improve the food while I was gone?" I attempt to poke my finger through the hard bun of my hamburger. I should've just gotten the damn fruit.

"You know that will never happen. Not even by the time our kids have to come here will they fix the grossness of cafeteria food. It's a way to torture us teens..." she replies, biting into her carrot. "I thought Hunter brought you something for lunch."

Hunter had brought me a turkey sandwich from my favorite deli with tomatoes and mayo. Just the way I like it. I think he's trying to fatten me back up from the weight I lost when I was recovering.

"He did, but I ate it for breakfast." I push the sad looking burger away and steal one of Riley's carrots.

Two girls from my chemistry class swoop in to take a seat beside me at the table. They make small talk with me as they dig into their lunch. Riley and I always sat alone at the lunch table, but now it's like everyone wants to sit with us. Not that I mind; people have been nice and not talking about the drama. I'm starting to wonder if this was how it was always supposed to be.

"Brooke?" I turn around to the sound of my name. It's April Stevens. She's a cheerleader, one of the other 'populars.'. The ones that don't belong in Kara's group and never were to those standards. Sure, they would hang out together, sort of stick together, but you could tell they weren't friends.

But Mr. Marshall told me April was one of the many seniors that helped come up with the idea of the anti-bullying program.

"Hey." April smiles and sits down next to me. She's twisting her fingers on the table and biting her lip looking anxious and unsure.

"Hi." I smile back. I can tell she needs to say something, so I wait.

"I know you don't want to talk about what happened, but I kind of wanted to talk about the new program."

I glance over at Riley who is still chomping on her carrot. She nods, giving me the signal that April is safe. "It's fine. What's up?"

"I wanted to say I was sorry. There are many of us that are sorry because we could have maybe stopped Kara's reign if we spoke up sooner. Stood together and fought, instead of acting like a bunch of scaredy-cats. That's part of why we thought maybe helping start this more aggressive anti-bullying program could be a way to do that now. It's just…" Her words wander off, and she glances down at the table.

"Go on. It's okay."

"Like, it sounds awful, but finding out what happened to you was a shock to everyone. Nobody could have foreseen they would go that far. It should've never gotten to that. But it was an eye-opener. You hear this stuff on the news, but it doesn't hit home till it happens to someone you know. I know with you sharing your story, that's if you want to, it could help shine the light on a big problem everywhere."

"Of course. I want to help as much as I can. I know Hunter and Riley do too." I'm more than willing to try anything, so maybe what happened to me doesn't happen to someone else.

"Yeah, they've been a big help already. I think it was Hunter that made us all see how peer pressure can be a bitch. We were all afraid of Kara and her pawns. I was one of them. Freshman year I dated John, right after they broke up. She hated me because she was trying so hard to get him back. He claimed he didn't want her, I would find out later, as you know, he never stopped doing her bidding." She scoffs and rolls her eyes. Then she suddenly goes pale and gulps. "One day, Kara cornered me and threatened me with publishing the nude pictures John took of me. I had no idea he took pictures of me."

I never realized how deep Kara's control went. It's insane to think about even after what she did to me.

"She told me she would tell my dad, who's in Congress. Not something that would be good for his political career, especially when she said she would load them on his computer…God, she really was a fucking crazy bitch," she snaps, and her pale cheeks are now fiery red as a few tears slip from her eyes.

It's easy to see how much her situation still pains her, just as bad as what happened to me in middle school. No one was safe from Kara.

"I caved to her control. I had to do what she wanted, stay away from people, never say a word about what she was doing. And I did it all in fear she would send the pictures. And no one likes the squealer. She would threaten anybody that would be her competition, as you know. Nobody spoke about it either, not till lately. I think most avoided getting in her way. They knew if you didn't want to be her victim you played chicken. We all stood back and let it happen because we were all too scared and didn't think we could stop her without her destroying us. So, I'm sorry Brooke."

I take April's hand and squeeze it. "It's not your fault. It's not anyone's fault but theirs. You didn't know what she was doing to me, just like I didn't know what she was doing to you. My own boyfriend didn't see it all, and even though Kara was a bitch, I never thought she would get to the point that she did. I didn't speak up either, not even to Hunter. Hell, he was afraid of them, so I think all we can do is move on, and you don't need to say sorry. This new program is a great start."

"Yeah, hopefully it will help someone else. Thank you for listening, Brooke. I'm glad you came back to school and aren't letting them hold you back. It's something to really admire. I think I would be hiding under my bed till I was thirty." She laughs and tucks a strand of her blonde hair back.

"Sometimes I think about it. I think everyone around here as made it easier."

"I'm glad. Maybe we could all hang out sometime soon?" April asks addressing both Riley and me sincerely. Boy, how the tides have changed.

"I'm down." Riley agrees and throws a half-eaten carrot back on her plate. "We can do something with no boys. I've spent too much time watching this girl slobber all over her boyfriend." She points her thumb at me and makes a gagging noise.

"Shut up, you." I wave her off with a giggle. She's so over dramatic—we don't slobber. "But yeah it could be fun."

"Awesome. I'll see you guys around." April leans in and gives me a hug, telling me thanks for listening again before she goes bouncing off.

Next to me, Riley starts laughing, and I twist my head back to my crazy best friend. "What?"

"Brooke, you're popular now." She waves around the cafeteria and everyone is looking at us, smiling, and giving me little waves.

"Um…yay?" I snort but join her in a bit of laughter.

This is definitely not the way I would ever want to get thrust into popularity. In a way, I know it's pity, but maybe I can use this new *superpower* for good instead of evil like those *other* people.

Erica Marselas

CHAPTER SEVENTEEN

"Never let anyone knock you down. You were made to rock. You were made to fight. Be brave. Be Fearless. Be powerful. Always remember you're stronger than you think you are. You will come out on top, and evil will lay at your feet."

Brooklyn

I survived my first two weeks back better than I ever pictured, but I'm glad it's over. I've never talked to so many of my classmates before in my life and my vocal cords need a rest.

After school I've spent most my free time working on the campaign, which has been dubbed "Stronger Together." Along with Hunter and Riley, I listened as people told their tales of being bullied and their ideas to stop it. I'm still flabbergasted by the unity of my classmates and the desire to do something that might end up changing how we deal with bullies. Because even though high school comes to an end, you still encounter bullies in the real world. Hopefully, now we can be better prepared to handle them by not letting them win.

I only wish it was as easy to do as it is to say.

Riley is walking with me out of school as she tells me all about her date with Billy tonight. The two have grown serious and more than just the casual hookup or *whatever* they were. Hunter is supposed to be meet me by his car to take me home, but he needed to clean out his *smelly* gym locker first before Coach Anders kills him.

I'm feet away from his car when the sound of screeching tires makes my heart race, my hands tingle, and my vision blur. I'm hit with a surge of Déjà vu, and I freeze in a panic. I grab Riley's hand, and she instantly stops talking. My eyes dart around me, wondering if anyone is about to jump out at me. There's no car, and I see a couple people looking at me through my fog. My chest tightens and I focus on Riley who is calling my name. No one is coming.

No one is coming.

Breathe. I tell myself and I release a strangled breath *No one is going to hurt you. No one is after you.*

"Brooke? What's wrong?" Riley's voice finally comes through the haze. I shake my head trying to brush off the feeling. I've been fine for weeks when I crossed this lot, so why is it bugging me now? Tears from the rush of adrenaline sting my eyes. I almost want to scream my frustration because I don't want to feel like this. They're gone. I'm safe. There's no way I can let this bother me. I've come so far.

"It was just…" I point out into the street where I heard the screeching car. "I don't know. I'm fine." I take some deep breaths as I try to calm my racing heart.

"No, you're not Brooke, you're sweating, pale, and you're crying." Riley brushes my hair back and sits me down on the curb. I brush the few fallen tears off my cheek.

"I just had a brief flashback. I'm okay, really," I tell her once I'm able to breathe again and my heart stops pumping out of my chest. "I think it's just the noise and where we are. Maybe because Hunter isn't here, and he's in the same place he was last time. I don't know, it just hit me suddenly." I look around me and take another deep breath. Most people have already left for the day, but there's still a few making their way out. I bury my head in my hands, not wanting anyone to see me. I don't need anyone asking me what's wrong.

"You sure?" Riley asks, rubbing my back. I nod.

I try to focus on what Dr. Fox told me a little while back to remind myself it's okay. *"No matter how strong you are, there's always going to be a moment that you remember the pain. You need to breathe through the moments, accept that they happen, and let them build to make you even stronger. Don't let the hurt hold you back from keeping you going."*

"Brooke?" I hear Hunter's frantic voice and when I look up, he's running over to me. He skids to a stop in front of me and falls to his knees before wrapping me in his arms.

I don't know why, but I giggle at his panic and my own. But he's here and I already feel much better.

He lifts my face and looks at me confused. "What are you giggling about?" Hunter glances over at Riley and she shrugs, just as confused as him. "Someone came and told me you seemed upset, so I rushed out here."

"God, someone saw that." I groan and cover my face. I know everyone knows what happened, but I don't want them seeing me be pitiful. Especially, after weeks of being awesome. The thought makes me giggle again.

"It was April and Mark, they said they passed you and you looked sick." Oh, well that doesn't bother me as much, and I guess it is kind of sweet they knew to get Hunter.

"I'm okay now, really. I guess I still deal with the memories of everything that happened that day, and when I came out here, all the triggers hit me at once. Dr. Fox told me about this...I didn't think it would happen."

Hunter lays a light kiss on my lips and brushes my

cheeks with his thumbs. "You sure?"

"Yeah. Let's not dwell on it. Please." I give them a smile and reach my hand out for Hunter who helps me stand. "Dust me off and let's go."

"You sure, Brooke?" Riley's forehead wrinkles in concern. "I can come over for a bit."

"No. You have a big date to get ready for. And I guess so do I." I look over at Hunter, wondering what he has up his sleeve, but I think I'm going to have to change his plans.

"Okay, well if you need me, call me." Riley pulls me into a hug and whispers in my ear, making me promise to call her if I need anything, no matter what.

"Riley, I can drop you off," Hunter offers, and Riley shakes her head.

"I can manage the few steps. Plus, it's nice out, and I'll be reducing my carbon footprint, firming my booty and all that. I'm fine." She dismisses him and says her goodbyes before going off to tighten her butt and save the world.

I slide into the passenger side of Hunter's car and he throws his gym bag in the backseat. He starts the car and the wretched smell of soiled clothes wafts through the car. "God, your coach was right. Those clothes do stink, Hunter. When was the last time you had them washed?" I pinch my nose and roll down the window to let the smell out.

"Yeah, sorry about that. They're from this week. I forgot on Wednesday to take them with me—and Thursday. And I never brought new ones in, so I sorta kept wearing them." He shrugs acting if it's not a big deal.

Boys are gross. At least he had clean underwear, I hope.

I wrinkle my nose and turn to him. "That's disgusting, Hunter. Is this something I'm going to help you with when we go to college. Because I'm not hanging out in your dorm if it smells like fresh skunk."

"No, you won't have to worry your pretty little head, Madame. I'm just not used to having an extracurricular that doesn't end with me being in the locker room. I'll just start taking them with me after class now. Because I'm going to make sure I walk out with you."

"Hunter, I'm fine." I sigh and throw my head against the headrest. The last thing I want is for him to always worry about me. "You can't always hold my hand. It was so many of the same things at once and maybe just hearing so many stories lately, it was bound to happen. I just need to keep working through it."

"Maybe I want to always hold your hand. Maybe we could super glue them together." He grabs my hand and intertwines our fingers. "They look pretty good together."

I break out with a goofy grin that I'm sure matches his. I have no doubt he might do it if he needed to. "You're crazy, but I love you." I lean over to kiss his cheek and then free my hand from his hold.

My phone buzzes and I yank it out of my bag to check it. There's a text from April, asking if I'm okay. I reply, letting her know I'm fine. Seeing this message, such a little, simple thing, reminds me I'm going to be alright because I'm surrounded by people who care.

"You have to think of all your positives, Brooke, even if it's only one thing. Negatives do exist, but they don't have to rule your life." My dad's words echo in my ear. Something he's been telling me for years, but now they mean so much more.

My phone buzzes again with an email I've been waiting for all week and I smile. "Where we going?"

"I thought maybe we could have a date night. I wanted to do this…." His mouth snaps shut, and I already know what he's going to say, but I press him to keep going. "Yeah, so, I wanted to do all the things we should've done from the beginning. Then afterward, I have dinner planned. Are you up for some putt-putt or laser tag? Then maybe a movie?"

"That all sounds wonderful, but I much rather go back to your place and—*you know.*" I brush my finger on his arm and bite my lip.

"Don't you want to go out? We spent most of our relationship indoors."

"*Annnnnd*? I remember many good times. All the make-out sessions, petting, talking. Plus, we can do them later or tomorrow before the party." I shrug, wanting to get him to his house. Like now. We have all day tomorrow before this huge party that's happening at one of Hunter's football buddy's house. It's so odd, me getting invited somewhere, and I won't have to worry about being the outsider.

"I just thought maybe—" He frowns and I rub his shoulder, trying to convey I do love it, but I need him more.

"Hunter, I love the idea, but I'm going to be serious. I haven't had your dick in almost a month and I don't mean when I had my hand wrapped around it. What I want is you inside of me, thrusting, ramming, *fucking* me. And I'm going to go nuts if I don't have it soon. Quit worrying about hurting me. I know my limits. Please…." I'm begging, pleading with him. I never thought trying to have sex, okay penetrating sex, with this man would be like pulling teeth.

We pull up to a stop sign and he looks me over. "I didn't want to hurt you."

"I know that," I sigh, "and I love you for it, but I think I've shown you that I'm more than okay. I'm going to get to the point where I drug you and take it…" I quirk my eyebrow at him.

"So, *no* putt putt?"

I could make many jokes right now, but I refrain.

"No. House, bed, now."

"As you wish." He smiles cheekily and I know he's okay with the change of plans.

After a change in direction, Hunter pulls up into his driveway and parks. He helps me out of the car and we walk to his door where I happen to notice the extra skip in his step. I'm excited to see my email was correct and the package I got for Hunter is sitting on his doorstep.

"What the heck is this?" He picks up the mysterious box with his name on it.

"I dunno, I guess you're going to have to open it."

He carries the box inside and sits it down on the end table, along with his stinky gym bag. He pulls me into his arms and kisses the side of my neck. I hum at the contact of his wet lips and his cool hand working under my shirt.

"Aren't you going to open the package?" My question comes out more like a moan with his hand under my bra.

"Later. I thought you wanted me to do something else to you," he whispers seductively in my ear, and it makes my whole body quiver.

"I do, but I'm also nosey and I think you should open it."

He groans and detaches himself from my body. "You know you're the most confusing woman on this planet?"

"I know. Let's just say I have a feeling I know what it is. Open it." I grab the box off the table and thrust it into his arms.

"You got me something?" He smiles, and his eyes shine bright like a kid on Christmas.

"Yeah, I feel like I owe it to you, especially after everything."

"You don't owe me anything, Angel."

"I think I do." I watch him as he peels the packing tape and opens the box. He pulls out the jacket and the box falls to the floor.

"You got me a new letterman?" His eyes widen in

surprise as he looks over the jacket and inspects each patch.

"Yeah. I regret cutting up the other one. I know you haven't ever complained or said anything about it, but I felt like I should have it replaced. I know it's not the same, though I think I managed to get all the same patches."

I ended up having to ask his mother if she had any good pictures of the front and back of the jacket. I was in luck when she did, but when I had to explain to her that I went a little psycho on the first one made for interesting conversation. But considering she knows everything that happened with Hunter and me that led up to my attack, she took it well. She made me feel better when she told me that if it had been her boyfriend or James, she might have done the same thing.

It's safe to say that Debbie and I have bonded.

I did have one thing made different. Where it says Evans on the back the print is bolder and done in gray stitching. His mom said that's what he wanted before, but they were unable to do it. It has his jersey number 50 on top of a football, the varsity patch, The W for Woodbine. An RB for his position on the team, and the mascot.

"This is great, Brooke. I love it, baby. Thank you." He grabs my hand and pulls me to him, capturing my mouth with his. "But you know what I want to do with this jacket right now?"

"What?" I pant, wanting his lips back on me.

"I want to fuck you, while you're only wearing my jacket."

I squeeze my legs together tightly at the thought and nod. "I want that too."

He places another soft kiss on my lips. "Go to my room, get ready, while I take care of my laundry, so my mom doesn't kill me." He winks at me before walking off.

I don't need to be told twice.

Stronger

I nuzzle my head into his chest, wanting to never move from here. I can't wait for college, so we can do this whenever, without having to worry about parents finding us. Hunter said that he's getting a private room, which his parents paid extra for. I know where I'll be staying almost every night and between study breaks. Hopefully, after freshman year we can get our own place. That's the dream, at least.

Hunter's fingers dance along my arm. "Are you sure you're still okay from this afternoon?"

I had a feeling he was going to bring that up again. I twist my finger inside his belly button, trying to avoid rubbing my hand along his now exhausted shaft.

"I am. I think I was just mad that it happened. I know it might happen again, but I'll survive it, one day at a time. I'll also talk to Dr. Fox about it." He kisses the top of my head and doesn't question it anymore. "How have you been doing?"

The last couple of days have been rough on him, hearing other people's stories. He did have a couple people upset with him; asking him how he could stand by his so-called friends for so long as they hurt other people. I knew as soon as it was said he felt ashamed. He ended up walking away for a few minutes to calm down, then when he came back, he told them his story and apologized. It was hard for them to believe that the all-star football player was bullied himself once, but once they knew, they had a better understanding. It was easy to see that the support group of the organization works and it's something that is needed. Soon, I think we will all start holding hands and sing kumbaya. I laugh inwardly. Okay, that's never going to happen, but it would be classic if it did.

"I couldn't be better, especially now." His eyes shine down at me.

"See, I told you, sex is what you needed." I place a kiss in the middle of his chest. I love how content I feel in his arms. How much stronger I have become thanks to him. Panic attacks be damned, I have everything I want. "I love you, Hunter. More than I thought I ever could."

"I love you. I only wish I could take back some of the things I did. Started this relationship off the right way," he muses, drifting off. I move and straddle his hips. I lay my body down on his, so our noses are touching, and my hands play with his hair.

"Our relationship is ours though and it started the way it was supposed to. It helped us both grow, so I see nothing wrong with it and neither should you."

"You're right." He grabs my ass with both of his hands and starts to move me against his hardening crotch. I know there's no way we're not going to go at it again, but I still need to get home and change. He's taking me out to dinner and has reservations at a fancy Italian restaurant downtown. Talk about romantic.

"If you think about it, our lives together have only started. Soon, we'll be out of this high school, getting thrust into adulthood. None of this stuff from high school will matter except me and you…"

His only reply is when he kisses me with pure, raw, unadulterated passion. I'm wrapped tight in his arms, as we reconnect once more.

I might not be one hundred percent better, but I'm stronger than I ever was before. There's still going to be steps back, battles to fight, but I'm not alone. I never was, but the difference now is I see the love, not just from others, but the love I have for myself. High school was just a part of my life—not the definition of what I have to live by. There are many more roads I have left to travel. If I do make a wrong turn and that road starts heading toward a cliff, I can't let myself fall off—because it's not the end. It was a lesson telling me to turn around and try again.

MAY

"PROM!!!!" Riley squeals next to me jumping up and down in her pink puffy dress. It's strapless and I'm worried the girls are about to bounce out with all the jumping she's doing.

"I know," I tell her calmly, so maybe she'll chill a bit.

"*Broookey*, you need to be more excited. This is our last big event. The final hurrah. In a couple of months, we're going to college. A million miles apart." I roll my eyes at her exaggeration. "If anybody deserves this magical night it's you...*and me*...dancing the night away."

"I am excited, but I think all the hairspray you put in your hair and mine has made me woozy," I tease. "And I'll feel better when my mom stops taking pictures."

"Never going to happen. Just wait till Hunter and Billy get here."

I shake my head and curse the day of the invention of digital cameras and being able to take as many pictures as you want. My mom has been clicking like crazy since I slipped into my dress, making me do different poses.

I didn't think at the beginning of my Senior year that I would be going to prom. I thought there was no way in hell I was going to want to hang out with a bunch of my classmates because at the time I wanted nothing to do with them. Nor did I think I was going to have a date, much less someone like Hunter.

Now, here I stand in my prom dress, an A-line, halter, floor-length, blue ombre Chiffon dress with the neck strap covered in rhinestones. I feel beautiful like I was always made to wear this dress.

My nightmares have stopped, and I'm completely healed physically—maybe somewhat emotionally. I've had a couple of minor panic attacks since the first one, but I've been able to shake them off. I only see Dr. Fox once a month now because I find working on the anti-bullying campaign is a better type of therapy for me. And it's also been working for Hunter. We've been helping others to learn to stand up for themselves. We're watching as all different cliques now get along and want to help others. All has been extra therapeutic. I'm glad that my experience with a bunch of jerks, even though it shouldn't have happened, could be turned into something positive.

The doorbell rings and Riley squeals again. She's going to make me deaf by the end of the night. My dad opens the door and greets the guys. My dad and Hunter have grown close since all the crap months ago. My dad treats him just like his own son. Our eyes meet, and I turn into a puddle of mush. His normally untamed hair is brushed back and he's wearing a Hugo Boss tux with a silver vest and matching tie.

"You look stunning, Brooklyn," Hunter says hungrily and brushes his lips across mine.

Yep, I'm a pile of goo.

"You're quite dashing yourself, Mr. Evans." He pins the corsage to my dress. It has an Iris and some Forget Me Nots around it, which match my dress perfectly. "Thank you."

"Pictures. Gather around. Then I want to do some outside," my mom yells, holding up her camera, and her face says she means business.

After about eight million pictures, and that might be quite literal, we're in the limo heading towards the hotel holding our prom. Hunter and I rented a room for the night for our own after party. A bunch of seniors rented a suite to throw a group party and it was my own mother that told me to get a room, so she would know I was safe. I have no plans of drinking or anything, but I was going to take advantage of spending the night with my man.

It's safe to say that I have spent the entire night dancing. Everyone is having a ball, there's been absolutely no stress whatsoever. Okay, there was a moment that our Principal had to separate Hunter and me for a moment because our dancing turned quite dirty and a little R-rated for a PG-rated prom. It's not my fault the boy can't keep his hands and lips to himself.

Dinner was some high-class buffet with steak, chicken, veggies, and potatoes. They also had a huge candy bar with every candy a person could imagine. Candy won over cake, somehow. I had more candy then I did dinner since the pig I date ate most of my meal. Thankfully, I wasn't hungry.

"I need to get out of these shoes," I tell Riley and stop dancing. Which is me just rubbing my ass on Hunter's crotch.

"Me too." Riley pulls out of her date's hold and kicks off her shoes. "Sweet relief."

I move to bend down, but Hunter stops me. "Wait, maybe we can go sneak up to our room really quick. You know, so I can have those shoes wrapped around my ears. Knowing you, you'll end up losing them after you take them off tonight," he says into my ear, but I think he said it a little too loud because Riley looks disgusted and Billy is cracking up.

"Uh-uh...you two are not leaving yet," Riley yells while Hunter is busy sucking on the side of my neck and squeezing my ass. He's going to leave a mark, but I don't care. Maybe we could sneak away for a couple of minutes, an hour...

"Geez, Evans, maybe Mr. Marks does need to hose you down." Riley pulls my hand out of Hunter's hold. Hunter protests his vacant arms. "I'm starting to wonder how you ever walk straight."

"I don't." I laugh and shove her shoulder. "And you're one to talk, missy."

"Maybe it's a good thing I'm going to a different college than you two. I don't think you would notice me even if I did go to Stanford too." Riley crosses her arms at me, pouting.

I shake my head at her. I am going to miss having this girl around. Who else is going to make me laugh all day? Sure, Hunter will, but it's not the same.

I pull my best friend into a hug just when Principal Marks comes to the microphone and the music fades. "Good evening, everyone. I hope you are all enjoying your night." Everyone cheers loudly and wildly. "Good to hear. It's that time of the night where we announce our Prom Court and our Prom King and Queen. You all ready?" He waits for everyone to calm down and starts with the King's Court, which is Gary, Mark, and Van; of course, Hunter's football buddies. Hunter hoots beside me and I roll my eyes. I get along with those three well, and none of them ever got along with any of the hateful four, which makes it easier. The three boys are given their sashes, then chest bump each other, making everyone laugh at their antics.

"Our Woodbine High Prom King 2018: Mr. Hunter Evans…" The crowd cheers at Hunter's name being called. He looks down at me, grabbing my chin and pulls me into a deep heated kiss. Cheers have turned in whooping sounds.

"Evans. Get up here," Principal Marks calls out, but you can hear the slight chuckle in his stern voice. I nudge Hunter away, and he gives me one last quick peck on my cheek before making his way to the stage.

Hunter is given his sash and his crown. Our eyes meet, and he blows me a kiss, making me feel as though I'm the only person in the room.

"Could that boy be any more smitten with you?" Riley whispers next to me, grinning.

"I dunno, probably," I joke back, my eyes never leaving Hunter's. He's sending me a clear message of what he's going to do to me later with only his eyes.

Did it just get hot in here?

"I hear wedding bells in their future," my friend, April, says in a sing-song voice, pulling me away from Hunter's lustful stare. "Think this dance would be good practice for the wedding…Instead of King and Queen, Mr. and Mrs." She laughs. "I want an invite," she adds elbowing me.

There's no way I'm going to be Queen. Hunter has always been popular, that never went away. Then my mind wanders to who will be prom Queen and dancing with my man. Although, as I look at the swarm of people gathered around the stage, I can't help but wonder if it even matters. As a class and as a school, they've been supportive and caring. I have friends I never thought I would have because the labels are gone. I didn't end up being outcasted further, I was accepted. I don't know how many people have told me that they aren't scared anymore, that they have someone to talk to, they have friends, and aren't being bullied anymore because of the new program. Although I know it's in part that the hateful four are now sitting in jail cells, I'm sure now they're the ones being picked on and eaten alive.

Principal Marks announces the names of the runners-up. As I watch Kasey, Marla, and Maya take the stage, I smile. None of these girls have ever caused me any problems. Their faces light up with how happy they are to be on that stage with sashes that say Prom Court. I can't help but clap and feel happy for them. It's something I bet they have been looking forward to their whole high school lives.

"Now for our Queen…Woodbine High Prom Queen 2018: Miss Brooklyn Turner." Principal Marks calls out and everyone turns to me. I stand there in shock. Why the hell would they pick me? Then a vision of *Carrie* comes to mind and I look up at the stage looking for the pig blood. But I know I'm overreacting.

"Brooke, go." Riley nudges me. I look to Hunter and he's waving his hand at me. The crowd cheers and chants my name. I walk towards the stage, still not believing this is happening. I'm like Laney Boggs from *She's All That*. The transformed nerd with new popularity, but I actually won the title, instead of the evil ice queen. Would Kara have won if she was here?

I guess the world will never know.

I get to the stage and Hunter grabs my hand. He's about to pull me into a kiss, but Principal Mark clears his throat and glares at him. "Put those lips away, Evans."

Stronger

Hunter rolls his eyes as I'm presented with a crown and a sash. We pose for a couple of pictures before Hunter and I have our King and Queen dance.

Ed Sheeran's "Perfect" starts to play, as Hunter leads me to the dance floor. Our classmates circle around us as we dance. I wrap my arms around Hunter's neck and he wraps his arms around my waist, our bodies as close as we can make them.

"I love you, Brooklyn. I wasn't sure I would get to have this moment with you."

"Hell, I never thought I would have this. I would have never thought I would be voted Prom Queen. Like part of me wonders if it's pity." As we sway together, I lay my head on his shoulder and inhale the smell of his cologne. I'm lost in the lyrics of the song and realize how perfect they are for us.

He lifts my head to look at him and his green eyes bore into mine lovingly. I smile thinking all the times he just aimlessly stared at me in class; that this man always saw me. That even if he feared what our classmates thought of us together, he still was true to his feelings for me. Thanks to him, he gave me the push to find out who I truly am and to start living again.

"Brooke, your win was not pity. You're the queen you always should've been. Just now everyone sees that." His hand brushes through my hair and he kisses me deeply, pouring every ounce of love into it. I really do love this man. He pulls away and moves his arms back to my waist, pushing me even closer to him, if that is possible, and our foreheads touch as we continue to stare at each other.

"I don't want or need to be queen...I just want to be Brooke."

"You are so much more than *just* Brooke..."

"Oh yeah?" I raise my eyebrow at him.

"Yeah, you're brave, remarkable, strong, smart,

adorable, sweet, humble, sexy, beautiful, a loving daughter, a loving friend, and most importantly, you're mine…"

"And you are mine."

EPILOGUE

*"Even the devil himself wouldn't be able to
bring me down again because I found my strength
and the ability to fly. To fly above all the hate, to fly
above all the negativity, and keep soaring to the life
I've always deserved to have."*

Brooklyn

Graduation Day

I approach the podium and look out to my fellow classmates. My eyes search the crowd and I find Riley. She gives me two thumbs up with a large grin on her face. That girl, I would be lost without her. I give her a tiny wave and search for Hunter. I spot him easily in the third row. He's smiling with his wild hair hanging out of his cap and his forest eyes staring right at me.

I thank every day that this football star came crashing into my life and stole my heart. Not only did he bring me out of my hiding, but I also saved him from his, and together we became stronger, better, and united forever, where no one else can tear us down again.

He blows me a kiss and my cheeks heat, but at the same time, the gesture relaxes me. The room hushes and all eyes are now on me. Taking a deep breath, I keep my sights on Hunter—my future, my strength—as I give the speech that closes out my official last day of high school. There's no going back, no do-overs, and I'm okay with

267

that because my final days at Woodbine High ended up bringing me peace and giving me my start in forever.

"My fellow classmates, after twelve long years, we've made it. Today is the beginning of our new lives, our future. We spent years learning, gathering knowledge to help us on our journeys. Some of us will become football stars, artists, writers, activists, moms and dads, construction workers, rock stars, engineers, or work the nine to five. No matter what job we take, it's important to be happy and never settle just because you don't think you can do better. You can always do better.

"I want you to think of your life now then think about what you want it to become. After you picture all that, now triple your potential. Ignore the 'I can'ts,' and 'I won'ts.' What you don't need in your future is negativity. Negativity is a pimple. It interrupts your life, it's a pain in the butt, and sometimes leaves scars. But once you get rid of it, things clear up, and you can walk around with your head held high. Having confidence and positivity is what makes you shine.

"Don't let what happened in your past bring you down tomorrow. I know, I know, that's easier said than done.

"As most of you know, several months ago I was involved in an incident with a couple of our former fellow classmates. Simply put, they were bullies. They craved to make my life and others' lives hell. I spent most of my high school years in the shadows. I didn't want to stand out because I was sick of being bothered. It's amazing how words can hurt, how they scar, or how they can turn someone that used to shine as the brightest star into someone that only wants to disappear. That was me. Then one day I met someone, a person that saw me for who I really was, and not some shell of a person the negativity turned me into. He started helping to make me feel like myself again. Sometimes it just takes one person to start seeing the potential you really have. You just need to believe it yourself.

"Then one day these bullies got told the harsh truth of who they really were from a person who knew them well, a person who finally saw he was allowed to stand up for himself and others. The ones that they put down now had a reason to feel brave because now everyone saw what they were. But instead of shaking it off and moving on, they sought revenge. In their revenge, they ended up throwing away their futures. Futures they could have had if they let the words of their embarrassment roll off their backs and remembered that they had the power to change.

"But wouldn't you know, their plot to destroy, actually ended up bringing us all closer together? Their vengeful act turned into over a thousand students advocating to stand up against bullies.

"We've started something that will help future students have a way to get help, maybe even something for our kids. We've built a foundation that proves we are all stronger together—working together as a whole and not against.

"Now we may never be able to get rid of bullies completely, but it's important to let people not feel alone, to be able to ask for help, and give these bullies harder punishments for their actions. We have been finding ways to stomp them down before they have a chance to hurt anyone to the point they want to disappear or maybe even take their own life. We also need to figure out why this bully is doing what they're doing. It could be they are going through hell that causes them to act out, but whatever the reason we need to try and help them. Hopefully, we can come full circle to help everyone to a brighter place.

"Remember when it comes to your future greatness—you helped build something amazing and know you helped at least one person...Me.

"I was lucky to have a good support system after my attack; my parents, my boyfriend, Hunter, my best friend, Riley, and their parents, but on top of that, I had you guys.

"I did my best to act strong, but I was increasingly worried about coming back to school. But thanks to you guys and your support, you kept me going and gave me faith in humanity.

"The system we helped build now not only expanded statewide but has become nationally recognized. Soon, it might be available in every school, helping others find faith and trust, once again. There's a chance for the ones that come behind us to potentially never live in fear the way we did. Feel proud of the greatness you have helped create.

"Class of 2018. Our futures are bright as long as we keep on shining."

As my classmates applaud and stand to their feet, I look at all the faces before me. We all made it through the vast wasteland of High School in one piece. Now it is time to start our futures, our true beginnings, and we are going to do it whole.

I am going to do it whole and stronger than before.

I plan to continue to share my story with others. I hope in doing so, it'll help someone else not hide from the pain others created, but that they can learn to be brave and keep their heads up. To keep fighting and win against evil. I might not have all the answers to what's going to happen next, but all I can do is step out into the world and try to live. There's always going to be obstacles, but I was given the strength and the love to power over them.

So, Brooklyn, meet world.

World, meet Brooklyn.

She's coming in swinging and she's never letting anyone take her down again.

THE END

Check out my other titles on Amazon:

I FOUND YOU

SO WRONG SO RIGHT

WATCHING YOU

PLAYING WITH FIRE

PLAYING WITH FIRE: THE CONLUSION

DIRTY LITTLE SECRETS

THE LOVE PLAN

Erica Marselas

ACKNOWLEDGMENTS:

To my husband: *Thank you for being the most supportive person in the world as I take on this publishing journey. For taking care of the rugrats so I can write and also reading every chapter against your will. (HA! I'm just kidding.) At least till the point where you get annoyed with me because I ask you every hour if you read the last chapter. Love you*

To the best group of women I know: **Denise, Lexi, Leslie, Melissa, Aakriti, Paula, Suzan, Helen, Colleen, Q.B, Carmel, Harlow, Gemini, Kelsey, Kristen, Rose, Danielle J, Erin, Danielle, Hala, Kelly H, Kelly R, and Jeanette**. *I would be lost without you guys! Thank you guys for always having my back, listening to me, reassuring me, motivating me, and helping my stories grow. I owe you guys more then you'll ever know!!! Love ya all.*

To my readers: **You guys are pretty flippin' awesome too. I love you guys. Thank you for coming along with me on this ride and enjoying the words I write. (then asking for more 😊)**

ABOUT THE AUTHOR

Erica is a wife, a mother of four, and a tequila drinking smart mouth. When she's not wrangling her children and trying to keep them alive, she's writing. She'll write anything from steamy erotica, to HEA romance novels because not all love stories are created equal. As long as she can dream it, she'll write it.:)

Erica Marselas

Living The Dream Through Words

"Dreams come to us when we sleep—but when you write them down, they come alive."

Made in the USA
Middletown, DE
19 November 2020